# *Laguna Treasure*

## *A Virginia Davies Mystery*

*D. F. Ciambrone*

Writers Club Press
San Jose  New York  Lincoln  Shanghai

# Acknowledgments

The author wishes to thank the following people for helping in a myriad of ways to help this book see the light of day.

My wife Kathy for her support, listening, patience and ideas My good friend Donna Todd for her critiques, ideas and being a sounding board and a good listener.

# **Prologue**

1933
Southern California coast

They came from the South, passing the evening summer sun, shimmering gold in the calm blue waters. The cotton sails of the craft sagged lifelessly under the placid, darkening sky. The puttering of the engine was the only sound as the boat slid through the water. The motor cut out and the white, two-masted yacht drifted another 20 yards before slowing to a stop. The splash of the anchor disturbed a seagull resting on the bow railing, and the startled bird took to flight.

Captain Anderson, adjusted an old, white officer's cap. He was a tall, muscular man and was dressed casually in a striped tee shirt and blue jeans. His tense grip on the old binoculars held to his eyes belied the casual garb. His eyes searched the sandy, surfless shore for the rendezvous point.

"Let's get this over with. And fast. Get those boxes up here quickly," he ordered.

A second, stocky man appeared from below deck carrying a high powered, Remington, 30-06 rifle. He took a station on the top of the cabin and surveyed the sea and beach. Two other men opened the forward hatch and began to bring boxes on deck. The smallest of the men, in his mid twenties with a slight build and blond hair, lowered the skiff into the water and motored around to the starboard side.

On the beach, a two ton faded green 1932 Ford truck—canvas-covered with a drooping right running board—backed its way toward the beach, and onto the hard-packed sand, remaining about 30 feet from the water's edge. The beach was nearly deserted.

Two husky men jumped down from the truck. Each man surveyed the beach noting every detail. About two hundred yards to the south, a couple walked down the beach, away from them. They were dismissed as not important. The slight traffic on the main road did not appear to offer any danger. No police were in sight. Spike, the driver and tallest of the two men, took a long drag on his cigarette and tossed it into the sea. Balding and overweight, the second man fingered the revolver bulging the pocket of his light jacket. They watched as the skiff, loaded with boxes, headed for shore, propelled by a muffled, Mercury outboard motor. The skiff rode through the slight surf and beached itself in the sand. Spike held the skiff fast on shore until the others secured it to the slightly sagging rear bumper of the truck.

Two men from the boat and the two on shore quickly unloaded the skiff. They carefully secured the heavy boxes into place in the truck with thick ropes then pushed the skiff back into the calm water. The two men from the truck remained on the beach and lit cigarettes and waited for their associates to return with the second load. Occasionally, the shorter man would walk around the truck, stopping to watch the road for anyone with anything but a casual interest in their presence. The skiff returned with the crew of the yacht and the unloading continued while the short man, leaning on the front of the truck, stood guard.

When the truck was loaded the crew of the yacht climbed into the rear and closed the canvas flaps behind them.

Captain Anderson turned to Spike, "After you get to the road, turn left. Go to the canyon road and head inland. About two to three miles you should see a dirt cut off on the left. Stop there." He too climbed into the back of the truck.

Spike drove the truck up to the paved highway and turned north a short way, before he turned east and headed down a twisting narrow road into the hills. After a few miles of slow driving, Spike pulled the truck off to the side of the road under a tall, live oak and stopped. He climbed down and walked to the back of the truck. The captain had already dismounted.

"I think we're close," said the driver.

Captain Anderson looked around. "The trail is right over there. We're doing fine." He gestured with his arms toward the mountain on their left, "Let's get up there while we still have some sun."

An eerie, moving shadow cast itself on the mountain as the sun rapidly set. The men climbed back into the truck and Spike turned the truck up an old dirt road that wound into the chaparral-covered mountainside. The scrub oak, tumbleweed, thistle and brown baked vegetation scratched the sides of the truck as it meandered up the mountain. Spike brought the truck to a stop a short distance from three caves. Two of the caves were small and further up the mountain from the third and largest one. The men quickly jumped off the truck and began pulling the canvas cover back.

"Let's get this stuff stowed before it gets too dark," yelled the captain.

The captain and the boat crew lugged the heavy boxes into the deep, musty cave. The men could hear the sound of an underground river running into a large opening toward the sea. They lit oil lamps. A large cavern opened before them in the shimmering light.

One of the boat crewmen stood looking at the smooth pool of water. "It's a damn desert outside and look at this. Who would have thought…?"

"Sight seeing's over…get crack'n, I don't want to be here all night!" yelled the captain.

Lugging the remaining boxes into the cave, the men placed them near the underground river.

Spike sat at the cave entrance to inventory the goods and to start a map of the area and cave. A small box on a rock outcropping slid off and fell to the floor of the cave. It broke open, spilling its gold contents. The men scrambled to the treasure. Spike, sitting at the entrance, heard the excitement and rushed in and picked up a large, round gold piece. He then walked back to the cave entrance to finish his map.

"Hold it! Hold it!" yield Captain Anderson putting his right hand on the pistol strapped to his hip. "Put all that stuff in a pile next to the rock. Come on mates, empty the pockets, we'll be back for it later. No one takes anything now. That was the deal."

The rumble began deep in the bowls of the earth. Hardly noticeable at first, the sounds grew, transformed into motion, as slow gyrations transformed into violent vibrations.

To the west, city streets buckled, brick chimneys collapsed through roofs of houses, water mains broke like so much dry spaghetti. Rails of the Santa Fe Rail Road twisted and writhed. Thirty miles north, in a few, terrifying moments, Long Beach was devastated.

In the excitement, the men failed to notice the ripples on the surface of the pool of water formed by the river. They didn't hear the growing noise—they didn't hear it until the earth started to undulate. Rocks in the ceiling fell, dirt and rubble tumbled into the cave. They never knew what hit them. Everything went dark, forever.

Buffeted by falling rocks and dirt, Spike, at the entrance to the cave, fell to the ground bruised and semiconscious. He crawled out of the cave entrance before blacking out.

A light damp morning fog hung in the sky when he regained consciousness. His head felt like an army had marched through it. He could still feel his side where the big rock had hit him that evening. The pain in his ribs felt like lightning was running through them. His broken left leg throbbed. His damp dirty clothes clung to him. The truck was on its side. He fashioned a walking stick out of a small tree limb that fell during the quake and slowly hobbled down the dirt road to the paved highway. With increasing pain, he limped along toward home. About a mile up the road he hitched a ride.

He stumbled into the house late in the day. Half conscious, his clothing torn, his body feeling like a hot iron was inside, Spike stuffed the gold piece and documents into a hiding place; he collapsed on the hall entrance floor. The cool, wood-flooring felt good next to his hot, bruised skin.

His wife ran into the entrance from the kitchen wiping her wet hands on her apron. Seeing her husband stretched out and bleeding before her, she screamed.

"What happened? Where have you been? I'll get something…call the doctor…" she stammered in confusion, with her heart racing.

He lifted his head and whispered, "Gold…I'm the only one left…the secret is in the…he time…you have the secret." He said no more. He was gone.

# Summer, Sixty plus Years Later
# Irvine, California

~ *1* ~

Virginia Davies sat on her apartment patio overlooking the pool area drinking iced tea and reading notes for her Masters thesis. The late morning sun brought out the underlying red highlights to the multiple shades of her shoulder length blond styling. She stretched. The already tight red tee shirt, with white letters proclaiming 'Sea Serpents Diving Club,' showed off the nicely proportioned bosom it tried to hide. She moved her long, tanned legs. Her cut off blue jeans were short enough for her to stick to the chair. Virginia was named after Virginia Dare, the first white person born in the New World, a name her father liked. People often tried to call her "Ginnie", but she pleasantly and unfailingly shifted them back to the name she preferred. She was beautiful, no dissenting votes. Hers was the sort of beauty that warmed the ideas of romance in some men and fueled the fires and sexual fantasies of others. Five foot six, and nicely tanned, she was a candidate for any men's magazine.

Sometimes, she was mistakenly assumed to be French. In fact her mother's parents were French, and she'd spent a lot of summers visiting them resulting in a better than working knowledge of the language. Her father, a bank manager, had been transferred around the western United States with the bank, so she received a first hand education in diverse life styles and histories of the region. This was her main reason for obtaining a degree in history and pursuing her Masters degree. Her eyes were surprisingly blue and unexpectedly bright and exuded intelligence and friendliness. She didn't dress or walk provocatively. Jeans or formal dresses, she turned heads. Today she had numerous admirers from the pool area below.

The unexpected ringing of the telephone startled her.

"Hello," she said in a low voice, thinking it may be her boyfriend.

"Hello yourself. How's the research going?" responded Abbey Mc Queen, an old friend and owner of Abbey's Antiques and Art in Laguna Beach. They had been friends for five years before, in college, when they both spent their junior year at Saint Ann de Buprie in Paris, France. They had become friends when they discovered that the food at the school wasn't fit for human consumption. They headed for the Left Bank and the Latin Quarter for Italian, where they spent the entire year existing on spaghetti.

"Not bad, just finding it hard to concentrate on such a beautiful day. What's up?"

"You still working on grandfathers clocks for your thesis?"

"Yeah. Why?"

"I got an old, and I mean old, grandfather clock in from an estate sale yesterday. Thought you'd like to see it since your thesis is about old clocks. It doesn't work, but it has nice dark mahogany and some other kind of wood for woodwork and a polished brass face and ornate black hands. Maybe you can identify its maker. Anyway we could have lunch…what do you say?"

"Sounds like a good idea. I could use a break. I'll drop by your place in an hour," Virginia replied and hung-up.

God, this could be exciting, she thought. I might actually get some hands-on study with a real Tall Clock. I wonder what exactly Abbey's got? It would be great if she had the history of it too. Where's it been, who's owned it. Well, just getting to study it close up would be good enough.

Virginia quickly folded up her files and returned them to her desk in the small living room. Her mind raced as she thought about the clock. I wonder how old it really is? If it is as old as I hope, this could be a real treasure for my thesis.

She picked up her black cat, Leo, from his sunny perch on the table and brought him into the apartment. Virginia found Leo as a rain soaked, half starved, ball of fir near a flood control channel the year before and nursed him back to health. Now Leo thought he owned the apartment. Stroking him, she thought of her doormat and how it summed up his opinion. It read, 'A cat and his support staff live here'. She watched as Leo trotted off to the bedroom.

Virginia closed the sliding glass door and locked it before grabbing her soft, brown, leather backpack and heading across the room toward the front door. Halfway she stopped, "Now. Where did I put those darn keys?" she asked herself.

Quickly scanning the small room; she spotted them among some quilt squares, fabric and fossils on the breakfast bar, the divider between the living room and the kitchen-dinning area.

"See yeah later, Leo," she said as she scooped up the keys and headed out the door locking it behind her. Virginia bounced down the stairs to the walkway and headed to her car. She unlocked the red Toyota Cresida, climbed in, opened the sunroof, started the car, and headed to Pacific Coast Highway, turning south to Laguna Beach.

The bell overhead tinkled as Virginia pushed open the door to Abbey's shop and entered a room crowded with too much furniture for its limited space. She maneuvered around dark, polished, wooden French Provincial tables and passed assorted wooden chairs, gingerly stepped around glass cases and high shelves loaded with glassware. An Oriental rug of blue and rose hues hung on one wall. Various old cabinets were situated to allow the light to glisten off the deep mahogany finishes and accentuate the intricate wood carving trim.

"Be right with you," came a loud cry from the rear of the building. A few seconds later by Abbey, emerged from a back room. Virginia noticed Abbey's brightly colored full skirt flowed as she hurried into the showroom. The Spanish style, off-the-shoulder white blouse and silver necklace complimented the skirt, and both accented her olive complexion, an inheritance from her Spanish mother. Raven hair just touched her brown shoulders formed the backdrop for her long silver and turquoise earrings. Her slight five foot three form seemed taller and Virginia recognized again that Abbey's presence was enhanced by her gregarious personality.

"Hi. You got here fast. Do you want to see the grand timepiece now or after we stuff ourselves?" Abbey held a towel, and briskly wiped her hands with it, removing the ever-present furniture polish.

"I'd like to peek at the clock, then eat, if you don't mind."

Together, they walked around tables with polished antiques and art displays to an even more congested back room where Abbey kept new arrivals and packaged sold items for shipment.

Light beamed in from high windows on the rear wall illuminating packing materials, figurines and paintings crowding the musty space.

Abbey pointed to a tall clock near the rear door. "There it is, what do you think? I got it from an estate sale in Pasadena. The only thing is, it doesn't work. That won't help selling it." Her tone merely matter-of-fact, without worry.

Virginia removed her backpack and pulled out her worn spiral notebook. She wound her way around crates and wooden picture frames to the clock and started to examine it. Her hands slid carefully over the cool wood. With these old clocks, thought Virginia, you could almost feel the history and stories they could tell. The clock was about seven feet high, made of dark mahogany wood. Virginia carefully released the latch on the front glass door exposing two large round brass weights and a polished brass pendulum weight on a wooden arm. The clock face was originally polished brass that was now slightly tarnished. The thin hands were ornate black iron. On both sides of the clocks' hood were small doors with decorative wooded lattice over cloth covers.

"Nice hood," mumbled Virginia.

"What's a hood? I thought it was something on a car."

"The top of a grandfather or tall clock that holds the clockworks and face is called the hood. This piece," said Virginia as she pointed to the smooth dark wood that stretched around the clock face.

She moved closer to the clock and squinted as she looked at the fine detail in the workmanship.

"It could be a Willard!" Virginia exclaimed. "Probably early to mid eighteen hundreds. Looks like it was well cared for."

"How do you figure it's a Willard, or whatever?" asked Abbey, "I don't know beans about clocks."

"The woodworking, style and the face. If it is a Willard, it will have the name engraved inside. Aaron Willard made these tall clocks, as they are called, in Boston in the early to mid 1800s."

"Is it rare or is there much of a market for it?" asked Abbey. "Antiques I know. Art I know. I'd better, my dad paid enough for my degree. But clocks…like I said, I know from nothing."

"These old clocks are collectors items." Virginia rubbed the smooth case. "Probably worth about two thousand to five thousand dollars. That's if it worked."

"Five thousand sounds like something I can relate to." She glanced at her watch. "Let's go to lunch, I'm starved." Without waiting for a reply, Abbey turned and headed for the front of the shop.

Virginia grabbed her backpack and followed. They left the shop and walked North along the beach on Pacific Coast Highway to Los Brisas. They entered the stone-covered patio area and sat at a table overlooking the curve of Laguna's Main Beach. Small waves broke gently on the shore below. The landscape looked Mediterranean with its white stucco buildings extending up the brownish hillside, curved sandy beach, complete with a boardwalk, and swaying palms. The gentle warm breeze ruffled the colorful umbrella covering their table. Their waiter, having spotted Abbey, brought them each a glass of White Zinfandel and menus.

After ordering, Abbey asked, "Would the Willard or whatever, help your research?"

Drawing circles in the white tablecloth with her fork, Virginia looked up,

"Yes, I think so, I'll need to examine the workings and see how the case was made. Usually I can only look at them. To actually be able to get into the workings and see the construction first hand will be great. They did excellent woodwork in those days, and we could verify the maker. How much would you want for it?"

The waiter returned for their orders. Abbey ordered a tropical fruit salad and tortillas; Virginia ordered a taco salad.

"I don't know, I'll have to think about it. If we could get it to work, that would be an extra plus."

During their discussions of the fashions displayed by other patrons, lunch arrived.

On the way back to the shop, they stopped in a couple of clothing stores on Forest Avenue, the kind that the well heeled frequent. Virginia and Abbey tried on fashions ranging from punk to preppy, western to expensively stylish.

"Darn it all," said Abbey in a shop that sold beachwear, "you can wear anything and look good. I have to be careful. If the stripes go the wrong way I look heavy; if it's not my color, I look like Hell. I should hate you. Oh well, as my mama always said, if you get depressed, buy something." Abbey bought a new white blouse and a pair of suede boots.

"Dad's inheritance comes in handy. Art dealers usually starve but at least it's fun," Abbey said as they entered her shop lugging her boxes.

"Tell you what, I'll loan the clock to you. Besides, what am I going to do with an old clock that doesn't work? Might be kinda hard to sell. Do you know anyone who could, maybe, fix the thing?"

"Oh Abbey…that would be great!" Virginia answered. "As to fixing it, there are some good clock repairers in the county that work on old clocks. I'm not sure about one this old, though. Now the task of the day is to figure out how on earth I'm going to get it home. I don't even know if it will fit in the apartment. I'll call Andy and see what he thinks."

She dialed Dr. Andy Clark's office with the College of Engineering at the University of California at Irvine. Virginia remembered the first time she went to Andy's house. He had invited her to a barbecue. She brought wine. Her past experience with single men's abodes meant she should get buster shoots before going. She was shocked to find his house in Laguna Hills clean and neat as a pin. Andy answered the door. She stared at a five foot ten inch frame in jeans and a sawdust covered tee-shirt. Goggles covered his glasses and a UCI baseball cap partially hid his brown hair and balding spot Virginia knew was there. She thrust a bottle of Zinfandel wine at him. He thanked her for the wine and hustled her into his woodworking shop in the garage. He found out about her love of animals and especially horses, and had made a small rocking horse especially for her.

She stroked the smooth, brown stained surface. It was beautiful. The attention to detail was exquisite. It must have taken him weeks to make. "It's beautiful Andy. I don't know what to say. Thank you."

"Don't say anything. Just give it a lot of love."

Virginia looked around the shop. In a corner, next to some shelves were diving bottles. On the shelf above them were regulators, a wet suit and assorted diving gear.

As Andy prepared the barbecue, Virginia wandered through the house. She stopped to admire a Kincade painting in his living room and beautiful landscapes by painters she didn't recognize. Two thick books rested on the coffee table, History of the Mississippi Delta and Bronze Age Shipwrecks in Turkish Waters. A faint whiff of smoke from the charcoal reached her nostrils. A fossil sat on an end table. She heard Andy in the family room fumbling with his CD player, followed by a serenade by Patsy Cline. She wandered into his den. Next to the computer was an edited manuscript for a novel he was working on. This wasn't what she had expected of an engineering professor. Andy was, in her mind, a Renaissance man.

"Dr. Clark." he answered.

"Andy! I'm at Abbey's. She has a beautiful old grandfather clock she is loaning me for my research!" Virginia yelled over the phone, unable to control her excitement.

"That's great, but why are you so excited about this clock? What's so special? You sound pretty jazzed over it," said Andy.

Virginia could hear amusement in his voice and the sound of shuffling papers. She lowered her voice to a normal tone. "It's just that it may be an old Willard and in excellent shape, a real find! These are usually found in museums." She paused then continued, "Only thing is, it doesn't work. I need help."

"For the kind of help you need, you should be dating a different kind of Doctor," he said, amusement still evident in his voice. "I know I shouldn't ask, but what do you need?"

"I can't get it home, and I'm actually not sure where home for it will be. It's huge!"

"I'll bring my truck and we'll figure something out when I get there. Can you wait until about four?"

She agreed, and after a few personal comments, hung up. She continued to gaze at the tall clock.

Virginia was still engrossed in examining the old clock when a load knock sounded on the rear door. A glance at the showroom cuckoo clock recalled it was 3:30.

"Maybe that's Andy," said Abbey.

She opened the door to find Dr. Andy Clark tucking his light blue Old Navy shirt into his jeans. He grinned, and looked at her through his wire-rimmed sunglasses. "Hello ladies. Your knight in shinning armor is here to save the day." His balding head was covered with a red baseball cap with UCI Anteaters written in gold on the front.

"Hi, Andy," Virginia called from the back of the shop.

Abbey stepped back to let him in and followed him to the middle of the workroom where she and Virginia had moved the clock. It looked mystical standing in the light streaming down from the windows above.

"The darn thing certainly is big," he stated. "Where are we taking it?"

"I don't know. I'm not sure it will fit in the apartment and still have room for me to work on it," Virginia replied as she stepped out from behind the clock.

"Well, if you want to store it and see if we can get it to work while you study it, how about my lab at school? It's big, the spring quarter is over, and it's secure. Anyway I'd like to see how it works myself. Maybe I could get it going."

"Sounds good to me," said Virginia. "Help us wrap it up so we don't hurt it in the move."


"Be careful ladies," Andy yelled, "You don't want to lose this thing on the steps."

Abbey and Virginia were carrying the bottom end while Andy lugged the hood of the clock up the concrete stairs leading to the engineering building and Andy's laboratory. Andy unlocked the laboratory door. He flicked the light switch with his right hand and quickly regrabbed the clock. They entered a room smelling of hydraulic oil and cluttered with tensile test equipment, Izod impact testers, hardness testers, tool lockers and boxes, and laboratory workbenches.

Carefully standing it up in the lab next to a workbench, he said,

"This thing weighs more than I thought, even more than at the shop." He sat on a lab stool and sourly looked at the old clock. "I clearly need to go to the gym more often."

Virginia removed the bubble wrap she and Abbey placed around the clock, and started examining it. Rubbing the smooth carved pillars on the side of the hood and the carved balls that adorned the top and corners, she mumbled to herself and ignored the others.

Abbey arched her back and stretched. "It's getting late and I have some things to do; do you want a lift back to the shop?"

"Oh. I forgot about my car. Do you mind?" asked Virginia.

"That will work out better for me, too," interjected Andy as he walked over to the clock. He carefully opened the glass front and started to remove the paper they had used to secure the pendulum and weights. "I have a couple of things to do and I'd like to look at this beauty some."

"If you find anything interesting, let me know," said Abbey.

Virginia kissed Andy. "Thanks for the help, you always come through for me, even with crazy stunts like this one."

With that, Virginia and Abbey headed for the parking lot and Abbeys' blue BMW. Abbey started the engine and they pulled out into the street.

"Yeah know, if Andy finds anything unusual, I could probably add a little mystery to it." Said Abbey. "A little intrigue never hurt sales."

# ~ **2** ~

Andy laid aside his finished paperwork and completed the grade forms for the spring quarter, then stretched his tall form fully erect. He looked through the window between his small office and the laboratory at the old clock standing next to a bench. He shifted his eyes to the clock on the wall above his messy desk. It was ten o'clock. "What the hell," he muttered, "It's late, but I think I'll take a quick look."

Moving a small chair stacked with books and papers closer to the bookshelves that lined one wall, he opened the connecting door and went into the laboratory.

He approached the clock and examined the woodwork and construction. His hands caressed the smooth surface. He adjusted his glasses to examine the wood working finer details. The quality and workmanship the craftsmen obtained can rival anything we can do today, he thought. And they did it all by hand, no power tools. Amazing. Inside a toolbox, Andy located a fine tipped screwdriver, a can of machine oil and a small hammer. He removed some notes from his pants pocket that Virginia had scribbled in the truck. Adjusting his glasses, he looked at her notes. She had sketched out how the hood of the clock was fastened and wrote a brief description of the workings and where the inscription would be if the clock was indeed a Willard. As he climbed on a short stepladder, he said to the clock, "Let's see what makes an old boy like you tick."

Undoing some newer looking fasteners, Andy pushed the top of the clock. "I think this is what Virginia said was the hood," he muttered outloud. The hood slid up easily to provide access to the dial and the clockworks behind. He examined the inner workings of the clock. The clock movement looked like a dead-beat escapement type, used in the early to mid 1800s, according to Virginia's notes. The semicircular pallet arbor seemed to be in very good shape for its age. There was a piece of paper stuck between the pallet and scape weight. Andy carefully removed the wad of paper and stuffed it into his shirt pocket. He peered further down inside the clock. There was another paper, even more yellowed with age and something that looked like brass wedged in the weight drive. Using some long nosed pliers he removed the paper and the metal item.

"Boy, you're pretty heavy," he said softly to himself.

The object appeared to be a medallion or coin and seemed somewhat worn but still shinny, surprisingly untarnished for having been inside an old clock. He placed the coin on a lab bench along with the pieces of paper. The paper was yellowing and had been torn. The ink was fading. He adjusted a nearby gooseneck lamp, pulled up a stool and examined the papers.

"This looks like part of a list of some kind and part of a map," he observed aloud out of habit. The pieces roughly fit together. He returned to his office bringing notepaper, pen and a magnifying glass back to the light. He pulled up a stool next to the bench and clock, examined the papers and copied them as best he could.

"This will help. At least it's more readable," he said. He studied the map: it was of somewhere along the ocean, but not readily recognizable. The list seemed to be an inventory of some kind but the items were not identifiable. They referred to boxes and some items he didn't understand. Folding up the copies and the original map and list, he mumbled to himself, "Virginia is going to go bananas over this. I wonder how much trouble she's gotten herself into this time?"

The coin item intrigued him. Obtaining a bottle of hydrochloric acid from a shelf, he said to himself, "Let's see if you are brass or what." He applied a few drops of the acid. Nothing happened!

He stared at the medallion. "Well, well, you're not brass after all. Thought you were too heavy for it. Anyway, if you were brass, you would be tarnished by now, **gold** on the other hand doesn't tarnish or react with acid."

Looking at his watch, he realized it was too late to call Virginia. He took the gold piece, the 'new' map and list and sealed them in a baggie, and placed them in the lab freezer.

"Since the cheapskates won't buy us a lock box, this will have to do…short of keeping them on ice," he chuckled.

He placed the original papers in a manila folder and left them on the workbench under the toolbox next to the clock. Gathering up his keys from the office, he turned out the lights, locked the door and slowly walked down the steps to the tree lined facility parking area. A warm, soft breeze ruffled the leaves. He could smell a hint of the ocean in the air.

Even at midnight there are people around, he thought, as he drove off in his black Ford pickup truck. He headed to his small house in Laguna Hills.

~ *3* ~

Abbey arrived at the shop with a cup of coffee in one hand and a small painting encased in brown paper in the other. Entering, she threaded her way through the tight collection of tables, statues and display cases to the rear of the shop inadvertently leaving the front door unlocked. Abbey began to unwrap the painting when she heard the front door bell tinkle as it opened. A man and a woman entered. They walked in and looked around, as if interested in the items on display but really looking for something else.

"Can I help you?" asked Abbey.

She took an immediate dislike to the man. Something about his manner made her shudder.

"My name is Charles Jameson III, and this is Ms. Sue Hill," he said. "We are looking for a grandfather clock that I believe belongs to me."

Abbey stared at him. She guessed he was in his early thirties and about six feet tall. His wavy blond hair was perfectly styled, not a hair out of place. She noticed his lightweight, cream-colored turtleneck sweater under a green cashmere sport coat. It seemed a little out of place considering the warm weather. His dark gray pressed wool slacks topped a pair of wing tip shoes. His posture stated that he was used to being the center of attention. This boy's oozing of money, she thought.

Abbey shifted her attention to his lady friend. Sue Hill was dressed in a navy blue silk dress that clung to the lines of her figure like oil poured over her shoulders and allowed to run down. The sleeves were short, coming just above her elbows. The pearl necklace looked like it set someone back a pretty penny. Abbey guessed her age to be about twenty-nine or thirty.

"I beg your pardon!" Abbey exclaimed. "If you are referring to the clock I picked up at the estate sale the other day, you are mistaken. I paid for it and it belongs to me. If you would like to purchase it, that's a different matter. Anyway, it isn't here right now, as you have obviously observed. What is your interest in it, anyway?"

"The clock belonged to my late aunt Shara," he stated with disdain in his voice. "And, it was sold by the executor of the estate before I had a chance to examine it or take it myself. I want it back."

"Well, it isn't here, I haven't decided what I want for it as yet. If you are interested, here is my card, give me a call in a few weeks," she responded firmly. She placed her ands on her hips.

"Would you mind telling me where it is?" he asked in a less authoritarian voice.

"If it's any of your business…it's at the university. A friend of mine's boyfriend is an engineering professor there and he is trying to get it to work. It was broken when I bought it. My friend is studying old clocks for her Masters and I'm loaning it to her," said Abbey.

"Well, thank you for your time. We will be back." He turned, took Sue's arm and left the shop.

Abbey went to her cluttered Louis XIV desk in the rear of the shop and dialed Virginia's number fidgeting while she waited for her to answer.

"Hi, I just had the strangest visitors. They said they wanted **their** clock back, can you image?" stated Abbey.

"Who were they?" Virginia asked.

"They said it was their aunt's clock and shouldn't have been sold. I told them it wasn't here and I may or may not sell it. They'll be back, I'm afraid."

"That makes sense. I was just going to call you. Andy called at the crack of dawn to tell me what he found in the clock last night. You'll never guess what! " she exclaimed.

"What was it? Gold by the sound of your voice."

"Actually, it was gold," Virginia stated. "He found a gold medallion or something, stuck in the gears and a list of something or other and an old partly-drawn map. I'm feeding Leo then heading over there. I'll call you after I've seen what he has."

Virginia whipped down the road to the university. She could feel her heart beat in anticipation of what Andy had to show her. Parking her car in a tree shrouded student lot, she bounded up the concrete steps to the brick walkway and ran across campus to the lab. Virginia pulled the heavy door open and entered. She hurriedly looked around for Andy.

Andy, with a headset magnifier on, sat working on the clockworks laid out on the lab bench. Tools were strewed about on the workbench. He looked up. "Hi, I've almost got it working again. These old clock makers were pretty shrewd. This thing's a work of art."

He got up from his stool, stretched and walked to the refrigerator.

"Before you say anything, wait and see what I have on ice for you." Andy opened the refrigerator door. Withdrawing a baggie from the freezer, he opened it and spread out the contents on a bench.

"Take a look at these. I figure one is some kind of list of materials someone hid. The other is a partial map. The original is over there in that folder. This copy I made is easier to read. See what you think."

Virginia looked at the list and map for a couple of minutes. "I don't know. It may be someplace around here. Here is the coast. This is a coast road and U.S. 101. Is there a date or anything? What's A Creek?"

"I don't know. That's what is on the original, as best I can tell. By the way, I'll have the clock running late this afternoon. Oh, yeah. This was also in there."

With an exaggerated flourish, he pulled the gold medallion from his pocket and gave it to Virginia.

"Wow! This is something. It's beautiful. What is it?"

"I don't know. Might be some kind of coin, maybe one of your history professors might be of help," he said.

"I'll take this stuff with me and show it to Abbey and see what we can dig up. Yeah know, you're right, maybe Dr. Gillette could help. I'll look into that too. It's going to be fun researching this thing and the clock. You know how I love mysteries, pirates and stories about buried treasure. Why don't you come by for dinner about six? I'll make your favorite, then we can come by here afterwards to see this beauty run and figure out what to do next."

She kissed him quickly and hurried out the door to her car.

Andy put the last screw back in place, set 5:30 on the clock and lowered the hood. As he climbed down from the stepladder, the door to the laboratory opened. Two men entered. The bigger man was dressed in a blue button down sport shirt. His right hand was in the pocket of his brown Docker pants. He had black wavy hair and a tan. The second shorter man had a green polo shirt and black slacks. He had short blond hair, and a fair complexion.

"Nice clock professor. You got it working?" asked the taller of the two.

"Who are you?" asked Andy.

"Allow me to introduce us, I'm Mr. Smith," said the tall man, "And this is Mr. Jones. Now, did you get it working?"

"Yes"

"Very good professor. Did you find anything interesting inside?" asked Mr. Jones.

"Nothing you two could understand. Where did you come from? Who exactly sent you?"

"Now, now professor, we can either be civilized or do it the hard way. Just tell us what you found. From your voice we can tell you found something interesting," stated Mr. Smith.

"Get out of here before I call the Police." Andy turned toward his office. He lurched forward as something hit him in the back of his head. He caught himself on a stool and tried to straighten up. Mr. Smith grabbed him by the back of his shirt and roughly pushed him into the wall. Andy fell to the floor; his chest and head felt like a truck hit them. Mr. Smith came up rapidly and kicked him in the kidneys. The pain shot through him like an electric shock. He moved slightly in agony.

"Now, exactly what did you find professor?" asked Mr. Jones.

"Go to Hell!"

"Not a good answer professor," said Mr. Smith kicking Andy in the jaw. The pain was riveting. Andy thought a root canal couldn't hurt this much. He lay on the floor and watched as the two men moved the toolbox and opened the manila folder containing the original map and list. Everything began to fade from view.

Virginia glared at the kitchen clock. "It's seven o'clock. Where is that bum?" Virginia asked Leo. "He isn't usually this late." She looked through the sliding glass door toward the pool, then paced back to the dining room table. Virginia had prepared his favorite dinner: Swiss steak, mashed potatoes, green beans and a lot of gravy. She had called the laboratory and his house to no avail.

"I wonder if he has had an accident in the lab?" She said to the cat. They weren't supposed to work in laboratories alone. All that equipment and chemicals could be dangerous. She rose and walked to the kitchen, moved Leo and picked up the telephone and dialed the university police.

"University of California Police," a voice answered, "Can I help you?"

Virginia told the officer that Dr. Clark was very late and had been working alone in his laboratory. She asked them to have someone go to the laboratory and check.

Pacing the floor, she kept glancing back and forth between the phone and the wall clock in the kitchen. It seemed like eternity. After waiting ten minutes, Virginia turned off the stove, grabbed her purse and left the apartment. Locking the door she hurried to her car and sped off to the university.

As she nosed her car into a parking space, an ambulance with its red lights flashing, wound up the wide walkway towards the engineering building. A cold shiver went up her spine. She ran up the steps into the building. God, I hope all this isn't for Andy, she thought. There were police cars, a fire truck and a fire department paramedic vehicle parked in all directions in the walkway area outside the building. The police were in the lab along with fire department paramedics. She shouldered her way in past a young police officer. "Just a minute, you can't go in there," said the officer as he reached for her.

"I'm Virginia Davies, Dr. Clark's friend, I called you," she stated weakly. "Where is Andy?"

"The paramedics are working on him, someone beat him up pretty bad," responded a short, red headed uniformed officer. "Looks like they were looking for something, place is a mess, even for an engineering lab."

Virginia wound her way past police officers busy taking notes and firemen. She entered the lab and noticed firemen around someone on the floor. Andy lay on the ground; an IV bag was attached to one arm. Bandages, oozing with blood, covered his face and right arm. A paramedic looked up at her. "He is doing pretty well considering the beating he took. We'll transport to Hoag. He may have some internal injuries."

The medics carefully lifted Andy to the stretcher. One fireman carried the IV bag connected to Andy as they wheeled him to the waiting ambulance.

The ambulance sped down the road to Pacific Coast Highway and north to Newport Beach and Hoag Hospital.

Speeding to the hospital, Virginia started to cry, visualizing Andy, wanting to tell him how sorry she was that he may have gotten hurt because of her. She kept wiping the tears from her eyes. Virginia parked her car in the parking structure and ran into the main entrance. She spotted the volunteer at the information desk.

"Which way is the emergency room?" she asked panting.

"Follow the red line on the wall," answered the woman. "It will take you right there."

She followed the colored line on the hospital walls to the emergency room. There were people sitting in the waiting room. Some had bandages, others seemed to be in pain or worried. People spoke in low voices. A nurse came out from a wide door calling a name. Virginia swept into the treatment area before the door shut. An orderly pointed to the room where Andy was being examined. An older doctor was treating Andy. A police detective was standing next to the doctor. Virginia noticed the badge on his belt said Lieutenant, University of California Police. Andy was trying to mumble something while the doctor and the detective argued.

"He isn't in shape to talk to you now," insisted the doctor.

"I need a statement…he was attacked on university property," responded the officer.

"How is he? When can I take him home?" interjected Virginia. The two men stopped and turned. Surprise was written on their faces.

"Who are you? How did you get in here?" asked the doctor.

"I'm Virginia Davies and he's my boyfriend!" said Virginia firmly. "I called the police because I was worried about him. How is he?"

"I'm Doctor Jack Rubbin. Your friend has had a serious beating. His kidneys and ribs are bruised, his jaw may be cracked and he has a mild concussion. Surprisingly, though, nothing appears to be broken. We're getting him cleaned and bandaged. We've given him something for pain and some antibiotics. He is also stubborn. Look at what he wrote."

He handed the clipboard that Andy wrote on to Virginia. It said, *'How do I get out of here? I feel like shit. Do I have to breathe?'*

"How bad is he? Can I take him home?"

"We need to do some more tests," answered Dr. Rubbin. "It'll take about another couple of hours. If everything checks out,

I'll give you some prescriptions and you can take him. I'd like to keep him overnight but he doesn't like our company."

"He hates hospitals."

The detective stepped forward. "Ms. Davies, I'm Lieutenant John Killroy of the University of California Police."

He was about five feet nine inches tall, short dark brown hair, and blue eyes. A brown tweed sport coat covered an open collared blue shirt. His tan Dockers topped a pair of brown moccasins. A gold badge was attached to his belt on the right side near the buckle. A conspicuous bulge could be seen under his coat on his left side. She thought he looked more like a professor than a police officer.

"I know Professor Clark somewhat from school. I'm sorry about the attack. We will do everything we can to clear it up. We have asked the local police for assistance. Some maintenance workers said they saw two men leave the building a little after six tonight. They were in a hurry. We got a sketchy description. Do you have any idea what they were after?

"No," she responded, not wanting to bring up the map and gold piece. "No, I don't know what they were after.

"Why was that grandfather clock in his lab? Any ideas?"

"He was trying to get it to work," she said sitting in a chair against the wall. "A friend loaned it to me for my research but it didn't work, Andy was going to try and fix it."

Kilroy looked at her. "Can I get you anything?"

"No, thank you. It was just a shock."

"Let's go to the little waiting room next to the emergency. I need to ask some more questions."

Virginia glanced back and forth at Kilroy then at Andy.

"We won't be far and I'll tell them where we'll be. Okay?"

After what seemed like minutes, Virginia glanced at the clock on the table between her and Lieutenant Kilroy. They had been talking for an hour.

"Thank you for your help. Here's my card, if you think of anything else, please give me a call." Kilroy shook her hand and left.

After he disappeared down the hall, she phoned Abbey and told her about Andy. She paced the floor for what seemed like eternity. A nurse brought Andy down the hall in a wheel chair followed by Dr. Rubbin.

"Well, nothing is broken. His kidneys, jaw and ribs were severely bruised. His head will feel like a base drum for a while. I'd like to keep him for observation but he would rather be with you." He smiled. "I can't say that I blame him. I have written some instructions and here are a couple of prescriptions and my card. Get the prescriptions filled before the drugs we gave him wear off. If there are any problems, call me at once. I'm not expecting any, but you never can tell. Keep him down for a few days. Good luck." Dr. Rubbin shook hands and turned back to the busy emergency room.

Virginia brought her car to the entrance of the hospital. She and the nurse carefully loaded Andy into her car. They left the hospital parking lot and turned north on a busy Newport Blvd. As the road changed into the Newport Freeway, Virginia noticed a white car that ran a traffic light to keep up with them.

"I think your new friends might be still with you," she said.

Andy turned slightly in his seat to look. "It's too dark to tell. Let's see if we can lose them before we get to my place. And, they're not my friends, it's your clock they seem to like. Oooh…my jaw is sore."

"I'll see what I can do, but we're not going to your place, we're going to mine. It's closer," she said. "And be quiet if it hurts. Men."

She sped up to 85, weaving in and out of evening traffic. Angry drivers honked, braked and swerved around her wild driving. The white car tried to keep up. At the last second, Virginia cut across two lanes of traffic to exit at Baker, causing cars to swerve off the road onto the dirt shoulder. Her shadow didn't make it.

"Amateurs!" she yelled. Her heart pounded in her chest. "We'll cut over to the 405 and get off at Culver. They'll never follow us…I hope. We'd better call your friend Lieutenant Killroy when we get there."

She drove frantically down the freeway, wheels squealing with each turn. An American Airline 757 roared over the freeway on its landing approach as they sped by the airport.

"You're going to get us killed…ooh," he said as the seat belt tightened around a sore set of ribs at her next sharp turn off the freeway. "By the way, they got the original map. It isn't very readable, but they got it. Sorry."

"So, why are they following us?"

"I don't know, but at the rate you're driving, they may watch us die."

Virginia wound through the parking lot of her apartment complex, pulled into her parking space and stopped.

Andy, gripping the seatbelt, said, "Can I open my eyes now?"

"And I thought you were a audacious adventurer. Let's get you upstairs and into bed," she said firmly.

She helped Andy upstairs and into her spare bedroom she used as an office. The room was small with light green wallpaper, a single bed on one wall, a tall white storage cabinet on the sidewall, a wooden desk under the window and a mirrored closet on the side they entered. She got him into the pajamas he left in her closet and settled him down under a quilt. He fell asleep as soon as his head hit the pillow. She took the prescriptions to the drug store around the corner at the strip center and returned with his medicine in a half-hour. She collapsed on her couch and dialed the university police.

"Lieutenant Killroy? This is Virginia Davies. On the way home from the hospital we were followed by a white Chevy with two men in it."

"Did it follow you home? Did you get a license number? Were you able to see them well enough to get a description?" he asked.

"No, we couldn't make out the men and we were too busy trying to lose them to get a license number. Sorry. They didn't follow us home. I lost them in traffic."

"Keep your doors locked and let me know if there are any developments. I'll have a patrol car frequent your apartment complex tonight," he said. "Thanks for the report."

Pulling up her kitchen chair, Virginia spread the list and map out on the table.

Leo padded out of Andy's room and hopped on the table.

"This appears to be along the coast, here is PCH or something like it. This looks like 101. A Creek & SJ, what are they?" she asked Leo. "SJ, maybe San Juan? Maybe not." Stretching, she got up and headed to her bedroom.

## ~ *4* ~

"I'm going to do some leg work. You stay here with Leo and rest," she told Andy.

Virginia folded up the list and map then retrieved the medallion. She stuffed them both into her purse and left for the City of Orange and the multitude of antique dealers that lined the shady streets.

A few blocks from Chapman University she slid her car into a parking space, walked to Glassell and turned towards Chapman Avenue and the dealers whose stores fronted the street. The stores were reminiscent of the 1920s and 1930s. Across the traffic circle on Chapman Avenue stood Watson's Drugs, with its' 1940s soda fountain and blue awning covering the sidewalk tables. Next door, on the edge of the traffic circle, was a red brick office building that had a hanging square clock outside. The sidewalks were brick and uneven. The traffic circle, home to a tree-shaded park, added a charm to the little community. Virginia recalled how she and Abbey used to come here on

weekends looking for treasures. It was in the middle of the traffic circle that Abbey decided she wanted to open her own
antique shop, only hers would be at the beach.

Entering each shop that handled coins, Virginia displayed
her medallion for appraisal

"It seems to be an old medallion of some type. Gold most
likely, but I haven't seen anything like it before," stated the first
dealer. "Sorry I can't identify it."

The next four dealers she went to said the same thing.

"The gold is worth about $1500," the fifth dealer told her. "It
could be worth more if we knew what it is, where it came from
and how old it is. The inscription looks interesting." Virginia
walked out of the shop.

As she strolled East on Chapman Avenue, she looked at the
medallion. What can it be? Funny, no one has ever seen anything like it before. Researching this could be exciting, a real
adventure. Well, there's one person I haven't tried yet.

At the drug store phone booth she dialed the telephone
number at the university for Dr. William Gillette.

"Dr. Gillette, this is Virginia Davies. Are you busy this afternoon? I need some assistance and thought you might be able to
shed some light on a mystery I have." After a brief discussion
she agreed to a three o'clock appointment at his office.


Her track shoes squeaked on the tile floor as she walked
down the hall on the second floor of the history building. The
still air smelled of old papers. The corkboards on the walls had
postings for part time jobs, Bible study classes and rooms for
rent ads. Most of the office doors were closed. Light streamed
out of the office at the end of the hall. The paper sign on the
small rectangular corkboard next to the office door said 'Dr.
William Gillette, Professor.'

Virginia stood in the doorway and peered into the large office. On the rear wall hung a large poster of a tropical island. The right wall had a large bookshelf stuffed with books, journals, small dusty statues and figurines. In front of the poster sat a large, cluttered, dark wooden desk with a worn, leather executive high-backed chair. Two file cabinets were to the left of the door in the corner with a potted plant of unrecognizable origin on top. Two wooden armchairs faced the desk. On the wall next to the desk were diplomas, certificates, and awards. Dr. Bill Gillette sat behind the desk reading a copy of Archeology magazine. Gillette was about 6 feet tall, with a full head of gray hair. His tanned face showed off his large brown eyes. He had a lean and fit look for a man of 55. Dressed in casual clothes, he looked more like a businessman than a professor.

"Hello, Virginia, nice seeing you again. What can I do for you?" Gillette asked as he put down a magazine. "You presented quite a mystery on the phone."

"I have something to show you. I can't place where it's from or what it is. Nor can anyone else I've talked to. I've been to a half dozen coin and antique dealers and they all struck out."

She removed the medallion from her backpack and handed it to Dr. Gillette. He turned it over a few times then picked up a magnifying glass. Adjusting his desk lamp he studied both sides of the medallion.

"Pull up a chair," he said absentmindedly. "This medallion you have appears to be Aztec. Probably from around the 1300s to early 1400s. The surface is slightly worn. I may have something here to help us,"

He pulled some books off the shelves and rummaged through them for a few minutes.

"Here we are, look at this." He pointed to a sketch in one of the books. "See how the image on this side of the medallion resembles the drawing."

Virginia compared the medallion and the figure in the book. "The medallion looks like the one here in the book."

"It sure does," he responded. "It looks like Centeatl. He was their god of corn. It was a ceremonial medallion, probably pure gold judging by the weight and appearance. Do you have any more?"

"No, just this one. It was with an old partial map and some sort of list. We got them out of an old clock."

"An old clock? Where did you get it?"

"An old friend, Abbey Mc Queen, owns an art and antique dealership. She got it from an estate sale. Now, even though they don't know about this, some members of the family want it back," Virginia responded.

"It may be part of a smuggler's treasure trove. During the 20s and 30s there was a lot of treasure hunting and smuggling," he said. "A lot of museums and private collectors paid well for artifacts, no questions asked. During the 30s there was bootlegging, which got a lot of attention, but smuggling was still there. It still exists today."

Virginia put her notebook back in her backpack. "Thank you very much for your help, Dr. Gillette. Wait until I tell Andy about this. This is getting more exciting by the minute!" She got up, shook hands with Bill and left the office. She stopped a few feet from the office door. Virginia felt goose bumps run up her arms as a quick chill ran through her. That's strange she thought. What brought that on? She looked for a telephone. Spotting a pay phone at the end of the hall, she hurried toward it.

Dr. Gillette watched Virginia run down the hall. He picked up the telephone on his desk and dialed a number. "Virginia

Davies was just here. She has a gold, Aztec medallion. If there is more, our problems are over."

Virginia dialed her apartment. She shifted her weight nervously from foot to foot until Andy answered. "Guess what? The coin is an old, Aztec, gold medallion from about 1300 to 1400. I saw its brother in a photo in one of Dr. Gillette's books! How are you feeling?"

"Nice of you to ask," he grumbled. "I'm fine, a little sore, but I think I'll live. The pain medicine and muscle relaxants seem to be working. What did he think about the map?"

"I didn't show it to him. I'm headed to the library. They have old maps, maybe something will show up. I'll see you later, take it easy. There is food in the fridge."

"Oh yeah, Lieutenant Killroy is on his way over to get a statement. Did you tell him about the medallion?" asked Andy.

"No. I just told him about the clock and Abbey, and how you were fixing it."

"OK," he said. "Just be careful."


Virginia hung up the phone and walked out of the building. The warm air brushed against her cool skin as she strolled down the eucalyptus-lined walkways towards the central library. As she entered the library, the cool air sent goose bumps down her arms. Virginia headed down the stairs to the map reference area. The reference area was devoid of people except for a librarian behind a desk in back of the counter. She presented her Grad student ID and a note from her advisor to the librarian on duty behind a counter.

"I need some maps of the Orange County coastline from about 1900 to 1941. Do you have any?" she asked

"We have some. They're not a complete set, though," answered the librarian.

The nametag on the librarian said Mrs. Ann O'Brian. She was in her mid-30s, five feet five inches tall, with shoulder length, wavy, chestnut hair and brown eyes and a figure not thought of with a librarian. A light brown blouse topped a short denim skirt. Ann showed Virginia which cabinet held the maps.

Virginia spread the maps out on a map table. The maps were USGS topographical maps. Virginia studied them carefully. She had no clue how to read all the funny lines of different colors. The symbols for schools, hospitals, fire stations and assorted other features she could understand. The lines she figured out indicated elevation, so hills were a series of semi-concentric circles. The shoreline was evident in some. None compared exactly with her map. There were some of the southern part of the county that were similar in certain respects, the relative shape of the coast, Alisio Creek might be A Creek, but she wasn't sure. She carefully placed the old maps back into the large, flat map trays in the blue storage cabinet.

"Thank you for your help," said Virginia. "The maps may have narrowed my search some but didn't do it completely. Do you know anyone else that may have maps from those years?"

"There's a Franciscan priest down at the Mission San Juan who is a nut about the history of the county and early California. He has maps there that we would die for. Hold on a second I'll find his name." Ann rummaged through a black index card box and came up with a dog-eared 3x5 card. "Here it is. His name is Father John Ross. Father Ross has a Masters in Archaeology of all things and is an interesting man to talk to. Tell him I gave you his name, we're friends through some associations we both belong to. I'm sure he will help you if he can."

Virginia wrote the information down in her notebook and walked to the elevators. As she entered the elevator and the doors closed, she noticed two men stroll to the librarian's desk.

Ann O' Brian looked up from her desk, smiled and said, "Can I help you gentlemen?"

"We would like to know what the young lady that was just here wanted and what you gave her," stated Mr. Smith.

"She wanted some old maps of Orange County. They are over there in the blue map cabinet," she said pointing. "I don't think they helped her much though."

"What else?" asked Mr. Jones.

Ann's stomach tightened, she suddenly got tense. "Nothing."

"We think otherwise," said Mr. Jones. He grabbed her by her blouse with his right hand and pulled her to her feet. "You tell me what else or we'll get it out of you!" With that he grabbed the front of her blouse with his left hand and pulled. The buttons popped off and it opened, exposing her white, shear lace bra. "Very nice," he stated as he looked at her, "Very nice."

His hand started to touch her right breast when the crack of a chair slamming against the floor and a shout rang through the empty space. They turned to see a male student running in their direction. He was over six feet tall and as broad as a moose, all muscle. He had long, red hair, light skin and wore a green tank top with jeans. The two men looked at each other. Jones released Ann and they hurried to the stairs and disappeared.

When the student arrived at the desk, he asked, "Are you all right? Wait until I catch those animals!"

"Don't go after them, you might get hurt. Please, just call the police," Ann said.

The University Police arrived in minutes. Ann recounted what had happened to the officers and praised the young man that had come to her aid. During the interrogation, Lieutenant Killroy arrived. The detective asked more questions and stopped abruptly when Ann mentioned Virginia's name. He took frantic notes and ordered a description of the attackers broadcasted to police agencies in the area.

Virginia looked at her watch then headed for her car. She drove to the Laguna Beach Public Library. She parked two blocks away and walked along the tree-shaded sidewalk. Her walk to the library, punctuated by stops in various dress shops and for an ice cream cone took the better part of an hour. She entered the library. The information desk was on her right.

The librarian looked up as Virginia approached. "May I help you?"

The librarian was younger than Virginia had expected. She was a tall thin girl with short, dark hair in her early twenties. The nameplate on the counter said Ms. Joan Franklyn.

"I'd like to see any old maps or history of the area, especially anything to do with underground rivers or caves."

The librarian looked at her for a second. "We have some books on our history but nothing about caves and rivers. There aren't any rivers around here. Just a couple of creeks that can sometimes look like rivers when it rains." She pointed out the books on the local history and geology.

Virginia piled them on a well-used wooden table.

"How about old smugglers operating in the area?" asked Virginia.

"There are stories from the twenties and thirties. During the war…the big war that is…the army had coast watchers to prevent people from sneaking ashore. Now it's drugs. I haven't heard of anything like that here though."

Virginia searched through the books to no avail. She had found four on smuggling during the twenties and thirties. Flipping through each of these, she saw nothing that came close to what she was looking for. They were mainly on bootlegging. She returned the books to the stacks and started to leave when Joan motioned to her.

"Have you tried the historical society? They might be able to help you." She handed Virginia a slip of paper with a name and phone number on it. "Call this lady, she might be of assistance to you."

Virginia thanked her. She went to the pay phone near the rest rooms and dialed the number on the paper.

A woman answered. Virginia introduced herself and explained that the Laguna Beach librarian referred her. She told the woman that she was looking for information on caves with water, and about smugglers from the twenties or thirties.

"I don't think we can help much. There were stories about smugglers and bootleggers, but no underground rivers. If you want to stop by I can show you newspaper articles from then about the smugglers and bootleggers."

Virginia asked if she could come right over. She hung up and started for the historical society. As she reached the door, the librarian was standing just outside looking at the main beach.

"Do you see that old man in the blue jacket, sitting on the green bench watching the ocean?" she asked Virginia. "His name is Thanos. He used to be a fisherman, then he had a restaurant here. He's retired, but loves the ocean. He has been here longer than anyone can remember. You might want to ask him about your caves."

Virginia thanked her and walked across PCH to the bench. The old man sat quietly, holding his cane, watching the breakers roll onto the beach. A seagull sang as he circled above the boardwalk.

Mr. Thanos looked up at the young lady standing next to him and smiled.

"Excuse me, are you Mr. Thanos?" Virginia asked the gray haired gentleman.

He leaned forward on his brown cane, "Yes I am. And whom may you be?"

"Mr. Thanos. My name is Virginia Davies, and I'd like to ask you some questions about the old days here, if it's all right. The librarian, Ms. Franklyn, sent me."

"I'd be honored. I'd get up but these old joints don't work very well anymore. Joan is a nice young lady. Very caring and sweet, especially to an old man with boring stories about the old days. Now, how can I help such a charming young lady?"

Virginia sat down next to Thanos.

"I'm interested in caves in the area that may have water running in them. Like an underground river. Have you ever heard of such a thing around here? I'm a student at the university majoring in history and this fascinates me," she added.

Thanos looked at her, then at the blue green sea. "The officials say nothing like that exists around here. The geology or something about the rocks isn't right for it." He smiled. "What do they know? Have they ever looked? There were stories, ones told by old men…like me…about caves, and one with a river in it. Smugglers use to use them. I've never seen it, or them…but too many stories to be wrong. There has to be some truth in them. Doesn't there?"

"Yes sir, there usually is," answered Virginia. "Did the stories say where the caves with the water are?"

"Not caves." He held up one finger. "Just one cave with water. Somewhere in the hills north of here. Probably on Irvine Ranch or State lands now. I don't know where. Sorry I can't help you. I never really knew for sure, just stories. At my age that's about all that's left. That and my Mary."

Virginia started to get up.

"You know, I just thought of something. There was a man, Old John, many years ago, found a skull and some silver trinkets up in the hills to the north." Thanos took off his glasses and rubbed his eyes. "He talked about treasure and pirates. Everyone thought he was crazy. I saw the silver things. Couldn't figure out what they were."

"Any chance Old John still lives around here? Do you know Old John's last name? Maybe I could find him," asked Virginia.

"Don't think it would do you much good. He died some years back. Heart, yeah know?"

"What happened to the skull and silver artifacts?"

"I don't know for sure. The skull he had for years. Later he sold it to some student or someone. Probably sold the other things too. Didn't have a family or anyone. Just a few of us old timers who he hung out with here at the beach or at a little spot down the coast. It's gone now, too. I never saw the little silver things again."

"Mr. Thanos, you're wonderful. Thank you very much," said Virginia. She leaned over and kissed him on his cheek. "Sorry to leave so soon, but I must find out if Old John was right."

"Ms. Davies," said Mr. Thanos, "Come to think of it, Old John did mention that where he dug up the skull…he thought he could hear running water. Maybe the same cave as in the legend. Who knows? My Mary says they're just stories. I hope it helps you."

"Sir, if I'm right, there may be more truth to your story than you can imagine. Thank you very much."

Virginia scurried to the historical society. They had copies of articles about smugglers. Two mentioned the use of caves for hiding smuggled goods. There were crude, simple maps in some of the old newspapers. The maps were for areas south of Laguna and weren't very good at that. None mentioned water.

Virginia sat back in a chair. The maps told of the use of caves by smugglers but made no mention of underground rivers.

With all the fuss about water in Southern California, if it existed, it would have been exploited by now, she thought. That is unless it is really a lost river. Mr. Thanos was her only direct local link. Now she really knew what mixed emotions felt like.

Virginia returned to her car and drove to Abbey's shop. Abbey was gone. Her assistant recognized Virginia.

"Can I use the phone for a second?" Virginia asked.

"Of course, Ms. Davies, anytime. It's right over there on Abbey's desk."

Virginia called the Mission San Juan Capistrano and arranged to meet with the priest the next morning. She thanked the girl and left the shop.

She opened the window in her car and drove north on PCH toward her apartment. While driving, Virginia kept recounting the conversation with Mr. Thanos. Here was a living verification of the existence of the cave, an underground river and a treasure. The sea breeze and Mr. Thanos lifted her spirits. She pulled into her parking space next to a large spot utility vehicle, shut off the engine, pulled out her backpack and headed for her apartment.

At home, she found Andy watching television in blue shorts and a faded green tee shirt. There were soda cans and pill bottles on the coffee table. Remnants of sandwiches and chips were on the floor. The air had the aroma of popcorn.

"Are we enjoying ourselves?" she asked.

Andy looked up from the chair with a sheepish grin, "How'd it go?"

"Good. She told him about her meeting with Dr. Gillette and the maps in the library. Virginia continued to explain about her visit with Mr. Thanos and the old stories. Then she mentioned Old John.

"Who's Old John?"

"He was a man who found a skull in a cave with water in it and some silver trinkets as Mr. Thanos called them. He said they were in the mountains north of Laguna Beach. Mr. Thanos thinks the caves are real. But, he doesn't know where they are. The real break may be a priest at the mission San Juan. He has a collection of old maps that may help; I'm seeing him tomorrow."

$$\sim \boldsymbol{5} \sim$$

The drive south to the Mission San Juan was easy compared to the commuter traffic jam on the northbound side of the freeway. She nosed her Toyota into parking spot under a sprawling pepper tree in the mission parking lot. Gathering up her backpack she strolled to the entrance of the Mission grounds. Since this was a church, Virginia had decided to wear her hair styled up on her head. She wore a white blouse under a black vest which topped a knee length black pelted skirt that whisked as she walked. She asked the attendant how to reach Father Ross as she dug into her backpack for the entry donation.

"Oh, yes Ms. Davies," he said. "Father Ross is expecting you. Please go on in; he's at the old mission pestering the men doing the restoration. They'll be glad to see you come."

She walked through the grounds past flowerbeds filled with fragrant roses as well as succulents. The mission had a peaceful, relaxing air about it. The sun was shinning on the brown chipped adobe buildings that once housed the kitchens and solder's barracks. The big rough wooden beams that held up the portico or covered walkway seemed to glow. Doves had made nests in the roof tiles of the structure and were cooing softly as she walked by. Inside the construction site a workman, holding a set of plans, waved his arms towards the front of the old church structure.

Next to him stood a Franciscan Priest, complete with brown hooded robes. He fit the picture of a friar with is stomach rounding the front of the robes. His short white hair seemed to stick out in every direction. Virginia guessed him to be about 60 to 65 years old. His face was jovial and kind. His emerald green eyes stood out against a tan wrinkled complexion. A bright yellow hard hat sat almost on top of his head. On the front was a sticker with a bright red cross. He saw Virginia coming and headed toward her.

"Hello, my dear, you must be Ms. Davies." He stuck his hand out toward her. "Nice of you to come."

"Thank you Father for taking the time to see me. I have a puzzle and I'm hoping you can help. There's a lot going on, isn't there?" she pointed to the construction. "And, nice hat, Father."

Father Ross chuckled. "It drives the Monsignor crazy. He doesn't think it's dignified. At my age, who cares? What's he going to do, fire me?"

As they walked through the grounds Father Ross gestured toward the old church and said, "It has been severely damaged by earthquakes over the years. Begun in 1797, it took nine years to build the church. It stood for only six years. On the morning of December 9th, 1812, during a mass, a big earthquake struck. The building crumbled and forty worshipers panicked and died. The Padres never rebuilt the church. The only church remaining was a chapel called Serra Chapel, the oldest building in California."

They walked to the old adobe office building that was part of the mission grounds off the central courtyard.

"As to my problem." She pulled the map out of her backpack. "This copy of a map was found in an old clock with a gold medallion from the Aztecs. I believe the map to be of somewhere around the area. However, the map is incomplete and probably drawn in the 1930s. I'm hoping you can help me pinpoint it better."

They entered Father Ross's musty office through small, thick wooden doors. He patted the door.

"The structure, doors and hardware are the original ones from the early days of the mission, the walls are three feet thick adobe, helps keep it cool," said Father Ross as they entered. "Please make your self comfortable. Would you like some coffee?"

"No thank you. This is an unusual office for a priest, isn't it?" she responded.

The office had bare adobe walls with pictures of St. Francis, the Pope, a family photo with the friar in it, a photo of the governor with the priest, and one of the Dallas Cowboys, again with Father Ross, and a large bronze cross. On a table under the window, on the wall opposite the door, were various artifacts, a big magnifying glass, brushes, dental picks, boxes and a hammer. The massive table, Fr. Ross explained, was made from wooden planks taken from a shipwreck off the coast in the early 1800s. The dark teak and oak table was polished but dusty. In front of it sat an old wooden stool. The large wooden bookshelf was crammed with books, magazines and small knickknacks. Next to it stood a new metal filing cabinet. Father Ross's desk, made of old carved oak, was cluttered with papers, books and a football. She sat in a chair in front of the desk.

"The pastor thinks I'm a little eccentric, which is fine with me." He hung his helmet on an old wooden coat rack. "I love the old things we are discovering about the mission and the area. Now, about your map."

She spread the map out on his desk. "This is a copy, the original was stolen. I think the area depicted is somewhere around southern Orange County, but I'm not sure."

Father Ross examined Virginia's map. He went to the cabinet and retrieved a map. He carefully unfolded it next to Virginia's. "This road map is from about 1933 or '34. Let's see if it helps any." As they compared the maps, it became clear that Virginias' map could possibly be part of what is now the inland section of Laguna Beach.

"See here where the road on your map looks something like PCH on this one. Here is the ocean," Father Ross said pointing. "These bluffs look about right. There are a couple of curves and streets ending on PCH that are close to your map too. This is as close as I can get for you my dear. I hope it helps. Smugglers probably drew your map. It only needed enough detail for them to retrace their steps and not tell anyone else where the treasure was located. As for the reference to caves, I can't help much. These old maps show some, but how accurate I don't know. There are a lot of small caves in the area even today. The road that is highlighted seems to be what is now Laguna Canyon Drive. It wasn't much in those days."

"How about the notation about water in the cave, a 'river'?" Virginia asked.

"I've heard stories about such an idea, but my geologist friends say it is hogwash. I'm afraid I can't help you much there," said Father Ross. "Tell you what, since you're a student and I'm interested in your little adventure, why don't you borrow these for a few days. You could take them to the area and check them out."

Virginia folded up the maps and thanked Father Ross, who walked her to the exit of the mission. Along the way he told her more about the mission and the restoration going on.

"I just thought of something. An old friend of mine is a geologist and contractor in Las Vegas. He told me of an underground river running under the Balley Hotel. It was the MGM Grand at that time. It wasn't just groundwater; it was an actual underground river. They found it when they were sinking footings for the construction of the hotel. Let me give you his name. He might be able to shed some light on your river." Father Ross wrote the name and phone number in Virginia's notebook.

Outside the mission she called Abbey.

"Hi. I've been doing some detective work. I think I've found out what the gold coin is that Andy found, and about where the map was drawn."

"Don't kill me girl, tell me about it!" exclaimed Abbey, "Oh. Andy got the clock going too."

"Who told you about the clock?"

"Andy did, he called a little while ago looking for you."

"It's almost eleven, why don't I meet you at the Jolly Roger for lunch at quarter to twelve?" asked Virginia. "I'll fill you in then."

They agreed.

Virginia found her car and drove to the coast highway. She headed north on PCH to enjoy the ride along the coast. She opened her sunroof, turned on the radio, and enjoyed the sea air that came wafting into the car. The bright sun warmed her skin as she leisurely drove, smelling the fragrance of the flowers and the listening to the music mixed with the muffled sounds of cars along the winding road. Virginia considered how she'd tell Abbey about her discoveries. She found a parking space on Ocean Boulevard and nosed the car in front of a parking meter.

She locked her car, plugged a handful of quarters into the meter, and walked to the restaurant, stopping to look at shop windows along the way. As she entered the Jolly Roger she saw Abbey waving at her.

"First tell me about the clock. Andy said it's running," Abbey said as Virginia sat down at their table.

They were sitting at a white cloth covered table set for four next to the window facing Pacific Coast Highway and downtown Laguna Beach. Virginia looked around the restaurant as if she had never been there before. She liked the motif. The Jolly Roger was decorated like an 1800s New England seacoast establishment. There were paintings of sea captains and sailing ships adorning the walls. The ceiling had large dark oak beams. A massive gray stone fireplace was set near a corner on one wall. The window seats were highly coveted because they allowed a view of the people walking outside. As she peered out the window, the pedestrians included blond surfers in baggy shorts, tank tops and baseball caps on backwards, young girls in bikini bathing suits, or shorts and bikini tops and business men in suits.

"Yes, he got it going. The gears or something were jammed with this," Virginia pulled the gold medallion from her backpack. "It is a gold Aztec medallion from about 1300. Andy found shreds of some sort of a list and parts of an old map, too. No wonder the thing didn't work. What I can't figure out is why someone hadn't found it sooner."

"Probably didn't care if it worked or not. May have just been a piece of furniture to them. Do you still have the map? What's it say?"

"Andy's attackers stole it. However, he copied it and hid the copy before the two thugs attacked him," answered Virginia.

"Who told you about the medallion?"

"I tried antique coin dealers without any luck. A professor at the university identified the medallion. It's supposed to be some sort of religious token to their corn god. The gold itself is worth about $1500. As for the maps, the library wasn't much help either, but, I got a lead from a priest at the mission…"

"A priest?"

"Yes, a priest at the mission, and stop interrupting! He has some old maps of the area and thinks our map is of somewhere around here," stated Virginia. "He gave me a contact in Las Vegas that might help too."

"A priest has contacts in Las Vegas?" questioned Abbey.

Virginia glanced up as two men in dark suits were seated at the table behind Abbey.

"What will you have ladies?" asked the waitress dressed in a buccaneer costume.

"I'll have a glass of white Zinfandel and a Caesar salad," said Abbey. "And put both of these on one check please."

"I'll have the same, but ice tea for me," responded Virginia.

"How is Andy doing? Have the police located the guys that attacked him yet?" asked Abbey.

"He'll live. He's been taking his pills and resting. He'll be as good as new shortly. His ribs were bruised pretty bad but nothing was broken," said Virginia. "He was going to have a friend bring his truck from school. He wants to go to his place this afternoon. The hard head will most likely go back to his lab tomorrow. He won't be moving very fast, that's for sure. The thing that's interesting is that his attackers must have been sent by the people that visited your shop."

"Did you tell the police that?"

"No. I didn't want them involved with the map and medallion. That would really gum up the works." Virginia poked her fork into the tablecloth. "If the treasure really exists, I'd like us to find it."

"What's next?"

"I plan on looking around here for a while then go home and study the map and my notes. Maybe I can narrow the search some. I'll try to contact Father Ross's friend, too…later. I have some shopping to do. I want to look at the clock some more. But, that will have to wait for Andy."

Virginia looked up just as the two men sitting behind them got up, paid their check and departed. They looked somewhat familiar, like she'd seen them somewhere before. She wrinkled her brow. Was it at the university? Oh well, it wasn't important.

Abbey and Virginia ate their lunch and left about an hour later. Abbey returned to her shop. Her part time assistant, Ann, completed the sale of a landscape oil painting as Abbey arrived.

"If you're going to be around a while, I'll get a quick bite now. If that's okay?" asked the assistant.

"Yeah, go ahead," said Abbey. After Ann left, Abbey picked up the phone on her desk and dialed.

"It's me. Virginia has a map to go with the medallion. She's almost verified that the caves and treasure exist and is trying to locate them. I'll stay close to her. If she's right, this could be big enough to be our last jo-…project." She hung up and leaned back in her leather, executive, desk chair. It seemed out of place with all the antiques.

She stared at the pile of correspondence and a photo of her dream. A sleek white two-masted sailboat in a brown wood frame stared back at her.

"Wine tastes on a beer budget. What am I to do?"

Virginia drove up Laguna Canyon Drive away from the ocean. She pulled her car to the side of the road. Small pebbles peened the underside as she slowed to a stop on the road's gravel shoulder. Parked under some eucalyptus and live oak trees she rolled down the window and let the scent of the eucalyptus and wild lilac waft in.

She peered out at the hillside next to the road. "You're up there somewhere," she said outloud. Her mind filled with pictures of pirates and smugglers from a bygone age. She wondered if her feelings now were what people meant by the thrill of the hunt. After surveying the surrounding hills, she pulled into traffic. Turning onto the freeway, she glanced at her rearview mirror. *That's funny. I'd swear that blue Ford's been behind me since the restaurant.* Virginia pulled into her apartment.

Andy left a note thanking her for the help and care: He was going home, he had some things to do there and he asked her to call him with the latest developments. She tossed her backpack on the kitchen table. The air conditioning was humming. Retrieving a bottle of water from the refrigerator, Virginia sat on her couch and dialed Andy's home number. Leo jumped into her lap.

"How are you feeling tiger?" she asked.

"Better, but very sore. It only hurts when I breathe or move. I figure I have nothing to worry about. Only the good die young, so I have plenty of time. How did your investigation go?"

"I talked to a very obliging priest. He even loaned me some maps. I'm going to check them out. He also gave me a contact in Las Vegas that may be helpful. I'm going to have some wine and do some reading up on Willards tonight. Might even hit the sack early. I'll call you tomorrow."

Virginia had little difficulty going to sleep. However, after two hours between the sheets her head began to throb and she had indecisive slumber. She finally mustered the energy to make her way to the bathroom for aspirin. It was nearly 2:30 in the morning when her fitful sleep was disturbed by a slight squeaking sound of a door opening. She knew the sound instantly. Someone was in the apartment with her and it wasn't Andy. He always called out in order not to frighten her.

Her eyes opened wide in the darkness of her bedroom. She heard the sound of muffled footsteps on the carpet in the living room. She lay motionless, listening. Again came the soft, barely discernible footsteps. Virginia moved slowly under the covers to the edge of the bed. She reached for the nightstand. Quietly she picked up the portable phone and pushed the on button. Nothing happened. She looked at the dark shape in her hand. Shit, she thought, the battery is dead. Why now? She dropped the phone on the bed, her hand now reached the drawer of her nightstand. Slowly and quietly she eased it open and removed the small 25-caliber semi-automatic Andy had insisted giving her. With the pistol firmly in her hand, she watched the bedroom door.

Through the living room window, a dim sliver of light shone down the hall, from a security light near the pool. Virginia fixed her eyes on the light and waited for several seconds. Nothing. No movement, no sound. Suddenly the shaft of light was broken. Someone had moved in the other room.

Virginia pulled back the sheet and swung her legs quietly over the edge of the bed. She stood up and tried to get her bearing in the dark room. Small beads of sweat peppered her forehead. She had never aimed a gun at any living thing before. She didn't remember if the gun was loaded. She felt for the clip in the handle. It was in place. Did it have bullets in it?

Dressed in a shear nightgown she considered her options. She could turn on the lights and aim the gun at the intruder, but with an empty gun, she might get herself killed. She could pull the trigger now and if it went off maybe it would scare the burglar and perhaps kill the person in the next apartment, not a good option. Could it shoot through a wall? Andy never said anything about that. What if it only clicked? That would be embarrassing as well as dangerous.

She felt for the button on the side of the handle to release the clip, so she could feel for the bullets. Without placing her hand under the handle, the clip slipped out of the pistol and onto the rug with a definite thud. She accidentally moved her foot and kicked the clip into the hall doorway. The noise made the intruder stop. Silence. The element of surprise was lost, the empty gun was useless and the intruder knew she was awake. She got down on her hands and knees and swept her hands in search of the clip. She crossed the shaft of light in the hall and moved into the shadows beyond when her hand came into contact with a solid object. The object didn't move. She felt a larger solid, with lightweight wool fabric of a man's pant leg above. Pangs of fear possessed her as she lifted up her eyes. A flash of light behind her eyes sent a jolt down her spine and the world faded to black

## ~ *6* ~

A blue Ford pulled into a curbside parking place next to the Mission San Juan. Mr. Smith and Mr. Jones got out. They buttoned their sport coats and walked to the mission entrance. Jones removed six dollars from his wallet for the entrance donation while Smith asked the gatekeeper how to reach Father Ross.

"He should be in his office about now. Just go through the fountain yard right there," he said gesturing, " to the south wing. His office door has a silver cross on it. You can't miss it.

The two men strolled across the garden.

"Good morning." Smith said to an older Spanish looking man dressed in khaki pants and shirt. He had a wide brimmed straw hat covering his dark hair. He was on his knees next to the flowerbed planting pansies. "Can you tell us where Father Ross's office is?" Smith continued.

"Si. Right over there," said the gardener pointing.

"Thank you," Smith responded.

"What the hell did you do that for?" asked Jones. "You trying to be noticed?"

"Just trying to look friendly. Anyway the guy at the gate saw us. And, we're not here to do anything anyone should care about. What's your problem?

The office door with the big silver cross stood ajar. Jones peered inside.

"Father Ross? I'm Mr. Jones and this is Mr. Smith. We'd like a word with you if you don't mind."

Father Ross looked up from his worktable. Smiling he said, "Not at all gentlemen. Why don't we go outside? It's such a beautiful day."

They walked out into the garden. Father Ross leaned on an old, split rail, wood fence.

"Now then, how can I help you?"

"Yesterday you saw a young lady with a map," said Mr. Smith folding his arms across his chest. "You helped her with some information. We would like to know what you told her and we want to see the maps you showed her."

"May I ask why are you interested in the young lady?"

"Professional business," answered Smith.

Father Ross narrowed his eyebrows. "What kind of professional business? You're not police."

Jones opened his jacket exposing the handle of a gun. "Look priest, just tell us what we want to know and no one gets hurt, comprendo?"

Father Ross stood up. "First, you do not come to a church and make demands! Secondly, I don't see that our conversation is any of your business."

"We don't care what you think, just tell us what we want to know, now!" said Mr. Jones.

Father Ross's body stiffened. His eyes became wide and blank. The front of his robe, in the middle of his chest, became wet. He fell forward on the ground. There was a hole in the back of his robe. Smith knelt down and looked at the priest.

"He's been shot." Smith looked around. "I didn't hear anything, did you?"

Jones unbuttoned his sport coat; his right hand slipped under the jacket as he quickly scanned the surrounding area. There was no one in sight, not even the gardener.

"Is he dead?" asked Jones.

"Yeah. We need to get out of here fast. Who the Hell would want to kill a priest? And why now?"

They walked cautiously across the garden and exited through the metal turn styles.

"How do we explain this one to Mr. Jameson? " asked Smith as the climbed into the car.

"I don't know," said Jones. "But we better be history before someone calls the police."

They drove a block down the street and parked in a strip mall. Entering a coffeehouse they ordered French Vanilla coffee and took seats at a small wooden window table with a view of the mission, to gather their wits and wait for the police to converge on the mission. Because they had not rushed away or done anything to draw attention to themselves, they hoped to leave, unnoticed, during the coming madhouse of emergency vehicles and spectators.

They watched as paramedics and fire trucks arrived within minutes. These were followed by sheriffs' cars. As the two men started to leave they noticed a University of California Police car pull up and a detective climb out. He talked to an uniformed deputy and went into the mission.

"Looks like a good time to make our exit," said Mr. Smith.

"I'm Lieutenant Killroy, UCI Police," he said, flashing his badge at the Sheriff's deputy standing next to the priest's body. "Who's in charge here?"

"I am," said a tall detective walking toward him. "I'm Deputy De Santis. Your people put out a notice about any strange occurrences and a Ms. Virginia Davies."

"What does Ms. Davies have to do with the priest's death? She didn't kill him I trust," said Kilroy.

"No. He was very much alive when she left here yesterday. Today he is dead. I thought you might want to know about this," said the deputy.

"Can you give me a rundown on what happened here?" asked Killroy.

"As best we can tell, at this time, two men came to see the priest, a Father Ross, about ten this morning. They were seen leaving about ten twenty. No one heard any shots or unusual noise. No witnesses of the shooting. A lady outside the mission thinks she saw two men get in a blue car parked around the corner about that time. She doesn't know the make, or where it went. The men in it weren't doing anything unusual so she didn't pay that much attention," voiced the deputy. "The suspect used a nine millimeter, probably with a silencer at relatively close range from behind. He never knew what hit him. Got him right through the heart. By the way, what's your girl," he glanced at his notes, " Virginia Davies, have to do with this?"

"Probably nothing. But lately, every time something strange happens, her name turns up. Where she goes, trouble usually follows. It seems there are some real bad characters one step behind the little lady."

As Killroy talked to the deputy a call crackled over his hand held radio.

"Unit five, go ahead."

"Lieutenant. Irvine Police responded to a fire rescue call at an apartment near the campus a short time ago. It belongs to a Ms. Virginia Davies. There was a break-in. She was found unconscious. You wanted to know when anything concerning her turned up," said the female radio voice. "Watch commander says respond code three at your discretion. 10-4."

"Show my 20 at Mission San Juan," said Killroy. "I'll respond code three."

He thanked the deputy and hurried to his car. He turned on the red lights, sounded the siren, spun the car around and rushed toward the freeway.

Lieutenant Kilroy swung his police car into a space between two fire trucks and parked. He climbed out of the car, observing that his was the third police vehicle in front of the multi-story apartment complex. Perched on the sidewalk and grass near the main entrance was a fire department paramedic van. He pushed his way through a small crowd and walked up the stairs to Virginia's apartment and identified himself to the Irvine Police Officer standing outside her door. "Lieutenant Kilroy," he said flashing his badge, "Is Sergeant Thompson still here?"

The large, red headed cop glanced briefly at the identification Kilroy displayed, and moved aside. "Yes sir, right inside."

Kilroy nodded and passed through into the apartment. He spotted Andy sitting on the couch and walked toward him. "Hello, Dr. Clark. How are you feeling?"

Andy slowly pushed himself off the couch and approached Kilroy.

"Hello Lieutenant, I'm doing pretty good, still sore in a few spots but otherwise okay. Thanks for asking. What brings the university police?

Not that I'm not glad to see a friendly face."

"Dr. Clark, you might say I'm interested in everything your young lady does. It seems that where ever she goes, trouble soon follows."

"What do you mean about trouble following Virginia?"

Kilroy smiled. "Let me explain. First you get attacked at the university, over something about that old clock that she has you store there, I think. Then a librarian is attacked after talking to your girlfriend. Then, a priest gets shot after talking to Virginia. Now, she is assaulted. There seems to be a trend here, wouldn't you agree?"

Andy nodded.

"How is she doing?"

"She has a bad headache and a cut on the back of her head," stated Andy. "She's pissed she didn't get to shoot the bastard,"

"That's all I need, her loose with a gun. Please don't go away," Kilroy said turning. "I'll want to talk to you after I've spoken to the Irvine Police."

He walked up to the detective in charge. "Lieutenant John Kilroy, UCI Police, what have you got?"

Thompson dressed in wearing blue jeans and a slightly rumpled blue shirt, his badge attached to his belt, stood next to the kitchen counter looking at his notebook. He looked up a Kilroy approached.

"Hello, Lieutenant, I'm Sergeant Thompson. What we have is a burglary and a young lady with more guts than brains. In a nutshell, she heard the break in, saw the shadow of the intruder, got her gun and dropped the clip. She got hit on the head while crawling around in the dark looking for it. Lucky she wasn't killed. We may know more after the lab crew finishes."

"Was anything taken? The apartment seems to be in pretty good order for a burglary."

Thompson consulted his notes. "According to her and her boyfriend, a Dr. Andy Clark, he's the one who called us, nothing seems to have been taken. Something seems strange about this. I think she's holding something back, maybe you can get it out of her. If you learn anything useful, give me a call.

Kilroy walked toward Virginia's room. "If I learn anything I'll call you, and the sheriff."

"Hello Ms. Davies, I understand you have quite a headache," said Kilroy. "Mind if I ask some questions?"

Virginia was stretched out on her bed, still in her nightgown. She opened one eye. "Hello Lieutenant. What brings the UCI Police here? Weren't the other cops enough?"

"You live within a mile of the campus, that alone gives me authority in this case," said Kilroy. "However, I've taken a personal interest. A lot of strange things have been happening around you and I want to know why. I think it has something to do with the clock in Dr. Clark's lab. I want you, or the good professor out there, to tell me about this little mess you've gotten yourself into young lady."

Kilroy and Andy put coffee on and waited for Virginia to join them at the dinning room table. Virginia walked into the room tucking a thin red tee shirt into a pair of brown shorts. She sat down, poured sugar into her coffee and smiled.

"What did you mean about strange things happening around me?" She leaned on the table toward the lieutenant. She took a sip of coffee as she listened to him.

"So far, in the past couple of days, Dr. Clark has been attacked and his lab searched. A librarian at the university was assaulted. A Father Ross at the Mission San Juan was killed and you were assaulted. Now, if I were superstitious, I'd say you're someone to stay away from. Mind telling me what is behind all of this?"

She dropped her cup. "Father Ross…dead! How did it happen? He was so nice. When did it happen? Who did it, do you know?"

Virginia slowly rose from the table and walked to the patio window and stared out at nothing. Tears ran from her eyes. A cold shiver ran up her spine. She turned and looked at Lieutenant Kilroy.

"What have I gotten us into?"

For the next hour she and Andy told Kilroy about the clock, maps and the gold medallion. Retrieving it from her freezer, Virginia showed the medallion to the Lieutenant.

Kilroy closed his notebook. "With what you've told me, it seems we should have a talk with this Mr. Charles Jameson III." He got up and walked to the door. Opening it he turned, "In the mean time, see if you can stay out of trouble, please!" He closed the door behind him as he walked out.

Andy put his arm around Virginia. "I think you need to go back to bed and rest."

"I'll rest if you call Abbey. We need to find that treasure before anyone else gets hurt," she said heading for her bedroom. She stopped at the threshold and turned.

"How are you feeling, Tiger? At this rate, there won't be one healthy person between us left to find the treasure."

"I'm feeling better. I'm taking it easy and the pills the doc gave me are helping. Now get."

As Andy called Abbey to fill her in, Virginia came out of her bedroom and walked to the patio. She had on a bright blue bikini bathing suit bottom and a towel draped around her neck covering her bare breasts. Virginia stretched out on the patio lounge. She removed her towel and closed her eyes. The warm sun felt good on her skin.

The warm sun relaxed her. It felt like Paris, when she and Abbey would sun themselves on their apartment roof. They would talk for hours about school, antiques, art, teachers and boys. She thought about the time they sneaked into the Roman bath ruins. The future was theirs for the taking. Life was simpler then. What had she gotten them into this time? Part of her wanted to quit. Another part wanted to find the treasure, if it existed. The adventurous side won. The sliding door opened. Andy joined her.

"Abbey thinks you should come to my place for a while, so your night time callers can't find you. She'll meet us later to go over the maps," said Andy.

Sitting up Virginia said, "I need to call that friend of Father Ross's in Las Vegas, Maybe he can help." As she started to get up the world seemed to spin. Everything got a streaked orange color, she sat down on the lounge. "Boy, a little bump on the head can really do a person in."

Andy helped her to her room. After a short rest she changed clothes and packed for a brief stay at Andy's house in Laguna Hills.

After unpacking her clothes, Virginia walked into the Andy's back yard. A five foot light brown stone wall enclosed it. Six tall, broad trees were spaced evenly across the rear wall. The grass was dark green without a trace of a weed. She enjoyed the smell of the roses, hibiscus, and gardenias that grew near the patio. The smell of freshly mowed grass hung in the air. Three small brown birds were jostling for space on the bird feeder hanging from a liquid amber tree. She picked up the cordless phone and dialed the number in Las Vegas that Father Ross had given her. After a few rings a man answered.

"My name is Virginia Davies. Father Ross gave me this number, I'm looking for a Mr. Neil Austin," said Virginia.

"This is Neil Austin, how can I help you Ms. Davies?" responded the voice on the phone.

"First, I'm sorry to have to tell you that Father Ross was murdered. The police are looking for the killers. I don't know how or why but there are two police agencies involved. Secondly, Father Ross told me you knew of some mysterious underground rivers. I'm looking for one and he thought you could help."

"I'm sorry to hear about the good father, he was an old and dear friend. Please keep me posted on their progress and about the arrangements. As for the rivers, I have identified a number of hidden underground rivers, or at least parts of them. I have some maps here in Vegas. Finding the rivers has been a hobby of mine. I think there's some mystery and adventure in them. You know, like where do they come from, where do they go? As a friend of the Father Ross, you are welcome to take a look at the maps that I have if you like. I'll help all I can."

After a brief discussion and setting a time, Virginia hung up and went looking for Andy. A rust colored wall to wall carpet covering the floor in the spacious family room. Green wallpaper topped the oak wainscoting. The sliding glass doors and windows had large brown shutters. The living-dinning room had the same carpet with over stuffed chairs, sofa and a large maple dining room set. The two bedrooms were medium size with queen size beds and dressers. The den had Andy's oak desk, chair, and messy bookshelves. Diplomas hanging on the off-white walls. There were framed photos on one wall. On his desk were papers in neat stacks, a Macintosh computer and printer, and a gold tri-frame photo stand. One photo was of her in a tee-shirt and shorts, the second one displayed her in a wet tee shirt getting out of his hot tub and the last one shown her topless at a beach in Mexico. *Will little boys never grow up?* she thought. At least they're pictures of me and not someone else, or Miss June. As she put it back on the desk, she heard a noise from the kitchen. She found him, his rear end sticking out of the refrigerator.

After lunch they made reservations to fly to Las Vegas the next day. At seven that evening, Abbey arrived. The threesome spread the map and notes out on the kitchen table.

"Okay, where do we go from here?" asked Abbey.

"Well, as close as I can guess, the treasure, assuming there is one, is somewhere in the hills around Laguna Beach. Where I don't know," said Virginia.

"After studying them carefully, and listening to what Virginia gathered from the people she talked to in Laguna, I figure the caves are north of Laguna Canyon Drive. How far north I haven't got a clue," stated Andy.

The trio looked at the maps and talked about Virginia's trip to Las Vegas. After Abbey departed, Virginia and Andy sat up for a while preparing questions for Mr. Austin and making a less detailed copy of their map to take along in case something happened on the quick trip.

*~7~*

The flight to Las Vegas from the Orange County Airport took a little over an hour. Andy rented a dark green Ford minivan at the airport. Virginia kept looking over her shoulder to see if they were being followed.

"Getting a little paranoid, aren't we?" said Andy, as he glanced at the side mirror.

They checked into the Excalibur hotel. Their 'garden room' on the first floor had a view of the pool. A three-foot high hedge surrounded their little patio. After opening the drapes and closing the shears they unpacked. Virginia called Neil Austin. He suggested they meet him at his office and provided directions.

An hour later, Virginia and Andy were seated in Neil's office, located in an executive office complex. The walls were painted a light brown. Photos, diplomas and licenses were displayed on a wall to their left as they entered. Neil's desk was facing the door with his back to the window. Bookshelves were on the adjacent wall. Against the wall behind them stood a drafting table and a computer stand with a large screen computer display terminal perched on the computer. The air conditioning gave Virginia a chill. Neil shook their hands and motioned them to sit down.

Neil Austin stood six foot six, two hundred and thirty pounds with thinning red hair, light complexion and green eyes. He wore a denim shirt and jeans topping a pair of gray lizard cowboy boots. A slight stomach hung over his black belt and oval silver buckle embossed with a steam engine.

"I was shocked to hear about Father Ross. He is…was an old friend," said Neil. "He was a good man with a love for life like few people I've ever known. Is there any word on who may have done this or why?"

Virginia looked at him for a second. She could see the hurt in his eyes.

"They don't know who did it yet. Like I mentioned before, there are two police agencies working on it. They think it may have to do with the reason we came to see you," said Virginia. "As I told you on the phone, I'm looking for an underground river that may flow under the Los Angeles area near Laguna Beach or Newport Beach. Father Ross thought that you might be able to help."

"I have been thinking about your problem. I don't know why anyone would want to kill over it, though. But since Father Ross thought it important, I think I may be able to help." Neil unrolled maps on the drawing board. "Let's take a look."

The first was a combination of Nevada and California and the second was of Orange County.

"Take a look at this map of the two states," he said. "You'll notice the blue lines I've drawn on it. These represent underground rivers. By that I mean real rivers. Masses of flowing water in tunnels, not slow moving ground water. Some run under or near Las Vegas as you can see. This one runs under a hotel here on the strip. We didn't know about it until we hit it putting in support pilings for the building. Some are further out in the desert. They seem to flow either towards the west or to the south."

"What about this one here?" asked Andy pointing to a set of blue lines starting near Los Vegas and traveling southwest towards Los Angeles.

"That one moves under the California desert and heads towards L.A. Look at the map of California. See where it seems to ends up? I believe it goes under Irvine and the northern part of Laguna Beach then out to sea. We have evidence of a river at various locations along the lines but it's never been traced it all the way. With the earthquakes and all, who can be sure it still flows in that direction anymore?" stated Neil. "If it's there, it should be about here," he said, flipping over to a third map under the one of California and pointing. The map encompassed Southern Orange County and the Laguna Beach area. The map indicated the probability of the river being under the mountains to the north east of Laguna Beach.

"Can I copy this?" asked Virginia.

"Better than that, you can have them all. I'm getting too old to tramp around in the hills anymore. If you find it, please let me know."

"Let's go to the casino!" Virginia suggested quickly as they pulled into the hotel parking lot.

"We can't gamble much," stated Andy firmly. He nosed the minivan into a space between two large RVs. "Why don't we go to the pool?"

"We can go swimming later. I want to try blackjack, and the nickel slot machines," said Virginia, like a kid in a toy store.

"The last time we were here, you almost lost your shirt." He glanced at her with sly look. "Figuratively speaking, of course."

"Of course. Party pooper." She gave him a downfall look.

"Okay. Stick to the nickel slots."

Virginia led Andy, by the hand, into the casino.

"Where are the nickel slots? There they are…see you later," she said with a mischievous grin. Virginia darted through the throng of people at the one-arm bandits.

Andy checked his wallet and meandered to the blackjack tables. He lost his allotment of gambling money in an hour. He spotted Virginia walking away from a cashier's booth.

"What did you do, run out of money?" he asked.

"Heavens no. I just cashed in my winnings. Guess how much?"

"How much?"

"Fifteen hundred dollars. I had them give it to me in hundred dollar bills." She held one up. "Isn't Mr. Franklin a handsome fellow? This trip won't cost us anything now. Want to go swimming?"

Andy shook his head. "You're unbelievable. You're the big winner, I guess we'll do whatever you want to do. By the way, how did you win that much on nickels?"

"I didn't. I won forty dollars on the nickel machines then switched to quarters."

"I had to ask…let's go swimming."

They wound their way through the casino to the hallway leading to the guestrooms. Andy opened the door to their room and cautiously entered. Seeing that the room was safe he motioned for Virginia to enter.

"Getting a little cloak and dagger aren't we, Tiger?"

"Better safe than sorry," said Andy. "Especially with everything that's been going on lately."

They changed into their bathing suits. Andy wore green and red surfer trunks that complimented Virginia's green bikini and sunglasses. His ever-present UCI baseball cap, and sunglasses finished his outfit.

Virginia found two lounge chairs and a small table near the pool, shaded by three large palm trees. She tossed a plastic bottle of suntan lotion to Andy and reclined on her stomach.

"Rub it on my back…please," she asked in a demur voice.

Andy opened the bottle and started to apply the lotion to her shoulders, then her back. He unfastened her top and applied more. Next he moved to her legs.

"Okay, roll over," he said with mischief in his voice.

"Very funny. Hook me up, you pervert. I'll do the rest."

"But…fronts are my specialty."

Virginia looked over her shoulder at him and laughed. He looked like a big kid with his hat.

"I know you like fronts…better be just mine you work on Dr. Clark. Go jump in the pool and cool your jets."

The pool water was warm enough to seem like a bath. Andy stretched out on an air mattress and lazily floated about the pool.

While changing for dinner Andy turned the television on to see the news. The local news carried a story about a geologist that was mugged outside his office and was in critical condition at a local hospital. His office had been ransacked and the police suspect robbery as the motive. As the news anchor said the geologist's name, Neil Austin, Andy shivered as goose bumps rose all over him. He hurried to the shower and opened the door.

"Get out quick! You won't believe what just happened! Neil was just attacked and is in critical condition at a hospital!" he said rapidly.

"Another attack? This means someone knew we were coming here." Virginia said stepping out of the shower. "This is getting crazy. Why attack poor Neil, why not us? Hand me that towel, please."

"I don't know." He handed her a beige towel. "We've gotten into more than I want to think about right now"

"We need to talk about it," said Virginia drying off. "Lieutenant Kilroy is right. Maybe we have something that they, whoever they are, want. If they had it, again, whatever it is, they wouldn't need us. We seem to be leading the pack. If they find it, they really won't need us. If you get my point."

"Nice thought," said Andy. "Keep trying to cheer me up. You're probably right. I wish I knew what it was that someone thinks we have. Why attack Neil, he was such a nice guy?"

"Wait a minute! The maps! I'll bet the guy who upset Abbey, what's his name…?"

"Jameson," replied Andy.

"Yeah. Jameson. I'll bet he's responsible."

"That's as good a guess as any," said Andy.

"Lieutenant Kilroy was going to talk to him. Doesn't seem to have helped much, does it? I bet the maps we just picked up are behind Neil's attack."

"You finish getting ready and I'll copy the maps," said Andy as he walked out of the bathroom. He abruptly stopped, turned around and walked back to Virginia and kissed her. She dropped the towel and looked at him with a blank stare.

"Nice work, Sherlock," Andy said as he patted her bottom and left.

Virginia could hear him humming in the bedroom as she applied her makeup and got dressed. We need to follow through with this, if not for the treasure as much as for Father Ross and Neil. Mother always said to finish what you start, she thought. Maybe a nice dinner and show tonight will help us relax.

On their way to dinner they placed a package in the hotel safe and mailed one to Andy's post office box.

As they walked to the casino entrance Andy said, "Any preference for dinner? And by the way you look great tonight, madam."

Virginia spun around showing off her long, flowing, black crepe pleated skirt, black lace tank top, and white blouse tied at her waist. Her blond hair bounced around her shoulders.

"Why not eat at the prime rib place here at the hotel and then go to the show at the Tropicana? You look good too sir!"

Andy gave her a small smile and swallowed. His blue, Docker pants were topped with an open collared, tan, Docker shirt with a small gold chain around his neck. They walked past the statues of medieval armored knights, side show games and video game rooms for kids. The tinny sounds of the slot machines and coins dropping into their metal trays made talking difficult. Cigarette smoke and the masses of people seemed to follow them to the second floor restaurant, Sir Galahad's. The restaurant's exterior walls were made of large stones, like a castle wall with stained glass windows. The inside walls were surfaced with dark wood with an open beam ceiling. A large stone fireplace adorned a wall. A suit of armor stood next to it. Swords, battle-axes and assorted arms adorned the walls. The table and chairs were heavy, solid, dark oak.

"We would like a table in the rear facing the door if possible," Andy said to the maitre'd.

Seated, Virginia said, "What do we do about Neil? The poor man was attacked because of my treasure hunt. I don't want to quit. I'd like to finish this, what do you think? Then again, maybe we should stop. I'm confused. I wouldn't want anything to happen to you."

"It isn't like you to give up easily. It isn't in your nature. Anyway, if someone else is after it, they might try and get you or both of us for the information we might have. Here comes our waiter, lets order and discuss this later."

Virginia ordered an end cut prime rib, asparagus and Yorkshire Pudding. Andy had a steak and baked potato. While waiting for their food, Virginia launched into a brief factual comparison of the real versus the Hollywood medieval times and their simulated surroundings.

"Boy you're original, steak again, why not be daring and try something new?" asked Virginia between bites of her meat.

"I like it. Anyway, you're daring enough for my tastes," Andy responded.

She kicked him.

After dinner, they strolled across the street to the Tropicana to see the Follies. The slight breeze was still warm. The air smelled of a tropical flower garden. The lights, streams of cars and noise added a sense of electricity to the air.

Standing in line for the show Andy put his arm around Virginia and said, "We'd better get an earlier flight tomorrow. Someone knows we are here, and they might know our flight number. Maybe we can throw them off by leaving early."

"Sounds like a plan to me." They moved up in the show line. Andy placed a fifty dollar bill to the matre'd. They were seated two rows from the front in the center. During the wait for the show they ordered drinks from a young, cocktail waitress. She returned shortly with their drinks and a message that she indicated was left at the door for Dr. Clark. Andy opened it. A computer print out read:

> *Leave the materials Mr. Austin gave your hotel front desk*
> *in an envelope marked Mr. Robins. Do not tell anyone*

*about it and forget the treasure. It would be a shame to not have the pretty lady live.Enjoy Las Vegas.*

He handed the note to Virginia. A cold sweat broke out on his forehead. The vinyl seats became hot and sticky. He looked at Virginia. She carefully folded the note, slid it in her purse, smiled and leaned closer to Andy.

"Not on your life, forget what I said earlier. We are in this to the finish. No son-of-a-bitch is going to tell me what to do."

"How can you be so casual? It threatens your life?"

"I have a plan. Let's enjoy the show."

"Another one of your plans? Now that's scary. I still don't see how can you enjoy the show after reading that note?"

"For one thing, what am I suppose to do? I'm in going to be just as jittery in our room as here. Only here, there are a lot of people, there's safety in numbers, I hope. Secondly, we paid for the show. I want to see it. They won't make a move until later, after they think we've given them what they want. So for now, I think we're safe. Don't you?" Virginia sat back in the booth and took Andy's hand as the lights dimmed.

After the show, they walked out of the hotel. The warm breeze caressed Virginia's skin. The smell of tropical flowers seemed out of place with the dense traffic and throngs of people wandering between casinos. Virginia took her tied blouse off and handed it to Andy to carry. The lace tank top allowed the warm dry air to wash over her. Her mood shifted to serious.

"When we get back to our place, we need to call Abbey and have her meet us," she said. "With what we have, I think we need to start doing some field work."

"I think we need to talk to Lieutenant Kilroy too," stated Andy. "We also need to figure out how to respond to the little note we got. By the way, are you trying to cause a scandal Ms. Davies? You look very provocative."

"Since they don't know what we have, we could give them anything. Do you have those maps we brought with us in the room? We could mark them and use them as dummies. And, I was hoping you'd notice."

"I don't think that will work. The map idea, I mean. We may be able to copy the one we have in the safe and mark it so it will be confusing. All it will do is slow them down," said Andy.

"It may buy us some time," said Virginia. "Have you been watching to see if we are being followed?"

"Yeah. But who could tell in all these people."

Andy approached the front desk and asked for access to the safe.

"The night manager is away from the desk at this time sir," stated the clerk. "He is on the grounds though, as soon as he returns I'll have him call you."

Andy and Virginia walked past the empty area to their room. Virginia went into the bathroom. Andy turned on the television to see if there was any news about the attack earlier and changed into shorts and a tee shirt, waiting for the front desk to call. He opened a small bottle of wine from the little refrigerator in the room and turned off the lights. Andy pushed the pillows up against the headboard and sat up on the bed. The room was dark except for the soft light from the television. The sheer drapes were drawn closed.

Virginia walked around the dressing area wall into the room. Her nude skin seductively reflected the soft dancing light from the television. She climbed on the bed and positioned herself on Andy. Her firm breasts blocked the television. Andy lost interest in the TV. She could be an erotic woman. Unwilling to be just the receiver of the stimuli, she like to be the aggressor as well.

The subtropical shrubs that partially hid the large sliding glass patio door, were the same shrubs that partially concealed the two men crouched there between the shrubs and the patio wall. The first man, Frankie, in his late thirties, tried to hide his five foot four inches tall and round frame in a dark shirt hanging over matching shorts. The dark blue baseball cap covered his balding head. He held a .32 caliber semiautomatic. The second man, Jim, slightly taller, was blond, mid twenties and muscular wore a nondescript dark colored shorts and shirt. They could easily blend into a crowd.

"Are they in the bedroom yet?" asked Frankie.

"I'll say, take a looka this!"

"Holly shit, they're going at it. Wow! Is she something or what?" said Frankie.

"You don't have that damned camera with yea either, do you?"

"The boss didn't say anything about pictures, he said to see that they put what that scientist gave them in an envelope and delivered it to the front desk, then waste 'em. Anyway I'd want a video cam. The hell with photos," responded Jim.

They crouched in the shrubs, open-mouthed until their knees hurt and watched.

"Why did the boss want to waste them? Seems a shame," said Frankie.

"Frankie..."

Jim poked Frankie's arm. He pressed his fingers to his mouth and pointed towards the pool area. People in swimsuits had congregated near the pool.

"Yeah, let's beat it. We'll tell the boss that his people in California will have to wait," said Frankie.

Jim and Frankie scurried to the corner of the hedge away from the pool and walked away, leaving two nearby guests to wonder the two men had been doing in the bushes.

Virginia swore as the phone rang. She rolled over across Andy and answered, "Yes?"

"Dr. Clark please, This is the night manager."

She handed the phone to a grinning Andy and rolled off of him.

"Dr. Clark," he said.

"This is the night manager, sir. The desk clerk said you wanted to get into your box. I'd be happy to assist you. I'm sorry for the delay."

"I'll be right there. Give me a couple of minutes."

"No problem, sir."

Virginia and Andy quickly put on some shorts and tee shirts and hurried to the lobby. After extracting the package, they walked through the casino then back to their room.

"See anyone suspicious?" Virginia asked.

"No and yes, I'm getting jumpy."

Safely in their room, Virginia cleared off the desk while Andy removed the maps from the package. Andy spread the maps out on the desk. He sat down and carefully added some marks, to the map, with a pen Virginia had taken from Neil's office. Virginia settled on the small couch and composed a note on a piece of paper with Niel's letterhead on it, describing the geology of the desert and a possible underground river near Newport Beach, the San Fernado Valley and Pasadena. She circled part of the valley.

"This and the map will give them something to keep their nasty little minds busy for a while," she said.

Andy pulled an envelope from the nightstand, stuffed the papers inside and sealed it. Virginia wrote Mr. Robins on the front.

They hurried across the pool area, through the casino, to the lobby and gave the envelope to the desk clerk. As they turned, Virginia heard the sound of a television from an office to right of the front desk area. An announcer was finishing a report about the death of Neil Austin.

"Did you hear that? Neil is dead."

"Yeah. He was a nice fella," stated Andy. "He died because of us. That thought really makes me feel sick."

"I know. How about just turning everything over to Lieutenant Kilroy?"

"That would be fine, but until they find out who is responsible, whoever is behind all this will keep going, find the treasure and be long gone before the cops get off square one. Then everything was for nothing," said Virginia. "We need to find it and turn it over to the authorities before too many more people get hurt. We owe it to the good Father and Neil."

Andy looked down and shook his head. "You're right. Do you know what time it is?"

"Yeah, about 2 am. Why?" answered Virginia.

"We have a plane to catch in the morning, I'm not sure we'll be awake in time."

"Not to worry love, I moved our reservations to noon from the phone in the bathroom while you were watching TV."

Virginia placed a call to Lieutenant Kilroy after breakfast.

"Good morning Lieutenant," stated Virginia. "I've got some disturbing news for you."

"Oh no. What happened? Are you all right?"

"Yeah, we're fine. We're in Las Vegas visiting a geologist, Mr. Austin, that Father Ross told us about. We saw him yesterday. He was attacked and died last night."

"Did you contact the local police?"

"No. We're coming home. I thought you'd be interested. There isn't anything we can tell them anyway."

"I'll call them. They may want to interview you two later."

Virginia and Andy left the Excalibur a little after ten thirty for the airport. They checked their minivan into the rental agency and walked to their flight gate under the watchful eyes of Frankie and Jim. As they boarded their flight Jim went to a pay phone.

"You can tell your client that the birds have flown," said Jim. "And the documents are in route."

$$\sim \textbf{\textit{8}} \sim$$

"You call Abbey while I get the bags," said Andy scurrying towards the baggage claim area. "I'll meet you at baggage claim."

Virginia walked to a pay phone and dialed Abbey's shop.

"Well, hello, stranger. If all it took to get a trip to Las Vegas with a cute man was a blow to the head, I'd hit myself. How'd it go? Win anything?" asked Abbey

"It went well. We got some information on underground rivers near Laguna. And, I did win at the slot machines and at blackjack, they're the only two things I know how to do there."

"Do you want to get together and go over what we have?"

"Yeah, Andy thinks we should look at what we've got and plan our next moves. How about this evening?" asked Virginia.

"Sounds good, see you at your place about seven."

Virginia hung up the telephone and hopped the escalator down to the baggage claim area. As she descended, she caught a glimpse of Andy pulling their bags from the baggage carousal. He joined her at the exit.

"Abbey will meet us about seven at my place," stated Virginia picking up her bag.

Retrieving Andy's truck from the parking structure they drove to his post office box and picked up the package he sent from Las Vegas. Virginia looked at the package resting on her lap. Neil may have been killed for what was in there. The thought of him and his dying struck her again. Her eyes filled with tears. She wiped a tear and opened the wrapping. Her hands were clammy as she removed the maps that Neil Austin had given them.

"Good thing we mailed these. Poor Neil, someone killed him for these. No telling what might have happened if they had been on us," said Virginia. "I can't wait to show these to Abbey!"

While Andy unpacked, Virginia stowed her bags next to the door. She returned to the kitchen as Andy spread the maps and notes on the kitchen table.

"The best I can make of this is that the area where our river should be is about here," he said drawing a circle on one of the maps. He pushed it towards Virginia.

"Looks good to me. It's consistent with what Mr. Thanos told me. He said the legend told of a cave with underground water about in that same area. That's about where Old John found the skull and silver too. We need to show this stuff to Abbey. She wants to help us search the areas we select. She's coming to my place about seven. Why don't we freshen up have lunch and look the area over before dinner. You're buying. We can meet her at my place then."

"What do you mean, I'm buying? That's all I ever do. Anyway, you're the big winner," said Andy, wide-eyed.

"Think of it as an investment. You've got so much invested in me, you couldn't afford to stop now. You might as well keep me. And for your information, that's not all you do," Virginia said smiling. She picked up her bag and walked out to her car with a sexy wiggle.

Andy shrugged and locked the door.

Virginia threw her bags in the trunk and drove to her Apartment with Andy following in his truck. Andy noticed a green BMW parked in the street outside of Virginia's apartment building. The man seated next to the driver used binoculars to watch the buildings and follow Virginia's Toyota as she pulled into her parking space. Andy noted the license number as he drove past.

As they entered the apartment he said, "Why don't you unpack while I get a beer? I'll meet you on the patio."

He watched Virginia go to the bedroom. Andy dialed Lieutenant Kilroy's number. He finished describing the car and its occupants to the lieutenant as Virginia walked into the room.

"Who were you talking to?" she asked.

"Lieutenant Kilroy, I told him about our trip and a car I saw watching this place. I saw it as I drove up. Didn't want to scare you."

"The green BMW? I saw it too. How are we going to go exploring with them following?"

"Well, we'll be on state and Irvine company land. Maybe they won't be able to follow us very far. Anyway, it is rugged terrain we'll be on. Kinda hard to follow someone without being seen unless you are trained for it. Let's hope they're not. That reminds me, we need to get permission to explore the areas we want. I'll contact the state parks department. I can use the university and my 'title' as a cover. You might want to try the Irvine Company."

"Why don't you call for a pizza while I change? We can have lunch on the patio and figure out how to get them to let us on their land."

As Andy called for pizza Virginia changed into brown shorts and a bright red tank top. She carried ice tea for herself and a beer for Andy to the patio. The warm gentle breeze felt good on her skin. She retrieved her sunglasses from the kitchen counter and sat at the patio table. Leo scampered back into the apartment. The pool area had three men sitting around it and two women were in the shallow end of the pool talking. She heard the doorbell sound, and a few minutes later Andy walked out on the patio with the pizza. As they ate, Virginia noticed two gardeners on the far side of the pool.

"Andy, do you see those two gardeners? That area they're digging in was worked on the other day. They seem more interested in us than work. Are you thinking what I'm thinking?"

"Yeah, I see them. You keep their attention while I go see what they're doing."

"How am I going to keep their attention and have them not notice you're gone?" she asked.

"I don't know, think of something."

He got up and took his beer with him. She watched him set it on the counter and hustle out the front door. Virginia moved to the lounge and slowly removed her shorts revealing a black thong bikini. She slowly removed her tank top exposing her bare breasts, and stretched out on the inclined lounge. That got the attention of the men and gardeners around the pool. Behind the sunglasses she watched as Andy approached the gardeners. He startled them as he spoke. The heavy-set gardener jumped up and swung at Andy. The second and younger of the two looked at his partner, then back at Virginia. As he turned to see what was happening, a tall muscular man from the pool area jumped him pinning him to the ground. Andy knocked the first one to the ground and sat on him.

"Who are you and what are you doing here?" asked Andy.

"We don't have to talk to you. You're not the police," said the young gardener. "You can't just assault people, there's a law."

Andy doubled his fist and pulled his arm back. "Watch me."

"I ain't talkin'."

"You'll talk to us, or what's left of you can talk to the police," said the young man from the pool. He flipped the gardener over and wrestled his arms behind him. The man's bathing suit dampened the gardener's uniform as he pulled the bent arm of the gardener further up his back.

The gardener screeched in pain.

"Talk or it comes off," added the fellow from the pool.

Andy leaned forward putting more weight on the man's chest under him. The gardener tried to push Andy off. Andy grabbed the man's arm and wrenched it backward across his knee. As he applied more pressure to the forearm, the man screamed. "Ease up man, you're going to break it!"

"No shit," said Andy. "We don't like being spied on. Talk!"

"We've got rights ya know."

Andy looked at the man, grinned, and put more pressure on the bent arm. "Right now you two got the right to talk or have your arms broken. Make up your minds fast, I'm loosing my patience." He tugged on the arm. The fellow from the pool did likewise.

"Okay, okay, we were hired to watch you and the girl and report where you went," grunted the second gardener. "There wasn't suppose to be any rough stuff. Ease up, man."

"Who hired you and how do you report?" asked Andy shifting his weight.

"We were hired by a woman. Ms. La France. I don't believe it's her real name. Short, had a bad, red wig on and a long dress. She paid us $200 each to watch you today. We call her every two hours. After each call she gives us a new number to call. That's all we know. Honest," said the man under Andy. "Just a quick $200."

"Let them go," said Andy getting up. "Get the Hell out of here. Oh, and tell Ms. La France if I find her she's toast!"

The small crowd that had gathered slowly dispersed as Andy walked back to the apartment. He watched the two spies run from the apartment complex rubbing their arms.

"Nice job of distracting. You distracted the whole complex. Couldn't you have thought of something a little less provocative?" he asked as he entered the apartment. "What would your mother say?"

"It worked, didn't it?" Virginia put her shorts and top on. "And why are you complaining now? You didn't mind before? And sir…about the topless photos you have of me in your wallet, and your den. Remember the beach?" Taking the pizza box and glasses to the kitchen she said, "Shall we head over to Laguna to scout our adventure? We can have Abbey meet us in Laguna for dinner." She turned toward Andy and snickered. "My mother doesn't have to know about my method of distracting the world. I won't tell if you don't."

"Okay. You win. I'll make reservations at the White House for seven. We should be done before then so we can spend some time looking at the shops," said Andy. "Don't forget a sweater for later."

After calling Abbey to tell her of their plans, they left the apartment and pulled out of the parking lot in Andy's truck. They drove down PCH through Newport Beach and the quaint shops of Corona Del Mar. As they drove by the state beach, they could hear the crash of the surf and smell the salt air. Traffic became heavier in North Laguna. Old seacoast houses, clapboard shops and art galleries surrounded them on both sides of the road. As they entered Laguna they turned east on Laguna Canyon Drive. Driving past shops, restaurants and the Laguna Playhouse, Virginia pulled out the maps.

"I don't remember any roads or trails on that side of the road, do you?" she asked nodding toward the North side of the highway.

"No, but that sketch was drawn over sixty years ago. Probably not much left of one by now. We should be getting close, watch the left side."

They drove the length of the road twice. They stopped three times at areas that looked promising. No luck.

"The old trail may be under a building by now or overgrown," said Andy. "We'll never see it."

"Pull up over there," said Virginia pointing to a parking area. "This should be close. We can look on foot from here."

"Okay. But don't get your hopes up." Andy turned into the parking area off the road. "Sixty years is a long time."

Andy pulled the truck in a dirt parking area and parked it against the railroad ties used as curbs. They locked it as they got out. Virginia was already to the edge of the parking lot facing the hills when Andy caught up.

"I'll start this way, why don't you go that way?" stated Andy, pointing to the west end of the lot.

They scouted the area for almost two hours. Virginia glanced at Andy every few minutes with anticipation as Andy squeeze between bushes and searched the ground for anything that looked like an old road or dirt trail. Virginia scouted the opposite end of the parking lot. She walked up a small footpath a shot distance. Her disappointment, when it stopped twenty yards up the hill, was evident even to Andy from across the parking lot. The combination of the hot sun and dusty trail made her thirsty and tired. Taking a break, Virginia sat on a log used as a curb next to the brush. She felt hopeless. Maybe it was just a legend after all. No treasure, no caves. As she glanced around, something unusual caught her eye. There, next to her, was what looked like a set of old ruts in the soil. She would have missed this had she been standing.

"Andy, Andy, come here!" Virginia shouted.

Andy ran to her, "Are you all right? What's the matter?"

"Pointing to an overgrown area she said, "I think this is our road. See the ruts? "

Pushing the brush aside, Andy and Virginia looked at what had been a dirt road many years ago.

"Good going, I'd have missed that," he said. "The location is about right for the map. Looking at this terrain, we'll need some equipment to go exploring. No point in getting hurt out here."

Virginia's heart raced. "When can we return? We need to tell Abbey. This is great! What do we need? When can we get the stuff?"

"Easy does it. I'll make us a couple of lists. We can get the stuff tomorrow and be back to investigate early the next day. If that meets with your approval?"

"That's great," said Virginia dancing around ahead of Andy as they walked to the truck. "Now, let's go look around Laguna. I'm thirsty, you can buy me a drink and a caramel apple."

The rest of the afternoon Virginia dragged Andy from one shop to another. They bought two caramel apples and ice teas. Virginia found a bench on the boardwalk facing the ocean. They ate their apples and drank the tea while Andy made the list of equipment they would need for their exploration. The sun was setting. The big red ball seemed to slowly slip into the dark blue Pacific. The sky had streaks of red running through a sea of light blue. The breeze off the ocean had picked up and the air had a distinct nip in it. Virginia pulled on her Bugs Bunny sweatshirt. Hand in hand they walked towards the White House to meet Abbey.

The White House, an established favorite in the beach community, was a white building with black letters announcing its location on PCH. The outside seating in front allowed for a better view of the ocean and people parading by. Abbey walked up as they approached from the opposite direction.

"Your table is ready Dr. Clark," said the Maitre 'd as he turned. "If you and your guests will follow me." He seated them at a corner outside table and took their wine order.

"Not bad service for a university professor. Just how much time do you spend here without me, Dr. Clark?" asked Virginia.

They ordered dinner and sipped their wine. The evening air was getting a slight chill. The sky was a rosy red as the sun sank into the sea.

Abbey leaned across the table and said, "What have you found out? I'm dying to get every last detail. How can I help? I feel like a stepchild. You two have done everything and suffered the consequences and I haven't done a damn thing."

Virginia described the past few days in detail. The attack on the geologist in Los Vegas and the pair of men watching Virginia's apartment startled Abbey.

"You have been through Hell and back. How did you get the guys by the pool to talk?" asked Abbey.

"Virginia distracted half of Irvine while a fellow by the pool and I nailed the bastards," said Andy.

"How did you distract them and half of Irvine?"

"I took off my tee shirt and shorts."

"What did you have on then?"

"Black bikini panties." said Virginia taking a bite of her salad.

"That'll do it. You must be more careful girl, we're not in France anymore." said Abbey. "What have you two decided to do, and how can I help?"

"We've prepared a list of everything we'll need for now to go exploring. You and Virginia can try and get Irvine Company permission to go on their ranch. I'll get the state parks department to give us a permit for their land. We need to purchase the stuff on the list too," said Andy cutting his steak.

"I'll buy the stuff on the list," said Abbey. " It's the least I can do. I'll call the Irvine Company first thing in the morning too. Maybe we can get the permit tomorrow."

## ~ *9* ~

Abbey said good-by and walked up the highway toward her shop thinking. She needed to call her partner with the news. This is getting better each day, she thought. She could already smell the money. Abbey unlocked the door to her shop. She wound her way to the alarm system control panel to turn the system off when she noticed the flashing green light. A voice spoke out of the darkness.

"Tell me how we're doing, my dear."

"I'll get the lights."

"No. Someone will notice us. How'd it go?"

Abbey sunk into a small rocking chair. "Very well. They may have stumbled onto something. We'll be exploring in a couple of days."

"Why so long?"

"We need to get permission to go on the land and will need some supplies," answered Abbey.

"Any word on the Jamason competition?"

"Yes. Virginia and Andy sent them a false map and notes. That should keep them off balance for a while."

"Good. Keep me posted. Remember, this could put us on easy street."

Abbey watched the dark figure walk to the door. As the door closed behind him, she muttered, "I'll remember."

# *~ 10 ~*

Virginia's answering machine picked up the call after several rings. "It's me, you're probably still asleep, or in the shower. Anyway I got us an appointment at the Irvine Company public relations office at ten thirty. I'll pick you up about ten. The man on the phone sounded like a nice guy and kinda young. Do you have a story for them yet? We can't tell them we are on a treasure hunt. See yea about ten."

Wrapped in a towel, Virginia played the message from Abbey. She dressed in a pair of tan cotton slacks, a white blouse, a red sport jacket and did her hair up in an effort to look sophisticated. She spun around in front of the mirrored closet doors. Looks pretty good she thought smiling. I hope we can pull this off.

Virginia walked to the front of the apartment complex. Abbey's blue BMW roared up to the curb. She noticed how striking Abbey looked with her long dark hair flowing over her shoulders above a light green pants suit. Virginia climbed in and they drove towards the Irvine Company headquarters. A green Chevy pulled into traffic behind them.

Abbey adjusted her center rear view mirror. "We've got company. I hope they're paid by the hour."

Abbey drove to the Irvine Company Headquarters building and parked in the tree shrouded visitors parking lot.

They walked into the reception area and asked for Mr. John Miller. The receptionist called his office. "His secretary will be right down. Please have a seat," she said.

Virginia and Abbey studied the old photos of the area including Laguna Beach, displayed around the room. The Irvine Company was one of the largest landowners in the Orange County area. The company had developed the City of Irvine as a model city. The University of California now sat on what once was Irvine Company land. Even today the ranch land holdings were immense. Cattle still roam the ranges near Irvine and Laguna Beach. A few minutes later, a secretary arrived. "Ms. Davies and Ms.

Mc Queen? Please come with me. Mr. Miller is expecting you."

She escorted them to Miller's office. As they entered, Virginia's eyes swept the office. The corner office was on the seventh floor of the building with glass windows providing a panorama of Irvine and Newport Beach. A potted palm decorated the far corner. A wide blond wood desk sat before the window with three chrome guest chairs set in front. A small table sat in a corner surrounded by two love seats.

As Virginia and Abbey entered, John Miller rose from his leather executive chair and smiled. Virginia figured he was about thirty-five, and about five feet eight. He had straight sandy hair and strong build. She chuckled to herself as he nervously adjusted his wire-rimmed glasses that covered large brown eyes. His smile broadened.

"Good morning ladies. Welcome to the Irvine Company," said Miller retaking his seat. "Please be seated. From our conversation earlier Ms.

Mc Queen, I understand you would like permission to do some exploring on part of our ranch. Is that correct?"

"Yes," said Abbey.

Virginia squirmed in her seat. "We would like to do some exploring for some artifacts we believe may be there. I'm a graduate student at UCI in history, and doing a thesis on the subject. Professor Clark, from UCI, will be with us. We'll be very careful."

"I believe you will. We have a good relationship with the university can let you on the ranch without much trouble. You'll have to sign some documents releasing us from damages should you get hurt. We'd also like to know what, if anything, you may find. As you are aware, anything you find on the ranch belongs to The Irvine Company and must be reported." Miller picked up a pen and fiddled with it in his fingers. "You will need to promise to leave things as you found them. Clean up after yourselves. What kind of artifacts do you expect to find?" He smiled at Abbey.

"We're looking for materials that may have been left by smugglers and bootleggers during the twenties and thirties. People usually think of them in the east. We had them here too," answered Virginia. "What did you think, buried treasure?"

Miller Laughed. "No, nothing like that. Researchers have found fossils here. I thought, maybe, that's what you wanted to look for. I've never heard of smugglers around here. Then again, I haven't lived here all my life either. This sounds much more interesting than fossils." He turned toward Abbey. "You will be careful I trust. I'd hate to see you get injured. It is pretty rough territory."

"We'll be very careful. What do we do next?" asked Abbey.

"We'll get you the proper documents in case our security, or the Sheriff, finds you on our land. We'll notify them so there shouldn't be any problems."

After the brief meeting, Mr. Miller's secretary escorted Virginia and Abbey to the legal department for their permit.

Walking out of the building Abbey said, "That was quaint. You told him what we are going to do and he went along with it. That was class!"

"Did you notice, he couldn't keep his eyes off of you?" asked Virginia. "You may have a new admirer."

"Yes. But I also noticed the ring on his left hand. Too bad. He was cute."

"Let's get going, we need to pick up our shovels and stuff from Andy's list," said Virginia. "There is an Army-Navy store in Orange that has what he wants. They're fold-up types the Army uses. Easy to carry."

As they drove to The City of Orange, Virginia called Andy from the car phone. "Hi, we got the permits. How did you do?" she asked.

"Great, We can go on the state park land and while I was at it I got county permission. Now we can go wherever we need to in the area. Where are you two now?"

"We are headed to the store to get the supplies. Abbey is buying them. We'll see you at your place."

They drove to the City of Orange, about ten miles from the Irvine Company. Abbey squeezed her BMW into a parking space a few yards from the military surplus store.

"I don't see our tail," said Abbey. "Maybe he couldn't find a parking space. Think we should wait for him?"

Virginia gave her a dirty look and opened the door. "Don't joke. Those men are dangerous. Anyway, they'll find us. Your car isn't exactly camouflaged."

"Yeah. And we're a little over dressed for an Army Surplus store," commented Abbey.

After purchasing the supplies, Virginia and Abbey drove to Andy's house. Andy unloaded the supplies into the garage.

"I'll make up our adventure kits tonight. We can get a start first thing in the morning," said Andy lugging the bags in the garage.

Abbey climbed into her car, leaned her head out the window. "I have some things to attend to. I'll see you tomorrow. Do we meet here? Do you want a ride home?"

"Yeah, we'll meet here," said Virginia, "No. I think I'll stay here tonight."

Abbey drove off with the car phone stuck to her ear.

"I'll change and help you," said Virginia walking toward the door.

"Stay like that. I thought we could go for an early dinner after I finish this."

"Okay. By the way, how long has that green Chevy been there," she said nodding.

"Right after you got here. Looks like you two picked up a fan club while you were out. Why don't you put our permits in our usual cold storage…just in case."

Virginia sealed the documents and maps in baggies and placed them in the freezer under a large frozen pizza. She placed some frozen waffles on top of the pizza and closed the door. That should do it she thought.

Andy completed the project of making 'adventurers' belts, from army web belts complete with army folding shovels, picks, waterproof flashlights, coils of rope and pouches for carrying small items they might find and canteens. Locking the garage, he went in to take a shower and dress for dinner.

"Andy," called Virginia from the bedroom. "One of the men in the car is missing, now what?"

"Not to worry my dear, I've got it covered."

He finished talking as the backyard sprinklers came on.

Virginia ran to the bedroom window just as a man in a dark, wet, suit climbed over the wall into a neighbor's yard. The neighbor's dog didn't approve. The man scrambled over the fence and ran from the yard to the waiting Chevy. The car sped off.

"Dr. Clark. What did you do?" asked Virginia as Andy stepped out of the shower.

"I rigged a motion sensor to the sprinklers. The main alarm system only works when someone enters the patio, garage or the house. This way I tend to discourage them before they enter. It's legal too. You should hear what happens if someone approaches the patio door."

Virginia walked to the sliding glass door in the family room and opened it. She walked onto the patio and strolled to the edge of the grass.

All of a sudden a load voice boomed from a speaker. "You are trespassing…leave now." A short time later the voice came on again, "You have been warned, repeat after me…'Our Father who art in heaven…"

Virginia returned inside and locked the door. Andy stood in the middle of the room dressed in a towel and his baseball cap. "What do you think?" he asked.

"You have way too much time on your hands Dr. Clark," she said. "I think you'll give any unexpected visitors a run for their money or have them die laughing." She smiled, "I hope you're wearing more than that for dinner."

Andy finished dressing. He strolled out of the bedroom pulling on a brown tweed jacket with elbow patches. Andy took Virginia's arm as they walked to his truck.

"Ya know," said Andy, "we may not find any treasure. Anything that may have been there, may be gone by now, picked over by people like Old John."

"I know. I think I've been caught up in the hunt," said Virginia climbing into Andy's truck. "Anyway, you know how I am about scavenger hunts and mysteries. Who knows? Maybe we're right and there still is a treasure after all."

"I hope there is," said Andy starting the truck. "How many people actually go on a real treasure hunt, much less find one. I wonder what was…or is?"

"Let's go slow so our shadow won't have any problem," said Virginia as they drove away from the house.

## ~ *11* ~

Abbey parked her BMW in the driveway next to Andy's truck and walked into the garage.

Virginia came out of the house pulling on a blue baseball cap and locked the door. She had her old hiking boots, blue jeans, and a green shirt…Virginia stopped and stared at Abbey. Dressed in denim slacks, brown shirt, hiking boots, and a wide brimmed straw hat, she looked like something out of a Banana Republic catalog. Abbey should be dating Indiana Jones, she thought.

"Good timing, we're almost ready," said Andy loading the supplies in the bed of the truck. With his blue jeans and red and black check sport shirt, he looked like a lumberjack. His UCI baseball cap was ever present. "We don't seem to have any uninvited guests, yet. I wonder what's keeping them?"

"Maybe it's too early for them. No self respecting crook gets up at this hour," said Abbey opening the door to the truck

"You know we shouldn't jest. They could be really danger-ous," said Andy.

"Well. So far I haven't seen anything to worry us, except maybe the note and Neil in Vegas," said Virginia.

Abbey placed her hands on her hips. "Are we going to stand around and talk or go treasure hunting? Anyway, they are most likely watching to see if you have any luck. It would be less effort to steal it from us than do the actual work."

They climbed in the truck and drove to the freeway and headed north. At El Toro Road they turned west for Laguna Beach. The morning was warm but overcast with coastal fog. The sight of deer on the side of the road punctuated the windy drive through Laguna canyon. Andy pulled his the truck into the deserted parking area near the place where the old road started and parked. He placed county and Laguna Beach City parking permits on the dash. They climbed out and unloaded the truck.

Two parking placards? Isn't that a little overkill?" asked Virginia as she slid out of the cab.

"I'm not sure whose jurisdiction this lot is in. Having both permits won't hurt."

"These belts were a good idea Andy," said Abbey fastening her belt. "Who gets the backpack?"

"I do," responded Andy.

"The old road or trail starts here and heads up the mountain," Virginia pointed. "We'll try and stay as close to it as possible."

Andy pulled out his machete. "I'll see how useful this is in the chaparral. Usually these things are used in the jungle. Remember, stay pretty close together."

The morning fog was gone by the time they reached the top of the first rise. The sun had a peculiar radiance, spilling down through a sky of blue white brilliance. There wasn't a cloud to be seen. The dry brush, tumbleweeds and sumac scratched their arms and legs as they hiked. Andy handed Virginia and Abbey small bottles of water from the backpack.

"Drink it slowly," he said. "We need to conserve it for later."

Virginia stopped near a large flat rock. She turned Andy around and carefully removed the maps from his backpack. Spreading the maps on a large rock, she studied them.

"Let's see...we should be about here. The caves, if they exist, will be about a mile from here in that direction," Virginia pointed.

Andy Looked at Abbey and shook his head. "Normally she can get lost on the highway with a road map and signs. Why are we trusting her with this?"

"Be nice," said Virginia in a sad but sultry voice. "If you don't, 'it'll be a long, and I mean long, dry, summer for you. If you get my drift."

"Which way did you say?"

Andy took the lead down the dusty trail and up the next hill. Lizards sunning themselves, watched as they passed. A hawk circled an unseen prey from high above. Virginia and Abbey stopped and applied more sunscreen.

They stopped under a cluster of live oak trees at the top of the next rise to rest. Virginia looked at the maps again.

"We should be pretty close, anyone seen anything yet?" she asked.

"No, but we don't exactly know what we're looking for," said Andy.

"We may need to be a bit closer to the side of the hill over there." Abbey looked at the hillside. "A cave would probably be covered with brush if it hasn't been used for years, wouldn't it?"

"Be on the lookout for snakes," said Andy.

"Great, he had to say that didn't he?" complained Abbey. "I don't like snakes. I'm a city girl."

They cut through bushes and climbed outcroppings. Dirty, and tired, Abbey opened her bottle of water and sat on a rock to drink. "What is that?" she said looking up the hill.

Andy climbed to the spot Abbey was staring and pushed some brushes aside. A small cave appeared. Andy pulled out his flashlight and a small caliber automatic. As he entered the opening he heard Virginia calling.

"Wait for me! You're not going in there alone."

Andy led the way as Virginia followed. The cave was dusty. Andy's light shown on some bats hanging from the top of the cave.

"It stinks in here," said Virginia. She looked up. "Is this thing getting smaller or is it just me?"

"No, it's getting smaller and it's dry too. No sign of a river. No sign of anyone has been here either. Let's go."

As they left the cave Virginia said, "Where is Abbey?"

Their eyes surveyed the scrub landscape around them. There was no sign of Abbey.

"Hi guys," yelled Abbey with half her body hidden in a rock structure about 20 yards to their right. "I found a second cave. Nothing here, you find anything?"

"No. But now we've found two caves. That's encouraging. The third one, if it exists, should be around here somewhere," stated Virginia.

Andy started looking further down the hill toward the clearing while Virginia and Abbey searched the sides of the mountain up hill from the two caves they had discovered.

A short distance from Abbey's cave, Andy started to wave his arms. "Well lookee here," he yelled. "Looks like this was a cave. The outline of an entrance can be seen, but there's been a cave-in."

Andy pulled his folding pick and started to pull rocks and pieces of tress and brush from the entrance. The heat beat down on his back and neck. Virginia and Abbey removed their shovels and dug the dirt from around large rocks. An hour later Andy pulled a couple of medium size rocks from the top of the rock pile.

Virginia peered inside. "It looks big enough for me to climb inside."

"I think the roof is okay, but be careful. We don't know how far the opening goes," said Andy shinning his light inside. "I don't see anything."

Virginia took her belt off. She took a drink of water, and with her flashlight in front of her, inched her way into the opening. Dirt covered her shirt. Small rocks nicked her arms. She scooped rock and dirt to the side as she crawled. She backed out pulling rocks to clear the tunnel. On her last trip about two yards of rock and dirt partially blocked her way to what seemed like a large opening. Her light revealed a cave ahead with rubble on the floor and what looked like standing room. The air was damp and musty. Listening she could hear water tumbling over rocks. Virginia slowly moved her light to get a better view. The beam reflected on a white surface. Her heart seemed to stop. Slowly she reached for the object. Her mouth went dry. "Oh…shit, just what I need, she thought. I hope this isn't a premonition of things to come. She pushed herself backward towards the sunlight. Andy grabbed her legs and pulled her from the dusty opening.

With a big grin on her dirty face, Virginia said, "I've found it. There is a cave in there and water. Oh yeah, this too." She reached back into the cave entrance and pulled out a skull. "Looks like someone didn't make it out before trouble hit. I hope we have better luck."

Virginia and Abbey sat on the ground in front of the cave with the skull while Andy worked the end of their tunnel near where

Virginia found the skull. She and Abbey picked up the heavy small gold figures Andy brought out and wiped off the dirt.

"Where did you find these?" asked Virginia.

He brushed himself off. "Near the end of the tunnel. What do you think?"

"We'll make a fortune selling this stuff. If it's Aztec like the medallion, we've got a fortune in there," said Abbey.

"It belongs to the Irvine Company, remember?" stated Virginia.

"Maybe we can work a deal," said Abbey soberly.

Virginia moved under a large sprawling oak and sat in the shade. Abbey and Andy joined her. They removed their belts. Andy retrieved the backpack from an outcropping near the cave entrance. The air was hot but the shade provided relief from the heat of the direct sun. A crow watched them from a neighboring tree.

"Let's have some lunch, we'll feel better after we eat," said Virginia.

Andy removed sandwiches, potato chips and three apples from the backpack. They ate lunch quietly and lay down on the soft carpet of leaves from the old oak. The crow called to them for crumbs.

Andy stood up and stretched. "I'll crawl back in there and see if I can enlarge the opening some."

"We can take turns," said Abbey gathering the papers and potato chip bags. Andy removed his shovel, pick and flashlight from his belt and approached the small entrance. He pushed the tools in ahead of him and started to crawl forward. After a half-hour he scampered back out. Abbey went in next. She worked for twenty minutes and emerged covered with dirt from head to toe. Virginia scooted in and worked for another twenty minutes. She climbed out head first, carrying a gold cross and a large gold coin.

"Where did you get those?" asked Abbey. "And, how did you turn around?"

"I got inside the cave where you can stand up. These were near the entrance. With a little work we should be able to open the entrance wide enough for us to walk in."

Andy worked the rest of the afternoon on the entrance with Abbey and Virginia providing water and temporary rest spells. By early evening, the cave entrance was open enough for a person to enter almost standing straight up. Their wet dirty shirts clung to them as they entered the cave. It was dark except for their lights and the little shaft of light from the entrance. Their flashlights illuminated an eerie sight. Scattered around the cave were skeletons, dressed in what appeared to be old-fashioned cloths. Virginia felt a cold shiver run up her back; goose bumps formed on her arms. She felt like crying and jumping for joy at the same time. This is what she had been after. Why wasn't she more excited? If these skeletons could talk, what history could they tell? Some day I'll investigate more of the history of the country that isn't in the history books, she thought. Playing pirate and treasure hunting were games she liked to play as a child. Who would have thought she'd really find a pirate's treasure? Virginia could see gold shinning in the beams of the flashlights. She felt like a kid again.

The air felt damp and musty. Andy found an old rifle lying under dirt and rocks near one skeleton. Broken boxes, their contents spilled on the cave floor and in the water, were clustered near the pool of water. Virginia was looking at the water rushing out of an opening in the sandstone formation and running over rocks to the large pool. Abbey looked into the pool. Her light shown on larger artifacts under the surface. Virginia and Abbey picked up the gold articles they could carry and took them outside. After several trips they returned to find Andy studying the pool and the cave structure.

"Just like an engineer, has to know how it works," said Virginia.

"Do all engineers do this?" asked Abbey.

"I think so. They're stuck at 13 years old. Still playing with toys and think girls are strange. They dress poorly, lack social skills, are intelligent and are in their own world most of the time. But they are fairly stable and loyal. My engineer over there is improving his color coordination and dressing, except for the hat."

"At the rate that the water is coming in, and the size of the pool, there must be a good size opening down there," Andy said, pointing.

"Most likely, it is partially blocked by rocks from the cave-in. That would explain why there are objects under water. The pool probably didn't exist until the cave in."

"That's nice. It's getting late and we're bushed. Let's go home. We can come back tomorrow. I don't think we should have any problem with looters tonight. Anyway, I need a bath," said Virginia.

"I'll second that," came Abbey's voice from the entrance.

Virginia took a quick inventory and packed a few of the gold articles in Andy's backpack while Abbey put the rubbish from lunch and their snacks in her belt pouches. Andy moved branches and foliage in front of the cave. It helped a little. In the dark, it might be hard to see, especially if you didn't know the exact location. As dusk approached they walked down the mountain towards the parking lot. Andy stowed the belts, tools and his backpack in the back of the truck.

"Let's go to the shop first. I can lock the treasure in the safe for now," offered Abbey.

Andy, with Virginia next to him, and Abbey by the passenger door, turned his truck onto Laguna Canyon Road and started for Abbey's shop.

"Looks like the adventurers had a good day. Wouldn't you say so, Mr. Jones?" asked Mr. Smith. "I wonder how Mr. Jameson is doing in the San Fernando Valley? It looks like they sent him on a wild goose chase."

"I can't wait to tell him and see the stupid look on his face. He was so sure that stunt in Vegas would get him what he wanted. Good thing those clowns in Vegas screwed up and didn't kill them. I kinda like the Davies girl anyway. She's got guts," said Jones. He turned on the headlights of the Chevrolet and pulled into traffic a few cars behind Andy's truck.

They Arrived at Abbey's gallery, locked the artifacts in her safe and set the time lock. Andy sat in a polished old chair.

"Watch the dirt, fella," said Abbey, "That's a real Chippendale your sitting on."

"A Chippendale?" He winked at Virginia. "I thought they were male strippers," laughed Andy.

"Okay, wise guy. I'll have you know Thomas Chippendale made furniture in England from the 1750s to 1785. Imitations come back in style at various periods, especially in the mid 1800s. The valuable pieces are from the period when old Thomas was working and the really valuable ones are of course his," stated Abbey.

"I'd better get off this one then. It's older than the Dean of Engineering. Let's go."

Andy drove south on PCH to Crown Valley Parkway and turned inland towards home. As he turned the corner toward his house, Andy fingered the remote control for the garage door opener. He backed the truck into his garage.

Virginia and Abbey helped unload the belts and supplies.

"Want me to drop you off at home?" Asked Abbey.

"Yeah, that would be nice. I'm pooped. I think I'll take a shower, make a sandwich and go to bed. What do we do tomorrow?" asked Virginia.

"After today, I think we will need some different equipment for our return to the cave, like lights and stuff. I'll make a list tonight. We'll need a larger truck and our diving equipment for the pool. I'll see you two in the morning. How about seven?" asked Andy.

"Seven? In the morning? If God wanted me to see sunrise he'd have scheduled it later!" said Abbey waving as she and Virginia walked to her BMW.

"Did you notice the green car as we pulled out?" asked Virginia.

"Yes, but it didn't follow us. I wonder why?"

## ~ *12* ~

Abbey's BMW pulled up in front of Andy's house. She noticed Virginia's red Toyota in the driveway between Andy's pick-up truck and a large white panel truck. The rear doors of the white truck were open. Through the open garage door, Abbey could see the tools and gear they had gathered. All around were battery powered camping lanterns, diving equipment, boxes, rope, yellow hard hats, gloves, crowbars, lengths of black iron pipe, packing cloths like movers use to cover large pieces of furniture and some unidentifiable objects she hadn't seen before.

Virginia's pony-tailed head popped out the rear of the truck. She wiped her hands on her gray sweatshirt. She had on blue shorts and scuffed hiking boots. "Good morning. We've started to load."

"Remind me to talk to God about scheduling sunrise later. Where did you get all this stuff…and…how'd you get it so fast?" asked Abbey. "Got any coffee?" Abbey yawned and tugged at her red Laguna Beach sweatshirt.

"Andy conned the dean into letting him borrow some of this from the university, some he had all ready, and part of it he got from friends. Not too bad for one night's work. Give me a hand with this stuff will ya? Coffee's in the kitchen."

Abbey looked around the garage. "Where is Andy?"

"He's down the street picking up some sort of waterproof packaging or something. He'll be right back."

They loaded the equipment Andy had stacked in the garage into the panel truck and closed it up. Entering the garage, Virginia fingered the remote control for the garage door. They walked into the kitchen as the big door banged shut and locked behind them.

"Coffee's a little strong now, but what the heck, it's got caffeine," stated Abbey filling a mug. "By the way, why is Andy getting water proof stuff? It hasn't rained for months."

"I'm not sure. Maybe for the things in the pond."

Andy returned and loaded the last of the hardware. He went into the kitchen for a cup of coffee and to round up the ladies. "I'll take the pick up, you two follow in the panel truck. Do we have everything?"

"I can't imagine what you may have left behind from the looks of the trucks," said Virginia.

Andy climbed into his truck and started for Laguna Beach. Virginia slid into the drivers' seat of the van with Abbey on the passenger side, and pulled out behind Andy. She watched as he put on his old Anteater hat.

"No tail this morning," said Virginia glancing at the mirrors. "I wonder where they went?"

"Who cares. Maybe they gave up. Or, it's too early for crooks, too. By the way, how are we going to get all this stuff up to the cave?" asked Abbey, "Or don't I want to ask?"

"We're going to drive up."

"Oh Shit, I had to ask!" responded Abbey biting her lower lip.

As they arrived at the parking lot, a white fog enveloped the trucks. It didn't improve Abbey's apprehension. She watched Andy gear down and start slowly up the old road, running over small bushes. His truck faded in and out of the fog. Abbey swallowed as she watched Virginia follow behind Andy's truck. They left the blacktop behind and plunged forward up the narrow gravel and dirt trail.

Virginia drove slowly along twin tire tracks at the center of the road, loose gravel stones ricocheted off the underside of the truck. At each switchback, she braked to a crawl.

Abbey held the handle on the dashboard. Her knuckles turned white. She looked straight ahead. God, I'll be glad when this is over, she thought. Oh shit! We still have to come down. God, I hate heights.

The road banked left then right as it wound its way up the hill between a shear drop on one side and a sandstone wall on the other. After a painstaking and jolting drive, the trucks came to a stop in a large flat area with dirt and scattered small shrubs around big oak and sycamore trees. The last of the lingering fog drifted among the treetops. They stopped. The caves were about twenty yards away.

"OK, ladies, let's get with it," yelled Andy as he got out of his truck.

"We've got a lot to do today,"

Virginia and Abbey climbed out of the panel truck and stretched. Abbey flexed her hands.

Virginia unlocked the rear doors as Abbey opened the sliding door on the side.

"How come this looks like a lot more stuff than we had at the house?" mumbled Abbey.

"Never mind that now, we've got to get this up to the cave. You'll love this stuff after we've started to dig out more treasure," said Virginia. "Now where did Andy go?"

Andy unloaded the pick up truck and moved the battery powered camping lights into the cave and turned them on. Next came the diving gear, cameras, and ropes. He assisted Abbey and Virginia with the gear from the panel truck and set up a staging area in the cave for the equipment.

"What's with the rubber boat and flotation gear?" asked Abbey.

"There seems to be some fairly large objects out in the pool. I think it will be easier to raise them and get them ashore by use of the floats than by brute force," stated Andy undoing a coil of rope. "The box over there," he added pointing, "has notebooks in it for recording our find. The tote boxes are for lugging stuff to the trucks."

The boxes in the panel truck took them the better part of an hour to unload and move into the cave. Virginia and Abbey photographed and made note of all the items then loaded small figurines from the cave floor into the tote boxes. When the first one was full Virginia tried to lift it. It wouldn't budge.

"For little things, they're heavy!" complained Virginia.

Laughing, Andy said, "It's gold, silly. It's one of the densest metals. It is twice as heavy as copper for the same size piece. You'll have to make several trips with fewer pieces in each trip."

Abbey transferred some of the figurines to another tote box. She and Virginia lugged the boxes to the panel truck and tucked them in the rear of the truck behind the two seats. They walked back into the cave for the next load.

Andy had rigged a makeshift A-frame and was pulling some larger objects out of the sand at the fringe of the pool. Smaller items he had moved to a pile near a rock outcropping.

Abbey found a couple of intact wooden crates. When she tried to move them parts of the wood fragmented. Finding a crow bar she opened the crates. Dropping to her knees in the dirt she said, "Holly shit! Look at these. There must be a king's ransom in here. These are beautiful. We'll have dealers and scholars drooling and bidding themselves into a frenzy." She ducked as an empty plastic tote box flew by her head.

"Load now, gush later," said Virginia. "The sooner we get this stuff out of here and locked up the happier I'll be. How about you helping us, Dr. Clark? After all, we're just fragile girls."

"Yeah, right."

We'll help you with the big stuff."

"Okay, okay." Reluctantly Andy abandoned his equipment and helped load boxes and packed the truck with small to medium size artifacts. The loading took most of the morning. Andy had pulled four good size statues from the pool. It took all three of them to pick up and carry the two jaguar figures to the truck. The second two statues of men with animal heads were dragged to Andy's pick up and hoisted to the bed.

Andy returned to the cave.

Virginia and Abbey pulled two picnic boxes from Andy's truck and carried them into the cave.

Andy had removed his shoes and wadded a short distance into the pool. "There are some more items in here. We'll need the floats and our snorkeling gear to get these."

"That can wait. We're hungry," said Virginia as she and Abbey unpacked the picnic baskets.

Andy wadded out of the pool. He grabbed a towel from a duffel bag and dried off. He walked to the blanket that served as their table and sat down. All at once his shoulders and arms felt the affects of lifting the heavy weights. He grimaced as he kneaded his sore muscles. Virginia got up to massage his shoulders as he drank an ice tea.

After eating Virginia and Abbey walked outside into the warm air and the mixed smell of the eucalyptus trees and salty sea air. Circling crows watched them.

Abbey looked in the truck. "For all the weight, seems like there should be more stuff."

"Don't forget, it is heavy and we're getting tired," responded Andy.

Returning to the cave Abbey helped Virginia repack the picnic baskets and took them back to Andy's truck. They scrambled back into the cave. Andy was assembling the winch to his makeshift retrieval system in the water near the edge of the pond.

"We should be able to lift whatever is down there and with the pulleys and rope move them close to shore," said Andy pointing to the makeshift equipment. "We can use these A-frames to drag them on shore. Virginia and I will go into the water with the diving equipment. Abbey, you will need to operate the lifts and pulleys with these winches I've rigged up. Let's get started."

Andy removed his shirt and shorts. His bathing suit was the color of a bright red crayon. He pulled on an iridescent orange wet suit and zipped it up. Virginia had removed her shirt and shorts. Her blue bikini was soon covered by another orange wet suit. They tugged on their green flippers.

"Where in God's name did you two find those suits?" asked Abbey.

"Sometimes visibility gets kind of poor, these tend to stand out so we can see each other," replied Andy pulled on his face-mask. "Are you ready ladies?"

Virginia and Andy wadded into the water and submerged briefly.

"It's not too bad," said Virginia, adjusting her mask. "I thought it'd be colder."

They swam a short distance to the floats and held on to the sides. Virginia reached into the floats and pulled out their snorkels, handing one to Andy.

"We'll take these ropes and canvas belts and tie the statues with them," Andy yelled to Abbey. "We'll signal you to start cranking the winches."

The two orange wet suits disappeared under the water. Every few minutes a snorkel would appear and a waterspout would shoot up. In what seemed like an eternity, Virginia's head appeared.

"Start turning the red handled winch," she said.

Abbey turned the crank. It didn't want to budge. After three more tries, the handle slowly turned. She cranked it until Virginia called to stop.

"Hold it there for a minute," called Andy as he surfaced.

Virginia and Andy tied a couple of new ropes to the belts around the statue suspended just under the surface. Releasing the ropes that pulled it to the surface, Virginia signaled Abbey to use the green handled winch to pull the statue to shore. This was easier. The pulleys creaked. The ropes strained under the load as the weight jerked toward the shore. When it was five feet from the edge of the pool, it stopped. The divers followed.

"We'll have to drag it out from here," said Andy. "I have a block and tackle set up to help."

He removed his mask and flippers and walked to a rope terminated with a hook. Fastening it to the belts on the statue he called to Abbey to turn the winch he had attached to the block and tackle. Virginia pushed as the rope and winch strained. The statue plowed into the sand as it moved to the damp dirt of the cave floor. Andy unhooked the rope.

"It's beautiful. This is going to keep some people up nights," said Abbey.

"Now that it's here, how do we get it out of the cave? By the way, what is it?" asked Virginia.

"On those movers dollies," said Andy pointing to dollies stacked by the cave entrance. "And I haven't the slightest idea what it is. It looks like a winged cat of some kind."

"Yeah, probably some kind of god," said Abbey.

Moving the dolly into place next to the statue, they rolled it on. Virginia retrieved some small diameter rope and tied the statue in place. Virginia and Abbey pushed as Andy pulled on a rope tied around the figure. The statue crept toward the rear of Andy's truck.

"OK, now what?" asked Virginia. "This thing weighs a lot more than we can lift."

"Don't worry. I have a plan," said Andy grinning. He walked back into the cave. He emerged a few minutes later with the A-frame and the block and tackle.

"We hoist it into the truck. And to think that my students don't appreciate mechanical advantage, levers and pulleys. They think it's all electronic! They should see us now."

They connected the ropes and Andy used the assortment of ropes and pulleys to hoist the winged statue to the truck. With the statue securely loaded, he closed the tailgate.

"There is one more statue down there, but I don't think we should go for it today. It's getting late and we need to put all this stuff away before it gets too late. We are out of room anyway. Why don't you drive the panel truck to your shop, Abbey, and start unloading this stuff into the safe while we clean up operations here?" asked Andy.

"You want me…to drive down this hill, alone? My insurance company hates me enough as is." She looked at the truck.

Coming up was bad enough, now I have to drive it down. How do I get into these predicaments? "Me, drive it down…now?"

"The sooner it's locked up the better," said Virginia. "We'll meet you at Andy's later and go for dinner. We can put our winged friend and the other stuff in Andy's garage tonight. No one will be able to move our winged…what ever it is."

"All right. But be careful, you two," said Abbey as she climbed into the truck. "I'll stop by my place after the shop for a shower and new cloths. No one will want to be around us at dinner smelling and looking like this."

Virginia stared at Abbey as she started the engine and slowly moved the truck forward. She stopped at the head of the trail. Virginia noticed Abbey stretch and peer over the steering wheel at the rough, narrow, road ahead. Abbey griped the wheel and slid her hands around it. She griped it again and slowly maneuvered the truck toward the path leading down the hill to the flat land and the highway below.

As Virginia turned toward the cave she saw a flash of light, like a reflection off a mirror. She gazed at the spot for a second. The light didn't reappear. Maybe it's my imagination, or an old bottle, she thought. That or someone is watching us. I'll be glad when the gold is in Abbey's safe. She broke into a trot to catch up with Andy.

Abbey slowly drove the truck into the parking lot at the bottom of the mountain and stopped. She wiped beads of perspiration from her brow and took a deep breath. She let it out slowly. Relief surged through her. The bottom at last.

Abbey wound her way through Laguna Beach on back roads to her shop. She pulled the truck up to her back door. Fumbling with her keys, she unlocked the steel outer door. She opened it, unlocked the rear door and propped it open. Abbey opened the side door on the truck and unloaded most of the gold and silver artifacts into the shop. She opened the truck's rear door, and with the aid of a dolly, moved the larger pieces to the shop. Abbey closed up the truck and went inside the shop. She picked up a note from her assistant. *Everything went well today, she wrote. Made some good sales. Money, checks and credit card slips are in the floor safe.* There was no floor safe. It was a code between them for a false compartment in a piece of furniture that they used to hold money and valuables until Abbey could put them in the vault. Abbey retrieved the day's receipts and opened the safe. The next two hours was spent stuffing the treasure and receipts in the vault. She locked the safe and set the time lock and silent alarm. She stretched; her muscles ached from the lifting of the gold. She picked up her phone and punched in a number.

The phone was answered on the second ring. "We opened the cave and I have some of the artifacts here. We need to contact our client."

Abbey finished her brief conversation, hung up and turned to leave. Standing in the doorway were Mr. Smith and Mr. Jones. Each held a snub nose, .38 caliber pistol.

"Nice shop, Ms. Mc Queen. I'll bet you keep the really valuable stuff in that vault. Sorry we couldn't be here before you went to the trouble of locking it. But that's just the way it goes. You know how traffic can be in Laguna," said Smith. "Now why don't you be a nice little lady and open it for us?"

"I can't. The timer is set."

"I'll bet with a little persuasion it can be opened. Now let's not cause any more trouble than necessary," said Smith.

"Open the damn safe. Do it before I loose my temper," said Jones pointing his gun at her head.

"OK, I'll try, but I don't think it'll work. Like I said, the timer is on," complained Abbey.

She spun the dial and dialed the combination. Next she inserted a key and turned it. The lever on the door didn't turn.

"I told you it wouldn't work! Why not come back after nine tomorrow?" asked Abbey in a shaky voice.

"Do you think we're that dumb? By then the police will be all over this place. No. We'll stay here until the damn thing opens. Try it again," said Jones. "I'd find a way if I were you young lady. My friend here likes good looking ladies like you, and the way it looks, he might have you to play with all night."

"Police! Drop the guns! Do it now! Put down the guns and put your hands on top of your heads! Now!" said a police officer from the rear door. A second officer walked in and picked up the guns from the floor.

"Boy am I happy to see you fellows," sighed Abbey. "I guess the alarm system really does work."

"We got the call a few minutes ago and were just down the street. Glad we got here when we did," said the first officer. The second policeman finished searching Smith and Jones. He read them their rights and handcuffed them.

"I'll take them to the car. Why don't you get the report?" he said.

The first officer questioned Abbey about the attempted robbery. After the brief questioning, Abbey promised to go to the station in the morning and sign a statement. The police left. Abbey made a phone call, locked up and drove the truck to her apartment. What else can happen, she thought?

~ *13* ~

Virginia walked into the cave. Her face was ashen. Andy looked up from a box he was packing.

"What's the matter?" he asked.

"Them," said Virginia gesturing backward with her head.

Charles Jameson and his girl friend followed Virginia into the cave. His light brown pants and shirt with a wide brimmed, dark brown, felt fedora hat made him look like someone out of a movie. Sue leaned against the sandstone cave entrance getting brown dust on her green blouse. She brushed her hands on her tan slacks and smiled. Jameson held a black nine-millimeter semiautomatic pistol at Virginia's back.

Andy looked at them as they entered the cave behind Virginia. Just what you'd expect for a well healed crook. Gucci all the way. Even the gun looks polished. "Leave her alone," Andy said sharply. "Who the hell are you? And, what do you want?"

"Nice to meet you professor. My boys said you were pretty smart and tough. Sorry we had to meet under these circumstances, but that's how it goes." Jameson sat down on a rock. "Now that I have my treasure. What am I to do with you?"

"You don't have shit, fella," said Andy. "It's in a safe by now."

"Not so my friend," stated Jameson. "My associates, I think you met them at the university not long ago, followed Ms. Mc Queen to her shop when she left. I'm here to take back what is rightfully mine. I'm truly sorry about her, too.

"If you did anything to her I'll see you in Hell for it, you snake!" yelled Andy.

"You might at that, doctor. But for now, I have plans for you. Why don't you two make yourselves at home? It will be home for as long as you live, which may not be too long."

Jameson and Sue backed out of the cave. Jameson fired two shots into the cave to ensure that Virginia and Andy stayed inside. He placed four small packages in the cave entrance and ran wires to the edge of the clearing. He fired two more rounds into the cave. As he connected the wires to an electronic device resembling a hand calculator, the scream of sirens could be heard at the bottom of the hill. Jameson looked at Sue and punched a code into the device. He handed it to her. She pressed a button and closed her eyes.

A load thundering noise rose into the evening air. The ground trembled. Birds fluttered, screaming into the air. Dust and dirt shot out of the cave as the entrance collapsed into a dense pile of rubble. The acid smell of the explosives hung in the air. For a long minute, Sue and Charles stood motionless. The sounds of vehicles approaching stirred their attention. They ran toward their Broncho.

Reaching for the door they heard, "Police! Stop where you are!"

They turned slowly. Two Laguna Beach Police four-wheel drive vehicles were in the clearing. The officers in the first car were standing next to it with their guns drawn.

"Hand on top of your heads and don't move," shouted the officer on the drivers side of the first police car. Two other officers, guns drawn, slowly approached Charles and Sue.

Jameson and Sue placed their hands on their heads and stood next to the Broncho. The officers approached on both sides.

"Turn around and lean against the car," said the officer on Jameson's right. "Spread your legs."

The officer searched Jameson. Standing Charles up, the officer pulled Charles's arms behind his back and handcuffed him.

"Put your arms behind your back," ordered another officer. Sue slowly lowered her arms and put them behind her back. He handcuffed Sue. One of the policemen turned Charles around and pushed him to the side of the Bronco.

"Looks like these two just blew the cave," said another policemen holding the detonation device and wires. "There's supposed to be a Dr. Clark and a Ms. Davies here too. Any sign of them?"

"No, and from what we got from the team at the antique shop, they were probably in the cave," responded another officer.

An officer walked around the front of the Broncho. He stood directly in front of Jameson. "Where are Dr. Clark and Ms. Davies?"

"We want to speak to our lawyer," said Charles.

"Have it your way. Mr. Jameson and Ms. Hill, you are under arrest for the attempted robbery of the antique shop in Laguna Beach and suspicion of the murder of Dr. Clark and Ms. Davies. We are also placing you under arrest for the illegal possession and use of explosives. That can also be a federal wrap if the US Attorney decides to get involved."

The officers read Charles and Sue their rights.

Two police officers lead Jameson and Sue to one of the police cars.

One officer opened the rear door. "Watch your heads," he said as they were eased into the rear seats.

They sat handcuffed in the back of the police car as the officers looked around the clearing. Andy's truck was there with a large gold figurine sitting in the bed.

"What the hell is that?" questioned an officer.

"I don't know," answered another policeman. "Looks like gold. I think we have an idea of why those two tried to do away with the Clark fellow and Ms. Davies."

The police officers examined the cave entrance. The clouds of dust were still swirling around. They searched the areas around the truck and near the trees fringing the small clearing. Another police car, with a red spotlight displayed, arrived and parked under a large tree. Lieutenant Killroy got out and walked up to Andy's truck. He looked at a uniformed officer standing next to the truck.

"Any sign of Dr. Clark or Ms. Davies?"

"No, lieutenant. We think they were in the cave when those two blew up the entrance. The caves around here are mainly sandstone. The explosion probably brought down the whole thing. We called for the rescue team. That's probably them coming."

A fire engine and a rescue truck, their red lights acting like beacons on the rocks and trees, rumbled into the clearing. The firemen scrambled out of the trucks. The police sergeant in charge talked to the rescue team. A fireman walked to the cave entrance. Using a pick he struck some of the larger boulders. More rubble fell.

"Doesn't look good Cap," said the fireman to a Captain from the engine. "We'll need a geologist to help with this one. That's if it isn't too late."

"We'll set up a command post and lights now, I'll call for more equipment and an expert," said the Captain as he turned toward the engine.

Killroy walked over to the Laguna Police sergeant. "Well, let's get Dr. Clark's truck into the station and we can figure out what to do."

"Are you all right?" asked Andy as he sat up coughing. "My ears are ringing."

"Yeah, I'm fine." Virginia rubbed her arm. "Lucky nothing very big hit us. Now what?

"I don't know. The dust in here is thick. The lights still work though. Glad I used battery lamps, this dust could have been a disaster with gas lamps."

Moving around rocks that had fallen in the explosion, Andy made his way to the entrance. "Doesn't look good. I wonder if anyone heard it? Abbey can't even tell them about us if Jameson was telling the truth. We're on our own."

A large boulder fell from the cave roof landing on a pile of rope. Smaller rocks rained down. A few small rocks tumbled to the cave floor near what was the entrance.

"I don't feel like dying in this place," said Virginia sitting on a rock. "How do we get out of here? If I'm going to die, I'd like to go fighting."

"You're sitting next to our only hope," said Andy. "The water in this pool has a fairly strong current. It's heading for the ocean. We could follow it underground to the sea. It might not work and we wouldn't be able to turn back. But, it's our only hope."

"You're kidding! Can't we dig our way out? We haven't the slightest idea of what's under there. We probably wouldn't make it. We probably couldn't squeeze through the opening in that pond! How do we get back if the river gets to small? It's dark under there!" she yelled hysterically. "I like digging." She picked up a shovel and started to sob. "I want to go home. Please tell me this is a dream and I'll wake up soon."

"Have you looked at what's blocking the entrance?" he said pointing. "Those rocks are big and there is a lot of them. To make things worse, we left the block and tackles, most of the tools and A-frame outside. All we've got are small shovels and rope. Not a lot to work with. And, in case you forgot, we ate all our food."

"Okay, Okay…I get the picture." She stared at the ground, then raised her eyes to Andy. "I still don't like it. Couldn't we wait and see if someone rescues us? "

"We could last a few days, if help was coming. But, I don't think any rescue squad is coming. Jameson said Abbey was dead, remember? She can't call 911. The Cavalry won't be riding over the hill to our rescue this time."

Virginia sat on the rock looking at the light reflecting off the pool. I wonder if the smugglers were trapped like this? They didn't get out. It took over sixty years for us to find them. How long before anyone finds us? She thought of her mother and father. How would they ever know what really happened. She felt empty inside. At least she was with her Andy and her neighbor, Donna, would take care of Leo. In spit of her craziness, Andy loved her. Please God, she prayed, not like this. She turned to see Andy on his knees staring at the water. She watched him in what seemed like slow motion as he rose and hobbled to her. He tenderly rubbed her neck. Why was he hobbling?

She turned her head and looked up at him. "What's the matter? Are you hurt?"

"I'm okay. I got a cramp where a small bolder hit me. It'll be okay."

For the next forty-five minutes, Virginia and Andy geared up and went over their plans. Communication signals were devised. Drills for inflating and deflating their vests and two floatation bags with supplies were practiced. The use of lights was agreed upon. Andy constructed a method to hold lamps to their hard hats.

They had made countless dives together in waters off California, Mexico, The Bahamas, Hawaii, and Florida. But none in caves or under the depths of the earth. Cave diving is dangerous even for those that are trained. Virginia and Andy had never experienced anything even close.

"Keep an eye on our depth gauge. We could go deeper than we think or come out in a deep part of the ocean. At least the water is warm enough to avoid hypothermia. We'll need to be ready for whatever happens," said Andy adjusting his flippers. "The small tank attached at our belts is pure oxygen. It's for decompression should we go below thirty meters. Let's hope they aren't needed. I rigged straps to these hard hats and lights. It could get rough."

Andy had rigged their air tanks to a harness around their hips to facilitate easier access through narrow passages. They checked their airlines, regulators and pressure gauges. Andy strapped a compass to his right wrist. Ropes fastened the floatation bags with supplies to Andy and Virginia.

Andy entered the pool first. He waded out about twenty feet then submerged. Virginia followed him. Andy swam toward the gapping hole in the rear of the pool and plunged down with the current. Virginia felt as though she were free-falling down a huge dark straw. The sides of the exit hole from the pool were smooth, as if they had been polished. She hadn't been able to see Andy below; the shaft seemed bottomless. Her heart raced. She cleared her ears as she descended. At the bottom she swam with the current until she saw Andy's helmet light. She turned on the light attached to her hard hat so he could see her. He was waiting for her flipping to hold himself against the current. Virginia glanced at the pressure gauge. It was holding steady at fifty meters. The water seemed to be to be sloping upward, with the pressure decreasing, relieving the fear of depth blackout. They moved with the current through the twists and turns of the river.

Virginia recalled that cave diving was one of the most dangerous sports in the world. There was Stygian blackness, the claustrophobic sensation and the silence, maddening silence and the constant threat of disorientation. Any or all of this could lead to panic and death. She remembered an article in a diving magazine that said twenty-six divers, in Florida in 1974, had died in caves. The thoughts sharpened Virginia's senses to danger. A series of fissures expanded and narrowed as the current swept them along. The current slowed. Virginia and Andy rose to what seemed to be a surface. Their heads splashed clear of the water.

The cave was large with air in the upper two thirds. Stalactites hung from the ceiling. The lights from their helmets illuminated rock with various colors. The only sounds were of water against the sides of the cave and drops falling from the roof. There were strings of dark rock running through the lighter browns and grays of the walls. Virginia knew they were volcanic in origin. Veins of quartz shimmered in the light from Virginia's light. The walls were smooth allowing them no place to land. Andy's light fell upon an opening at the far end of the cave. The current was taking them toward it. They drifted toward the opening. The entrance had a different, muffled sound. As they drifted down stream the sound became louder.

Andy spat out his regulator mouthpiece and called to Virginia. "Be ready to inflate our vest, I think we're headed for rapids." He replaced his regulator.

A thunderous roar echoed through the passage. Virginia began to panic. Her worst fear was to be swept through unnavigable rapids and be smashed against rocks or go over a waterfall. She had the sudden vision of going over Niagara Falls. She hated roller coaster rides because of the feeling she got at the sudden, steep drops. The roar was deafening, magnified by the acoustics of the cavern. She felt her heart stop as Andy passed into the mist and disappeared.

Virginia watched with paralyzed fascination as the mist and spray enveloped her. The roar was increasing. She braced herself for the tumbling fall. The fall never came. The thunder came, not from the river plunging over a presepres, but from a torrent that crashed down from openings above. She was pummeled by the falling deluge that burst from a gaping hole in the roof of the passage. She spun around in the torrent. The spare air tank hit her in her left side. The blow caused her to spit out her regulator just as her head popped to the surface. She turned over and looked up at the deluge and replaced her regulator. Virginia was baffled by the large amount of water under such an arid part of the country. Most of the water for Orange County was from an aqueduct. The rest of the county's water was comprised of slow moving ground water, not a raging river.

Once through the mist, she could see that the passage had widened into another cavern. More stalactites were ever present. Mineral deposits had formed delicate gypsum flowers and wild colored stalagmites. She brushed against one slightly scratching her right leg. The beam from her light caught sparkling crystals spotting the walls. It was as showcase. They dove with the current into the timeless dark as they left the cavern. Their illumination was fading as their batteries weakened. The dark river opened on another cavern. Andy pulled a pouch from a rope tied to his weight belt. He removed a piece of tape covering a small handle and pulled it. A loud hiss filled the cave as the compressed air inflated a small raft. They climbed in and removed their regulators.

"We should dump these tanks and use the reserve ones we've been pulling," said Andy.

Virginia quickly disengaged her tanks and replaced them with two that were in the floats she had been pulling behind her. She dumped the used one over the side. Andy's followed. She changed the batteries in her lamp and helped Andy restrap his helmet. The going was smooth for a while as they skimmed over shallow pools and bottomless crevasses. In one stretch it took all their concentration and Virginia's moving her weight in the raft to avoid ever-present rocks. The next curve had more cataracts. The ceiling changed from twenty feet above them to just enough headroom for the rubber raft to fit.

The raft hit the wall of a small cavern where the ceiling merged with the surface of the water and stopped.

"Looks like we go for a swim from here," said Andy.

Virginia fell backwards into the water and waited for Andy. He jumped out of the raft right behind her. They dove to the exit where the current picked up. They seemed to be sloping up again. The rush of the water propelled them faster. Virginia glanced at her pressure gauge. Twenty-five meters. She looked ahead. The only light was the blur of diffused light from Andy's hard hat.

Suddenly the water changed. The current died. The water was colder and tasted salty. She was in the ocean. Virginia looked around for Andy. Ahead of her was a smudged light bob-bing in the blackness. She swam toward it. Andy reached out and caught her arm. Together, they slowly rose to the surface. At fifteen meters Virginia pointed to the depth gauge. They held the fifteen-meter depth for what seemed like an eternity. The rest of the assent went smooth. Virginia's head broke the surface. She inflated her vest and saw Andy follow suit. They were riding on three-foot swells. The cool salty air smelled reassuring. The lights of Southern California appeared in the distance.

"Where are we?" she asked Andy.

"From what I can see, I'd say we were about three miles south of Main Beach and about a little over a mile out. That would mean we traveled about five to six miles underground. And we lived to talk about it."

Virginia shuddered and screamed as she twisted in the water.

"What's wrong?" asked Andy.

"Something very big just brushed against me. After all we've been through I don't want to be fish food."

"We'd better take off the helmets and lights," said Andy. "We'll attract every fish and critter within a ten mile radius."

Virginia pulled off her hard hat. She looked at it then threw it as far as she could, watching the light spin in the air and splash into a wave. Andy's followed.

"Let's make for shore. We can figure out what to do next when we get to dry land," stated Andy.

They swam toward shore, alternating between swimming and floating on the swells. Andy pointed to the south. They swam south for a hundred yards to avoid the surf pounding on the off shore rooks and cliff that loomed at them. The surf propelled them to a small section of sandy beach. They swam to shallow water then lumbered ashore. Virginia collapsed on the sand. She removed the air thanks, vest, weights and her flippers.

All at once, she started to cry. Andy removed his gear and sat next to her and held her, brushing his hand over her wet hair.

"We made it. We're safe. It's okay. It's okay," he said softly. "Somebody up there seems to like us. You're all right."

Virginia stopped crying and sat starring out to sea. She looked up at Andy. Her Andy. He was safe too. They made it. The feelings of wonder and relief flooded through her. Virginia looked into Andy's eyes. The look that exchanged between them said it all. No words were necessary to tell them how lucky they were. She opened the watertight pouch she had strapped to her waist. Inside she had a telephone credit card, a Master Card, ATM card, keys, driver's license, student ID and a twenty-dollar bill.

Looking at it she said, "Shit, no comb."

Andy opened his pouch and removed his ATM and credit cards, license, his faculty ID, a couple of keys and two twenty-dollar bills, then returned them. He removed his wet suit and strapped the little pouch back on. Virginia did the same. She shuddered as the cool sea air struck her bruised skin.

"This isn't the time to be in a wet bikini," she said.

They bundled up their equipment and trudged up to the road.

"Wait here, I'll use that pay phone to call a cab," said Andy.

"Don't be silly, let's just check into that little hotel across the street for the night. I'm cold and I don't think we're going to have much luck with a cab at this hour of the morning. It's late. It's dark. I'm tired and hurt in places I didn't know I had."

They lugged their equipment across the street and entered the hotel. The lobby was empty, almost eerily so, as they entered. The desk clerk rose from a chair behind the front counter and watched, with fascination, as these two strange people entered.

The small hotel was decorated as an English Inn complete with dark open beamed ceiling and overstuffed chairs in the lobby. The hardwood floor was covered with area rugs of deep greens, browns and burgundy.

Andy and Virginia dumped their equipment on the floor and walked to the counter.

"Can I help you?" asked the clerk, dressed like an English butler.

"Yeah. We'd like a room for the rest of the night," said Andy.

"Oh…Do you have any bags?" He eyed Virginia.

"No. Just our gear. How about the room?"

"How will you be paying for it, sir?"

Andy reached into his bag and pulled out his Master Card. The clerk took the card and ran it through the credit verifier. It checked out. He handed Andy a registration card and fumbled for a room key.

As Andy finished the card the clerk said, "Do you have any other ID? One with a photograph."

Andy glared at the small clerk and handed him his faculty ID with his photo on it.

"Oh. Sorry Dr. Clark. You and the young lady seemed kind of strange coming in at this hour. Please forgive my apprehension. Here is your key. You're in room 107. I didn't think you'd want to carry those tanks and things up stairs. "

"No problem. We must look like something out of a science fiction movie. We've been through a lot. Thanks for the room." They dragged their gear down the carpeted hall toward their room.

Virginia took the key and opened the door. She turned on the lights and helped Andy pull the diving equipment into the room. It was airy and good sized, with a queen size bed covered by a green and brown comforter. Across from the bed stood a low, dark wood, dresser topped with a large mirror. The TV rested in a large maple armoire. A small love seat, a stuffed chair, and a desk and chair set were near the sliding glass door. The telephone sat on the desk. Andy closed the drapes as Virginia went into the bathroom. A few seconds later Andy heard the shower running. He opened the bathroom door and followed Virginia into the steamy shower.

"You've got some nasty bruises. Do they hurt?" she asked gently touching one on his leg.

"Only if someone touches it."

Virginia came out wrapped in a towel and hung up their bathing suits to dry. After Andy dried off, he walked to the bed and climbed in. He noticed that Virginia was already asleep. Andy sat on the edge of the bed. He thought about what had happened and Abbey. Those bastards are going to pay, and pay dearly for what they did. Fatigue settled in. He had trouble keeping his eyes open. He lay back on the bed and pulled the covers up. He went out as his head hit the pillow.

$$\sim 14 \sim$$

John Kilroy reached for the telephone as he sat up in bed. As he picked up the receiver, he glanced at the clock. 8:00 am in little green numbers stared him in the face.

"Kilroy," he said with a groan. God, can't a guy have a day off?

"Lieutenant. It's Bill. We got ourselves an interesting case."

Bill Rubin was Kilroy's associate and partner on the university police. Rubin stood about five foot ten, weighed two hundred pounds with short blond hair. He called from the station.

"Have you been there all night? It was what…one a.m. when we finished up last night? What's so important that it can't wait until I get there?"

"It's about Dr. Clark and Ms. Davies."

"What about them?"

"It seems they aren't dead."

John swung his legs out of bed and stood up in a flash.

"What are you talking about? The geologists and rescue boys said the cave in was beyond hope. How did they get out? Where are they? Are they hurt? Bill, what the hell happened?"

"I don't know. The credit card company reported a use of Dr. Clark's credit card during the night. We checked and found that Dr. Clark and a woman answering Ms. Davies description checked into a hotel in South Laguna Beach. They were gone by the time officers got there. The clerk said they looked like death warmed over when they checked in. They had been diving and were wet and disheveled as he put it. Seems they dove and swam out of the cave. Turned up way the hell south of Laguna. Anyway, they're out but we don't know where they've gone or how. At least not yet. It looks like they went to Dr. Clark's house, but left."

"Okay, I'll be in shortly. Notify the banks and credit card companies that if their cards are used, they are to call us at once."

"Should we have them put a hold on the cards?" asked Bill.

"Hell, no. I want to know where they are so we can talk to them. With the treasure found, I'm sure Ms. Davies will try and see her friend to get some of the treasure that is in the safe. We'll talk to her and Dr. Clark then. Let them rest for now, wherever they are. It will be interesting to find out how they got out won't it? See you shortly."

He walked to the vanity and turned on the cold water. His wife got up and stood next to him as he splashed cold water on his face. He looked in the mirror at her. Sue had short black hair, olive skin and big bedroom brown eyes. Her nightgown was a short, pale green, lightweight cotton. John could make out the silhouette of her figure as the light from the bed behind her shadowed her body. Not bad for having two kids, he thought.

"What's going on dear? " she asked softly, touching his forehead. "I thought this was your day off."

"Last night we were wrapping up a case involving a professor and a student that were killed in Laguna Beach. They were blown up in a cave."

"How awful. Was it the same professor and girl you told me about?"

"Yeah. I liked them. It really bothered me that they were killed. Well it seems that somehow they managed to get out and ended up swimming ashore in South Laguna. How they got there we haven't a clue. I can't wait to ask Ms. Davies about this stunt of hers." Smiling with a mischievous grin he added, "I'm really glad they made it. The prof is a nice guy, a good teacher and an interesting fellow. Ms. Davies is a real character. She's smart, outgoing, pretty and a little nuts. From reports, and what I've seen, she's always into something or another. No wonder the professor likes her."

"I'll put the coffee on. Looks like it is going to be a long day," Sue said as she headed for the kitchen. Turning she said, "Take care of them dear, there may be more to this than you know."

Kilroy looked at his wife in the mirror. I wish she wouldn't do that, he thought. She's usually right.

## ~ *15* ~

The sun crept in between the edges of the drapes. Virginia woke up rubbing the sleep from her eyes. She went to the bathroom and washed her face.

"Not a pretty sight girl," she said blurry eyed to herself.

"I wouldn't say that," stated Andy leaning on the doorframe. "We need to get dressed and get a ride to my place. We can figure out what to do there and get into some clean clothes."

"Yeah. But at least my hair looks better than it did last night." Pulling on her bikini she added, "I hate to wear this in the lobby. I'd wear the wet suit but it's still wet, cold and clammy. I guess this'll have to do. I bet some old lady will look down her nose at me."

"Don't worry about it, " said Andy. "You look fine. Anyway you won't see them again anyway. It'll add local color to their visit. Most tourists think Californians are a little strange anyway."

"You're probably right, but I still feel funny."

Andy called for a cab. They dragged their gear to the lobby. Andy checked out as Virginia watched for the cab. A few tourists, wandering into the lobby from the elevators, stared at them.

The cab arrived in ten minutes. The driver and Andy stuffed their diving gear into the trunk of the taxi. Virginia enjoyed the morning sun and sea air as they rode, with the windows rolled down, to Andy's house.

"You know how good it feels to be able to see the sun again. Last night I wouldn't have bet my last nickel on it," said Virginia. "I can't wait to see if Abbey's okay and talk to my folks, eat a hamburger and see my apartment."

"Yeah. And wait 'til we tell lieutenant Kilroy about Jameson and his girl friend. What they did is attempted murder. I want to see them fry."

"I'm just glad to be alive."

Andy put his arm around her and held her close for the remainder of the trip to his house.

Andy opened the garage and with Virginia's help, stowed the diving equipment. Virginia went into the house as he put the air tanks away. As Andy finished and closed the garage door, he heard Virginia call from the kitchen.

"Coffees on! How about some breakfast? I'm starved."

"Smells good," said Andy. "Pour me a cup while I change into something more comfortable."

Andy walked into the bedroom. He picked out a pair of slacks and a green Polo shirt and laid them out on the bed. He went to the bathroom and brushed his teeth, then filled the sink with hot water while swirling his shaving brush in its soap mug. The brush made lather that overflowed the shaving mug. He applied it to his face and began shaving as Virginia entered carrying his favorite mug filled with hot coffee.

As Andy finished shaving and rinsed his face, Virginia said, "I just found out that you and I are dead, but Abbey's alive. The police got the thugs that tried to rob her at the shop and they got Jameson and his friend for killing us. It was just on the TV news."

"Wait a second. Were dead? Of course. The explosion was enough to bring down the cave on top of us. The authorities would think we were dead. By the way, you're a pretty cute ghost."

"I think we should call Abbey and tell her we're alive, don't you? We'd better call our folks too. Until now, I didn't think of us as news. Or dead."

"Yeah, let's get dressed, call our folks, then we can call Abbey or go to her place."

Andy dressed in the slacks and shirt he had laid out while Virginia washed her face and ran a comb through her hair. Virginia put on a pair of denim shorts, tee shirt and running shoes.

While Virginia was dressing, Andy went into the kitchen and called his parents. After the initial shock, they were extremely happy that he and Virginia were alive. Virginia kept motioning that she wanted the phone. Andy assured his parents that he'd tell them the details of how they got out as soon as he saw them.

Virginia followed suit and called her parents. They broke down and cried when they heard her voice. She told them that no one but them knew that she and Andy are alive and well. She briefly described their escape and said good-by. Next she called Donna to inquire about Leo's care. Reassured that he was living like a king but missed her, she dialed Abbey's shop. The line was busy.

Virginia looked at Andy sitting at the table eating cereal and drinking another cup of coffee. "The line's still busy, let's take my car and drive over to Abbey's."

"We don't have a lot of choice," he said sipping coffee. "The police have my truck with the statue in it. This is going to be fun to explain. A lot of people will want to claim the treasure, we're dead, but not dead, oh-boy."

Virginia and Andy climbed into her car. She started the engine and opened the sunroof. They drove off toward the coast highway with the radio on an 'oldies' station. The smell of eucalyptus and hibiscus drifted in through the sunroof. As they approached the coast, the overhanging fog put a chill in the air. Virginia found a parking place a block from Abbey's store. They walked toward the shop.

"What do you think Abbey will say when she sees us?" asked Virginia.

"Beats me, but knowing her, I don't think she'll faint."

As they walked past the rear alley, Andy stopped. His face reddened.

"What's wrong?"

"The truck I rented is still here and those guys are loading it with the larger pieces of the treasure. Let's get around front and see what's going on."

They hurried to the front of the store and peered inside around the edge of the display window. Abbey was inside. A tall man with gray hair was talking animatedly to Abbey. His back was to Virginia and Andy. Two other men in tee shirts and jeans were loading the treasure into the truck. One of them had a gun stuck in his belt. The man with the gray hair started to turn and walk toward the front door.

Andy grabbed Virginia by the arm and pulled her into a tee shirt and bathing suit store next to Abbey's shop.

"Why would Abbey be loading the truck with armed men?" asked Andy. "If they were guards, they'd be in uniform. I don't like the looks of this."

The man left the antique shop and walked past the store where Virginia and Andy were concealed behind a rack of bikinis.

"I think he just went by," whispered Virginia. She turned. "What are you looking at? You're not supposed to be enjoying this mister!"

"This is a cute little number," he said holding up a small bikini and grinning. "Want to try it on?"

"Oh, behave yourself. Let's go."

Virginia led Andy out of the shop. They walked back to the window in Abbey's shop and peered in. Abbey was giving direction to the two men. Virginia and Abbey opened the door and walked in.

"Hi. This place has old thing that are supposed to be haunted, so we're here from the dead to haunt, too," said Virginia.

Abbey turned. She stared at Virginia and Andy for what seemed like eternity. She turned ashen. "What are you doing here? I thought you were dead. The explosion killed you."

"She doesn't seem too happy to see us does she?" said Andy.

Abbey walked to her desk and sat down. Smiling, she opened a side drawer and removed a small caliber, semiautomatic pistol. "If you're dead, I can't go to jail for killing you can I? Please sit down while I figure out what to do with you."

"Who the hell are they?" asked the larger of the two workmen as they entered the shop through the rear door.

"This is Virginia and Andy. They are the ones, at least she is, that found our treasure. Oh, please excuse me, Virginia, Andy, this is Roger and Mike. They work for me and are assisting me in selling the treasure."

Roger was the bigger of the two men. He looked about twenty-five, dark brown wavy hair, five foot ten, with blue eyes. His tan contrasted the white tee shirt that stretched across his muscular frame. Mike was five foot seven, about the same age as Roger, with black short hair and a physique like a body builder.

"Sorry you had to drop by. I'm going to have to keep you two on ice for a while. I never did like actually killing someone," said Abbey. She pointed at Roger and Mike. "But they don't mind. Tie them up. We'll take them to my cabin off Ortega Highway. No one knows they're alive so they won't be missed. After we move the stuff, we can dispose of them."

Virginia starred at Abbey with a blank look on her face. "Why are you doing this? I thought we were friends."

"The answer is easy my dear," responded Abbey, "It's for the money. The art and antique business is up and down. Mostly down. Daddy's money had been sustaining things, but not forever. This treasure you and Andy stumbled on will go a long way in keeping me in the life style I'm accustomed to. The black market in art and antiquities pays better than the art gallery trade. When you mentioned at the cave that this belonged to the Irvine Company, I realized I was going to have to do something with you. Your untimely death in the cave was a stroke of luck for me, until now."

Mike put a pistol in his belt next to his left hip and pushed Andy and Virginia into the storeroom. Roger pulled about six feet of white nylon rope from a cabinet. He picked up a box knife from a worktable and cut the rope in half. Mike turned Andy around and yanked his arms behind his back. Taking a length of the rope from Roger he tied Andy's wrists.

"Sit here and don't make trouble," he told Andy as he pushed him to the floor.

"You're next little lady," said Roger. "Turn around and put your arms behind your back."

Virginia did as she was told. Roger tied her wrists and tested the knots. She watched Abbey answer the ringing phone. Roger pulled the ropes tighter as she heard Abbey tell Lieutenant Kilroy that she hadn't seen Virginia. She thought that Virginia and Andy were killed in the cave. She hung up and looked at them with pursed lips.

## ~ *16* ~

Mike pulled Andy to his feet. Roger opened the rear door of the shop and held it as Mike prodded Andy and Virginia out into the alley. Roger opened the rear door to the panel truck Abbey used for her shop and pushed them inside. Virginia heard the door lock behind them. Roger and Mike climbed in the front. Roger started the truck and drove out of the alley into traffic. He turned south on the coast highway, joining the morning traffic. Ten minutes later the truck turned east on Crown Valley Parkway toward the interstate. After a windy ride they swung down onto the southbound side of Interstate 5. Reaching the city of San Juan Capistrano they exited the freeway and started the windy trip up Ortega Highway. Andy and Virginia managed to sit up against the right side of the truck next to each other.

"Any ideas?" she asked in a whisper.

"Not yet. I think I'd like a weapon to take on those two."

"Quiet back there, you two!" snapped Mike.

Silence fell over them for the rest of the trip. Twenty minutes later the truck turned off the main highway onto a dirt road. The truck bounced over ruts and swayed around curves with tree branches scraping the sides. Pebbles pinged against the wheel wells and underside. Virginia could taste dirt as the truck kicked up the fine dust covering the road. The truck came to an abrupt halt, knocking Virginia to the floor. She followed the sounds of Roger and Mike as they crunched the gravel walking around the truck.

Roger opened the rear door of the truck as Mike pulled the gun from his waistband and pointed it at Virginia and Andy. "OK you two, get out and be quick about it."

Virginia and Andy slipped out of the truck and looked around. In front of them was a log cabin with a wooded porch and stone steps in front. On the left of the cabin was a brown clapboard shed that doubled as a garage. Next to the shed was a propane tank with white steel and concrete posts around the perimeter. To the right of the cabin was a water well and pressure storage tank. The area was surrounded and shaded by large live oak trees.

Roger pushed Virginia toward the cabin. "Move it you two. This is home for a while, but don't get to use to it. You won't be around long enough to enjoy it."

The soft needles underfoot released the sent of pine as they walked to the cabin. Two mockingbirds fought a blue jay for some seeds near the propane tank.

Entering the cabin Virginia walked into a large living room. On the right was a large stone fireplace. On the floor in front of the fireplace sat an Indian rug flanked by red and orange plaid wing chairs. There was a green couch in the center of the area. A small table was set in the front window with two wood straight-back chairs. The room had a polished hardwood floor with area rugs in strategic places. The kitchen and dinning area was to the rear. The dinning area had a large maple table with four Captains chairs. The pantry was next to the kitchen. A door, to the left, lead to a hallway, the bathroom and three bedrooms.

"Are you going to untie us?" asked Virginia.

"Only to eat and use the bathroom, honey," Roger answered. "Now into the room on the right."

Mike led the way to a bedroom. Roger shoved Andy and Virginia into the room. "Might as well get comfortable. This is your new home and final resting place." He backed out and locked the door.

Virginia sat on the large double bed with a green quilt over the top. Four pillows were stacked against the wooden inlayed headboard. She looked around at their new surroundings. An over-stuffed chair sat in a corner next to the widow and a floor lamp. A wooden dresser sat next to the door. A closet door was on the right. It could have been a cozy room, under different circumstances.

Andy walked to the widow. Through the light curtains he noticed the nails holding the window shut. "We're not getting out this way, that's for sure".

Virginia walked to the door and yelled, "Hay, guard, untie me I need the restroom!" She smiled at Andy.

Roger unlocked and opened the door. "Hold your horses, I'll untie you." He turned to Andy and said, "You stay there on the bed." He untied the rope and led Virginia to the restroom.

Virginia examined the bathroom carefully. The window over the shower was too high and too small to do them any good. There was nothing in the medicine cabinet or Pullman drawers. She flushed the toilet for the effect and opened the door. Roger was waiting.

He escorted her back to the bedroom. He turned her around and started to tie her again when Virginia said, "Why are you tying us up? The two of us are no match for two armed men, or are you two wimps?"

Roger glared at Virginia. He looked back and forth at the two of them, sizing up the situation. "Yeah, I guess you're right. You can't go very far with us here and when Gus arrives it'll be three of us to watch you and your boyfriend. Can't do any harm." He shoved Virginia into the room and told Andy to stand up. Roger untied Andy and started to walk out of the room.

"Can we have something to read?" asked Virginia.

"If you're bored we'll let you entertain us and have your boyfriend here watch."

"Like hell you will. How about something to read, you pervert?" snapped Virginia.

"Yeah, Yeah, I'll get you something. Keep quite until dinner, will ya?"

Virginia turned. Tiny drops of perspiration dotted her forehead.

"What did you do that for?" asked Andy. "You trying to get us killed?"

"I think we need to keep them off guard. Not let them think they are getting to us. Shit, I'm scared. I thought the river was bad. This is worse," choked Virginia.

Roger returned a few minutes later with three magazines.

Virginia climbed on the bed to look at a magazine. Out of the corner of her eye she watched Andy rolling the magazines. "What are you doing?" she asked.

"I don't know. Hoping for an inspiration, I think."

"I hope something comes soon. The bathroom isn't our way out. How do I get us into these messes? This is about as bad as it can get. These guys plan on killing us."

"Things looked pretty bad yesterday and we survived. Let's not give up yet. We'll think of something."

Several hours later, Virginia heard a car pull into the yard and the door to the cabin open. She and Andy heard another person entering.

Virginia went to the door and put her ear against it to listen. After a brief time she abruptly jerked up. "I'll teach that SOB something."

"What happened?" asked Andy.

"That new person must be Gus. But Roger told him I was a cute, dumb blonde! Dumb blonde! That arrogant ass hole. I'll show him who's dumb. Get us out'o here, Dr. Clark."

"I'm working on it. We now have a crude weapon against one of them but we need a gun. I have an idea. Come away from the door and I'll explain it." Andy explained his plan, as little of it as there was, to Virginia.

"Why do I have to be the distraction? You always have the fun."

"Talent, my dear."

At six o'clock they were brought to the kitchen. "You can cook us dinner, honey," said Mike. "There are five for dinner. Have you met Gus yet?" He pointed to what Virginia thought looked like a great ape with clothes. Gus was five foot six, muscular with hair all over his body. He didn't say anything, just leered at Virginia. Goose bumps ran up her spine.

In the kitchen she found hamburger and frozen French-fries. Taking her time she prepared dinner. She used the end of her blouse she had untucked as a towel for her hands. Virginia glanced at the thugs in the living room. Mike channel surfed the six channels they received with the roof antenna. Roger, perched on a barstool, watched both Virginia and the television. Gus seemed half-asleep in an overstuffed chair near the fireplace. The only knives she was allowed to handle were butter knives as she set the table for three. After the thugs ate, she and Andy got to eat while the three guards watched. Virginia and Andy were returned to their room and the door locked.

"Well, there wasn't much we could do out there, was there?" said Andy.

"I don't know. I got a screw driver and a pair of pliers," said Virginia as she pulled them from the waist of her shorts. Her loose blouse hiding them from view. "The screw driver could be a weapon."

"Let's stick to the original plan. The screw driver adds a new dimension, but let's still go with the plan, such as it is," said Andy.

About nine, Virginia called for another trip to the restroom. She asked for towels to take a shower.

"Why would you want to take a shower now?" asked Gus.

"I always take a shower at night. It might be my last, the way you guys have been talking."

Gus pulled a towel from a cabinet next to the bathroom and handed it to her. Virginia went in the bathroom and took a shower making a lot of noise. She dried off, wrapped a towel around herself and gathered up her clothes. Gus let her out and walked her to the bedroom door. He opened the bedroom door and followed her in. Andy was standing near the door as they entered.

"How about you professor? Need the facilities?"

As he asked, Virginia turned and let the towel slip a little, exposing her left breast. Gus's eyes got as big as saucers as he stared at Virginia. Andy lunged forward with a magazine rolled into a tight cylinder. He hit Gus in the throat smashing his Adam's Apple. He twisted the magazine as it started to unroll. The paper slashed Gus's neck to a bleeding pulp. Virginia dropped the towel and lunged for Gus, pulling the gun from his belt.

Gus grasped his throat. He tried unsuccessfully to call out as he fell to his knees.

Andy chopped the sides of Gus's head over his ears. The eardrums popped. He watched Gus stiffen as the pain raged through him. Andy pulled the pistol from Virginia and hit Gus over the head.

Gus lost sight of Virginia and consciousness at the same instant. He hit the floor with a dull thud.

Andy pulled the door closed.

Virginia pulled on her clothes. "Okay. Now what? What a mess, I'm glad I don't have to clean this up," she said as she watched blood seep from under Gus. "Is he knocked out or dead? That was quite a job you did on his neck."

Andy leaned over and felt for a pulse on Gus's neck. He looked up at Virginia, "I think he's dead. I don't feel so good."

"You'd feel a lot worse later when they killed us. Let's get out of here and worry later. Where's Mike and Roger?"

Andy pulled himself up by the edge of the bed and moved to the door. He turned the knob and cracked open the door. "Mike seems to be in the kitchen getting a beer or something," said Andy peering around the doorframe. "Looks like Roger must be outside, probably smoking."

"Let's go for it before they miss Gus."

Andy led the way down the short hall. Virginia kept one eye on Mike. As Mike stuck his head in the refrigerator they made for the main door. Andy twisted the handle; it opened without a sound. Roger was walking by the two vehicles smoking a cigarette. He was facing the woods away from the cabin. Andy and Virginia ran to a clump of bushes near the closest car. Andy kicked some loose rocks.

Roger stopped in his tracks. He slowly turned and swept the area with his eyes. His right hand rested on the handle of the pistol in his belt. He walked closer to the bushes, listening for a sound. He stood three feet from their hiding place. Not hearing anything, he walked to the cabin.

"Where is Gus?" he called out as he entered.

Virginia and Andy ran to the nearest car and climbed in. Andy started to fumble under the dash for wires to start the car.

"No time." called Virginia. She pulled the screwdriver out of her shorts. With the pliers she pounded it into the ignition key slot. She grabbed the handle of the screwdriver with the pliers and twisted the lock. The car started. She sat back as Andy started to pull away.

"Where did you learn to do that?" asked Andy. "Wait. I don't think I want to know. Oh, shit!"

The rear window shattered as a bullet ricocheted off. Virginia heard two more thuds as bullets rammed the rear of the car.

She grabbed the gun in Andy's belt and turned.

"What do you think you're doing?" yield Andy.

"That ass hole is shooting at this dumb blonde. He's going to get his." She aimed the. 357 Magnum out the rear window with both hands and fired three quick shots. The roar of the gun was deafening. The smell of cordite filled the car. One shot hit Roger and spun him around as he fell. Mike ran to the door and started shooting. Bullets hit around the fast moving car. Virginia ducked down in the seat and rolled on the floor as Andy swerved around the dirt road. They hit the solid pavement of Ortega Highway and raced west.

"Keep any eye out for your friends," Andy yelled.

Virginia climbed back on the seat and watched the rear. No one seemed to be trying to catch them. Andy drove to the freeway taking the north bound on ramp.

Virginia's hands were shaking. "I think I shot someone. I've never done anything like that before. What if he dies? I killed him."

"I think we may have killed Gus too, remember? Try and get hold of yourself. We had no choice," said Andy. "Let's pay a visit to friend, Abbey," he said. "Mike may have called her by now so we may need the last of the shots in our gun."

"They can't call out," sighed Virginia. "The phone is in the kitchen. I took the guts out of the mouth piece and put it at the bottom of the garbage container while cooking dinner."

"How did you do that with them watching?"

"The only other thing most men have on their minds, besides sex, is food. As I put dinner on the table, they lost interest in me, for a while."

He looked at her, "You're good, I think I'll keep you around."

"You'd better. If you try to leave, I'm going with you."

They drove to Crown Valley Parkway and took it west to the coast. The evening air was cool and damp along the coast highway as they headed North to Laguna Beach. Wisps of fog moved in from the sea. Dense patches were interspersed with sections of clear spots. The fog became denser as they approached downtown.

"We'd better ditch this car as soon as possible," said Virginia. "We don't want to have to explain the holes and that screw driver to a cop."

Andy parked the car on the street a couple of blocks from Abbey's shop. They walked along the streets hand in hand like a couple of lovers to avoid suspicion. The damp fog and salty air wet Virginia's hair into a limp tangle of yellow strands and curls. They rounded the corner of the alley behind Abbey's shop. Andy's rental truck was still there. A large dark-haired man was placing a lock on the rear door and talking to someone inside the shop. Virginia's car was in the parking space a short distance away, where she left it. Andy crouched next to a trashcan at the end of the alley.

"I'll watch here, looks like some action going on. Go around front and see if you can spot anything from the window. Be careful."

Virginia went to Pacific Coast Highway and walked towards the shop. She passed the bikini shop and slowed down. The lights were on in the rear section of the antique store. Virginia could see shadows of people in the back room and one man in the rear of the showroom. Out of the corner of her eye, Virginia spotted the second car from the cabin driving up PCH toward the shop. The damp fog suddenly felt ice cold against her skin. She turned and walked quickly back to the corner. She turned up the side street and darted across to a dark corner between two buildings.

Andy heard her run and watched as she motioned for him to be still.

The car turned the corner. It moved slowly up the street. It stopped a few yards from Virginia's hiding place. The driver was intent on someone walking further up the street and accelerated. The person crossing the street fifty yards ahead was blonde and had a similar color top and shorts on as Virginia. In the dark, with light from the street lamps diffused in the fog, it was hard to tell who it was. The driver didn't wait for identification. The racing automobile swung sideways and hit the walker like a fly swatter. She flew ahead and smashed into the pavement.

The car sped off into the night and fog. Virginia stood in he shadow horrified. That poor girl died because someone thought she was me, she thought. She felt sick and vomited. She felt herself shaking. All this for the treasure and money. Rage replaced the horror she felt. Virginia watched the road; half expecting Mike to return to insure the victim was indeed dead. Carefully she darted across the street to Andy. He looked shell-shocked.

"That could have been you. In case I haven't mentioned it lately, I love you."

"I know," she said as she huddled close to Andy. "I'm scared, and mad."

"It seems everyone has left except for Abbey and two men," said Andy. " Maybe we could get your car and the truck and get out before they have a chance to come back outside."

"I left the screw driver in the car back there," Virginia said. "Hang on here and I'll go get it." She spirited away from their hiding place and walked in the shadows to where they had left the car. She retrieved the screwdriver and pliers and returned to the shadows of the buildings and trees that lined the street. Almost as an afterthought, she walked back to the car. Virginia picked up a rag from the rear floor and wiped the steering wheel and door handles. She threw the rag in a waste container on the sidewalk. Thoughtful of the city, she thought.

The fog was getting thicker. She blended into the night. Half a block away from the car she saw diffused red and blue beams swing repeatedly through the fog. A police car was stopped next to their escape car. The officers were looking at the window and bullet holes. The parking meter read expired. They'll probably ticket it for the meter she thought. If they go another hundred feet they'll find that poor girl. She decided not to draw their attention. Carefully she threaded her way down the street to Andy.

"If we're going to do something, we'd better do it soon. There are cops up the street and they've found our car."

"Well, no time like the present," said Andy. "Abbey got a phone call just after you left. Maybe Mike told them you're dead. One of the men left. It's just two of them now. "

Andy led the way as they maneuvered up the alley in quick movements from dumpster to dumpster. Andy looked in the cab of the truck. The keys were in it. He motioned for Virginia to run for her car. As she rounded the front of the truck Abbey stepped out of the shop door.

"You! Mike called and warned us that you escaped, but he assured me that he had killed you here in Laguna. I guess I'll have to do the job myself," she said, as she thumbed back the hammer and pointed a baby Beretta at Virginia. "Where is that boy friend of yours, my dear? Might as well finish him off, too."

A large man in a sweatshirt and jeans stepped out of the shop door.

"Unlucky for you we got Mike's call," he said pulling an automatic from is belt. "I thought he said he killed her. What is she doing here?"

Andy stepped from behind the truck firing a shot that hit Abbey in the chest. The magnum slug picked her up and flattened her against the wall. Blood streamed down the front of her shirt. Her heart, blood and pieces of bone blew a gaping hole out her back. The man in the door raised his pistol as Andy shot him. His head disintegrated into the shop.

"No! It can't be…it can't…oh, God, no." Virgiunia felt her stomach retch.

Andy yield, "Go! Get your car and go! Now!"

Virginia picked up the baby Beretta and Abbey's cell phone that dropped from Abbey's purse and ran to the car. She reached under the fender and pulled the magnetic key holder out. She fumbled with the box dropping the spare key on the ground. On the second try she jabbed the key into the ignition starting the car. The car jumped as she backed out of the parking space and sped down the alley and up a side street away from PCH. She looked in the rearview mirror. Andy was behind her in the truck driving without lights. She could hear sirens. Turning onto a residential side street she parked the car. Andy pulled in behind her. She locked her car, climbed into the truck cab and hugged Andy. He was sweating. His hands were shaking. She could feel his heart pounding in his chest.

"Keep down, we don't want a passing police car to spot us. They'll be all over the place now," said Andy, his voice shaking.

Virginia slumped down in the seat and leaned against Andy. "My Good, what have we done? That was Abbey. Andy, she was my friend. How could money become so important that she'd kill me over it? What happened to her? I don't understand." She started to sob.

Andy put his arm around Virginia. "I think she had grown accustomed to a life style that was beyond her reach as a legitimate art dealer. She was a small fish in a big pond. Her income wasn't cutting it and her dad's money wouldn't last. The black market seemed to be the answer. It probably was as addictive as drugs. God, I feel sick. I've never shot anyone. I'm not even a hunter, for God's sake. I've never killed anyone or anything before tonight. Look at us. We're mass murderers. I don't know if I'll ever stop shaking or get over it. I'm sorry it came to this. I liked Abbey."

"I know. I don't understand. She was going to kill me, in cold blood. We went to school together. How could see? I can't believe we got away from professional killers. Even so, I'll never get over tonight."

Andy kissed her as they settled down in the truck for the rest of the night. "Tomorrow has to be better."

# ∼ *17* ∼

The fog lightened as the first light of day tried to cut through. Lights were on in the houses around them. The damp morning smelled of the sea. Virginia stretched. Her muscles ached. She felt Andy stir next to her. She thought of Abbey. Their days at school in France, the fun they had going on spur of the moment outings to Santa Barbara. She remembered when Abbey opened the shop, how proud she was of her friend. The way Abbey lived, Virginia had no idea there were money problems. Business seemed good. She was always off to estate sales and traveling to obtain new works to sell. Who would have thought Abbey could be working the black market. Virginia pictured Abbey holding a gun on her. The thought made her shiver. Would Abbey have really shot her? A tear fell. I'll never know. The mental picture of Abbey, with a bullet in her and the blood made her stomach tighten. Andy shifted his body next to her. Virginia looked at him as he sat up straight and yawned.

"Good morning, Tiger. Things seem to have quieted down from last night. Any ideas on what to do next?"

"I thought about it some last night. Things really got out of hand. I'm sick about Abbey. It seems like a bad dream. The sight of her with that gun aimed at you just sent me over the edge." He wiped his hands on his pant legs. "I have an idea. I'll drive this thing to the university campus. I can get a temporary parking pass from the information booth. No one will think of looking for it there. We can get some clothes and breakfast and rest up in a motel until we figure out what to do next. I'm afraid to go to either of our places just yet. I'd like to know whom else Abbey was working with. With our luck they are watching our houses now," said Andy with more resound than he had last night.

Virginia climbed down from the truck and followed Andy in her car. They turned north on PCH through Laguna Beach. There were police cars and fire trucks around Abbey's shop. The street next to her shop was blocked by police cars as the officers were looking at the street where the girl was killed and their escape car was parked. They followed the traffic through Laguna Beach and continued north along the coast. The fog hugged the coast up to the hills. Virginia could hear the pounding of the surf, smell the salt in the air and feel the dampness through her open sunroof.

The cellular phone on the seat next to her rang. Virginia picked it up.

"Hello?" she said.

"Hi," answered Andy. "Isn't technology wonderful?"

"How'd you get a phone?"

"It was on the table just inside the door. I grabbed it as I was running out last night. It must have belonged to the other guy or was how they use to stay in contact."

"I don't know about you, but last night still has me shaking," stated Virginia. "How many times are we going to almost get killed?"

"Yeah. And killing someone, both of them, even in self-defense, makes my stomach turn. I can still see them both as the bullets hit them. I don't know if I'll ever get over it."

"I wonder if Roger is Okay? I think I hit him at the cabin, but I think I just knocked him down," added Virginia.

"With a .357 Magnum, what would be a slight wound with another gun, can be fatal. A shoulder wound can tear an arm off for example. Then of course there is the little matter of Gus. That cabin will keep the Sheriff busy for a while. There was nothing on the news about the cabin though. Maybe the police don't know about that yet."

"You'd think a neighbor would have called the Sheriff. The gunshots alone should have brought them. It sounded like a cannon. If Mike was after us, then Roger is either dead or at some flaky doctors office. A reputable doctor will report a gunshot wound," said Virginia. "I'll see what's on the news station." She turned on the radio and set the tuner for an all news station. "Call me back in a few minutes."

After six minutes, the news of the killings in Laguna Beach was on. Still no mention of the killings at the cabin. Virginia's phone rang.

"Nothing on the cabin as yet," said Virginia.

"I don't know if that's good news or not," stated Andy. "Leave it on, maybe you'll hear something."

They proceeded through Corona Del Mar to Jamboree Street in Newport Beach. Andy turned east toward Irvine and the university. The streets around the university were deserted at the early morning hour. Andy turned into the main entrance. The information booth had just opened as he approached with the truck.

"I need a parking permit for this thing for three days," he said as he presented his faculty ID. "It'll take that long to unload and find a home for all this stuff." The young coed operating the booth filled out a temporary parking permit, and with a big smile, handed it to Andy. He placed the permit on the dashboard and drove toward the humanities area parking lot. The truck fit nicely between two large fan palms, obscured from the street and most traffic by large oleander bushes. He locked the truck and waited for Virginia to pull up.

"Need a ride, big fella?" she asked as the car came to a halt next to the front of the truck.

Andy climbed into the car and buckled his seat belt. "No one will see it here and the campus cops will even look after it. Let's go shopping. I don't think we should go home just yet. Abbey had others involved and they could be looking for the truck, and us, by now. Let's dump these phones, too. They can be traced if we cut across cells. Then, of course, we have the police to think about."

The phones were pitched into a trash can at the parking lot exit.

They drove, without speaking, off the campus onto the streets around the university.

Virginia drove north on Culver Drive to the San Diego Freeway. "Where to?" she asked.

"Let's take the 55 freeway to Main Place Center. It should be well enough off our usual path to avoid trouble and we can pick up some things there we'll need for the next few days. This will give us some time to think."

Virginia drove up the freeways to the shopping center. It was still closed.

"How about we stop for breakfast and plan while we wait for the center to open." She swung the car into a Denney's restaurant and parked. "I haven't seen anyone following us. Did you?"

"No. I think we're OK for now. What did you do with that little gun you took from Abbey? The one you lifted off Gus has only one shot left. I hid it under the seat in the truck."

Virginia lifted her shirt to show the handle of the Beretta sticking out of her shorts. They walked into Denney's and took a booth near the door and in sight of the car. No one paid any attention to them. Andy ordered French toast, orange juice, bacon and coffee. Virginia ordered scrambled eggs, crispy bacon, orange juice, hash brown potatoes, and coffee.

"After we buy what we need, where should we go and for how long? What about the stuff in the truck?" asked Virginia.

"I got a parking permit for three days. I thought we'd come up with something by then. As for where to go, I haven't a clue. We can't go near Laguna, your place or mine, and probably should stay out of Newport Beach as well.

The waitress brought them their breakfasts. Virginia attacked hers as if she hadn't eaten in a week. Andy plowed into his French toast. Finishing breakfast, they walked slowly to the car.

"We still have time to kill. Do you want to drive around a while?" asked Virginia.

"No. And could you use another word besides kill? The less we move around, the harder it will be for any of Abbey's playmates and the police to find us. Let's go in the mall. The stores aren't open but the mall walkers are there doing their exercise walking. We can get some exercise."

"Just what I need after the last two days," grumbled Virginia as they got in the car. They drove the block and a half to the mall. Virginia drove around the parking lot until she found a spot between cars that appeared to belong to mall employees and parked.

They entered the mall through the center ground floor entrance. The mall had two stories with exposed painted steel beams arching far overhead supporting a translucent cover. The morning sunlight streamed through. The bright colors of the steel support columns and the large potted plants gave the appearance of a science fiction location instead of a shopping mall. Middle aged women and older men wearing tennis shoes walked at a fast pace around the mall viewing each shop with interest as they sped past. Virginia and Andy joined the rear of the procession. The next hour was spent walking over every foot of both levels of the mall.

Sitting down on a bench in front of a video store, Virginia said,

"I'm pooped. These old people have more stamina than I gave them credit for."

Andy joined her. "Yeah, but they haven't been through what we've been through either. We shouldn't look like we are in a hurry. We need to blend in with the surroundings to avoid standing out."

They walked around the shops, looking in windows, until ten o'clock. When the stores started to open, Virginia headed for Nordstroms. She bought a red pullover top and a white blouse, a pair of denim shorts and black slacks. Andy bought two shirts, underwear, socks and a pair of leather moccasins. Next he selected some tan Docker slacks and a brown leather belt. On his way out he bought a brown fedora hat and a small suitcase. Virginia met him at the second floor store mall entrance.

They strolled down the mall to Victoria's Secret. Virginia bought underwear and a nightshirt. They headed for the CVS Drug Store for cosmetics and shaving gear, They picked up other necessities such as tooth paste, tooth brushes, combs, hair spray and aspirin.

At Ocean Land, Virginia stopped to admire the widow display. "If we're going to be holed up somewhere, there may be a pool. We might as well get some bathing suits." She strolled into the store with Andy trailing behind.

She examined three racks of bathing suits before selecting two to try one. Virginia started to look for Andy. He came shuffling up behind her.

"I like the green one," Andy stated with a grin. He held a green mans bathing suit in his hand. "We'll match."

"Great." Pointing to a chair next to the dressing rooms she said,

"Why don't you sit over there while I try them on?"

Virginia tried on the red suit first. She didn't like the way it fit. She came out of the dressing room to model for Andy. "This is cute but if I raise my arms, the top can come up too far. Thought you'd want to see it though."

"Raise your arms."

"Pervert!" she said returning to the dressing room.

The green one, Andy's choice, looked pretty good. She padded out of the dressing room for Andy to have a look.

"Very nice. I like it. Do you want two?"

"No. One's enough. I know why you like it. There isn't much to it. I think a man must have designed it."

Andy paid for their suits. "Anything else we should get?"

"No. Let's start thinking of where to go next."

They walked toward the mall exit. As they passed an electronics store they saw Abbey's antique shop on the large screen television in the window. The commentator was describing the scene of a double murder. The police were trying to see if there was a tie in between this grizzly murder and the murder of a young woman about the same time a short distance from this shop. He was saying that police were calling it a murder-robbery. Police were not disclosing what might have been stolen. A witness stated that two people were seen nearby at the approximate time of the killings. The camera swung around the crime scene. Virginia spotted a university police car in the background. The reporter mentioned that one of the victims had a gun and was probably shot because of it.

Virginia looked at Andy. "They didn't mention anything about the truck or the car. That's something."

"Not necessarily. They won't talk about things that are close to the case or anything that would help the crooks. In this case, us."

"I did notice one thing," said Virginia. "The university police are on the scene. Do you think Lieutenant Kilroy is there?"

"I'd bet on it. We'd better try and get some money from our ATMs. They will know where to find us by the use of our credit cards. They'll know we were here in no time."

"Great, so they know we're alive and where we have been. Now they know we bought stuff here. Don't they use your credit card at hotels even when you pay cash? How do we avoid that, Dr. Clark?"

"Look at this from a positive point of view," said Andy as they walked to the exit. "Maybe the police suspect us, maybe not. The other side doesn't know where we are either."

Virginia stopped in her tracks. "What other side? I feel awful about Abbey and the others, but…you mean there could be more? Oh…shit…"

"It is quite clear that Abbey was selling the stuff to someone. It's clear Jameson and company wasn't our only adversary. Maybe her client's another dealer, perhaps a rich private collector, an unethical museum buyer, who knows. You can bet on one thing. They'll want the goods and may have paid for them, or given Abbey a down payment. Either way, someone else wants what we have. I suspect that they even know who we are and where we live. Right now, they don't necessarily know where we are. The police are a worry, but they have rules they usually follow. The other guys don't. Now let's get out of here before they show our pictures or something."

They walked to Virginia's car. Andy placed their packages in the trunk. He opened the new suitcase and placed their purchases inside. Closing the trunk, he casually walked to the side of the car and climbed in the passenger seat next to Virginia.

Virginia sat in the seat staring ahead. "I've been scared before, but this has really gotten me unnerved. Look, I'm shaking and it's warm in here. We've got the police and some unknown crooks after us with no place to go. On top of that, I lost what I thought was a close friend. How could she try and kill me? It just doesn't seem right. I get all weepy and shaky just thinking about it. What had to happen for her to go so far? Now we're running for our lives. Now what? What have I gotten us into now? And that poor girl Mike hit with the car. She didn't do anything. Andy…I'm scared!"

"I know," he said. "We need to keep level heads about us right now. We've pulled through a lot up to now. I don't see any reason we won't get through this, too. There is a Bank of America around the corner, let's go over there and draw some money out of our accounts. I have an idea as to where we can go for a day or two while we get things in order. Remember, the police still think we're dead. I hope. "

"Not for long I'm afraid," said Virginia as she backed out of the parking space.

Virginia drove to the Bank of America. She got two hundred and sixty dollars while Andy pulled out three hundred.

"Okay, we've got some money and in a short time the police will know that, too," said Virginia. "How do we hide out, without using our credit cards?"

"What a genius you are!" exclaimed Andy. He kissed her. "We don't us **our** cards, we use my university Master Card. By the time anyone traces that one, we should have moved. They aren't issued by name, just AUTHORIZED AGENT. The university is a bureaucratic mess anyway. Even if they were looking for a university card, which I doubt, it will take time for the university to trace who has the card. Department assigns them to users. The university actually helped us this time."

"We'd better leave here. We've been here too long," said Virginia, with renewed spirit. "Let's go to Rancho Mirage. It's only a couple of hour drive. We may even enjoy it for a little while, and it's not close to here. I would think anyone looking for us would look near here, near where we live. And, they have a quilting store."

"Sounds like a plan. Let's get gas and head out. At a time like this, you worry about a quilt store? And why a quilt store? By the way, what do you think of my hat?" he asked placing a light brown fedora on his head.

"You and your hats! If you can recall, with that absent-minded-professor brain of yours, I've taken up quilting as a hobby."

"You don't have enough to do?"

"Everyone needs a hobby. Now lets get going."

The drive took two hours including a brief stop for lunch at a hamburger stand. They pulled into the Marriot Las Palmas about noon. The temperature was 112° degrees. The hotel has a desert-Spanish motif. The entrance was covered with twelve foot, massive, carved wooden doors. The lobby, decorated in southwestern fashion with thick open beams and a large stone fireplace, looked inviting. Beside the fireplace are two big overstuffed couches. The entrance to the dining room is to the right of the fireplace through more massive doors. The gift shop is to the left. The air conditioning felt good against their skin. Andy registered them at the front desk. Virginia went to the gift shop and picked up a newspaper, sun block and a blue girl's baseball cap. She met Andy in the lobby.

He gave her a room key. "We're in one of the rear buildings, number seven, second floor overlooking part of the golf course. We're well away from the road."

Virginia drove to their building around a landscaped broad driveway and through the Spanish style buildings well set back from the roadway. She nosed the car into a parking space in front of the two-story building with their room. They unloaded their new cloths and toiletries. The room was large. It had a queen size bed, table and chairs, couch with coffee table and a dresser with a TV on top of it. The closet was around a corner next to a big bathroom with a large shower. The rear wall held a large sliding glass door opening onto a small patio. The patio had a lounge, small table and two chairs.

Virginia slipped into her new bright green bikini and went out on the patio. Andy changed into a pair of Levy shorts and a red Polo shirt and picked up the newspaper. He joined Virginia on the patio.

"I was thinking, don't say it, when I think we get into trouble," said Virginia. "But, like I was saying, if we have another set of bad guys after us, we'd better keep any eye out for anything out of the ordinary. Don't you agree? Or am I being overly reactive?"

"I think your right. But I don't think anyone followed us here," said Andy. "That doesn't mean they, whom ever they are, can't trace us as well as the police. We'd better keep our guard up."

Andy picked up the newspaper and glanced at the sports section. Over the top of the paper he watched a foursome play on the palm-lined fairway below. None of the golfers seemed to take notice of them.

"I've been thinking," said Virginia turning over.

"Not again." said Andy, smiling.

"As I was saying, who would be after us? Someone Abbey was doing business with right? That could be almost anyone. We'd need her records to have any idea who would be after us. With the police all over the place, we wouldn't stand a chance of getting to them."

"Not just that, but illegal sales wouldn't be listed in her normal records," said Andy. "She wouldn't want an accountant or the tax people finding any files, to say nothing of the police. We really don't have much to go on. After a day or two we will need to go back. Maybe there aren't any other bad guys, and the police may not suspect us of anything."

"If that were the case why were the university cops there?"

"You believe in the Easter Bunny?"

"Cute. You're getting pretty red. We should go in. I think it's getting about time to change for dinner anyway. "

Virginia changed into her new red pull over top and denim shorts.

"You look smashing, sir," she said as Andy came out of the bathroom. "Where are we going for dinner?"

"I thought we'd go to Tony Roma's and maybe see a movie. What do you think?"

"Sounds good to me," she replied as they walked out of the room.

They drove down highway 111 to Palm Desert and Tony Roma's for ribs. The evening air was still warm. The outside dining area had small misters sending a cooling fog over the patio. The water evaporated overhead cooling the dining area. The strolled inside for a dinner of pork ribs, corn-on-the-cob and beans, in the air-conditioned, desert motif, dining room. After dinner Andy drove a short distance to the Palm Desert Mall's movie complex. The movie was just starting as they arrived.

After the movie, they slowly drove north on highway 111 to Bob Hope Road and their hotel. Entering the room Virginia noticed the red message light on the telephone flashing. She dialed the lobby for the message.

"Shall I read the message for you or would you like to pick it up," asked the hotel clerk.

"Just read it to me," answered Virginia as she motioned to Andy to join her.

"The message says, *We know you've got the merchandise. We can deal nice or otherwise. We have paid for it once but we are willing to reward you, somewhat. Contact will be made by the pool tomorrow.* That's all it says. Can I help with anything else?" asked the clerk.

"No thank you," she said and slowly hung up. Her heart pounded in her chest. Shaking, she turned to Andy. "Did you hear that? How did anyone know where to find us and so fast? How did they know we had the treasure?"

"We were either followed or the culprit is someone who knows us."

"That or Abbey did a lot of talking."

"Almost anyone associated with your little treasure hunt has been killed, except us, and that has been shear luck that we're alive," said Andy. "Who do we know that has knowledge of our adventure that is still alive?"

"Lieutenant Kilroy for one, but I seriously doubt it's him," said Virginia changing into her nightshirt. "There's Mike, the last one at the cabin who shot at us. I can't think of anyone else.

And, how would Mike know to find us here?" She turned down the bed. "There has to be someone else, but who?"

"Good questions. Maybe if we sleep on it an answer will come. Good night," he said as he climbed into bed.

"Andy…Andy," whispered Virginia as she poked him in the back.

Andy opened one eye and looked at the clock next to the bed. "It's 1:30 in the morning, what do you want?"

"We have company…I think."

All of a sudden he was awake. As he sat up he said, "How do you know and where are they?"

"They are one person, I think. He is sitting in a car in the parking lot outside our room. I looked out the door a couple of times and there he was, smoking. I saw the cigarette tip glow. What do we do now?"

"Call the front desk and have them send security," said Andy walking to the door. "I want to take a look so don't turn on any lights." Andy released the security chain and twisted the deadbolt open. He eased the door opened slightly without a sound and peered out. Below in a dark sedan, faintly visible from the lights gently illuminating the parking lot, was the mystery person. As Andy watched two cars approached. All of a sudden the car was illuminated in the lights from the two security vehicles spotlights. Two armed officers approached the car. As Andy watched the commotion below a police car arrived. The security men removed the cars' occupant and searched him. The police officers and security men appeared to be questioning the man for what seemed like forever. The suspect was handed over to the police. Andy closed the door and turned around. Virginia was gone. The drapes covering the sliding glass door to the patio were moving in the warm desert breeze. He moved the curtains. Virginia was on the patio leaning on the white iron railing, looking into the dark at the golf course.

"I thought I'd see if this side was being watched as well."

"Have you seen anything?"

"No. But unless the watcher is smoking, I guess it would be hard to tell if anyone was out there. How do they know where we are. If it were the police, they'd have picked us up by now. He," she said gesturing toward the door, "obviously shouldn't have been here or they wouldn't have taken him away."

"It means that who ever it is knows that we like to come here," Andy stated in a low voice as he sat on the lounge. "They haven't pulled something because they don't know where the treasure is."

Virginia moved to the lounge, removing her nightshirt she straddled Andy. "I can't sleep."

Andy reached for her as she lowered her body to his. The sounds of crickets and night birds were the only thing to be heard above the squeaking of the lounge. The dry desert breeze washed across her nude body as she made love to Andy. She stood up and leaned on the railing facing the golf course.

"Tomorrow will be interesting"

Across the seventh hole of the golf course, a lone figure snapped pictures with the infrared film and telephoto lens reflex camera.

## ~ *18* ~

Andy walked out of the bathroom wrapped in a towel. Virginia was sitting on the bed in her tee shirt and shorts. "What's taking you so long, Dr. Clark?"

He dressed quickly. They walked across the cool green grass by the pool toward the lobby and restaurant.

Virginia kept looking around for anyone suspicious. A knot formed in her stomach. A hotel employee vacuumed the pool. Where are they? Who are they, she wondered?

The restaurant was busy. They took a window overlooking the golf course and a second pool. They took their time eating breakfast, watching the lounges around the pool slowly fill up with vacationers.

"I haven't seen anything out of the ordinary, have you?" she asked.

"No. But I don't know what to look for either," said Andy. "This is getting on my nerves. We don't know who is after us. What will be traceable to Abbey's activities and death? Are the police looking for us? Are we in danger or not? So far, every place we've been someone's been hurt or killed. We've been through more in the last couple of days than most people do in a lifetime. We had to kill a friend and people we don't know. Look at me. I'm still shaking.

"I thought of something," said Virginia. She took a sip of coffee. "What if we gave the treasure to the Irvine Company or the police? Then who ever was after it would have the authorities to deal with and not us."

"Do you want to explain all that's happened to the police, right now? Things are really messed up. The idea has merit; we need to think it through. For now, let's go get ready and sit by our pool as the message said."

They returned to their room and changed. Andy stuck the Beretta in a newspaper he picked up in the lobby on the way back to the room. With towels slung over their shoulders, they walked to the pool area and selected two lounge chairs in shade provided by two tall palms. Virginia dove into the pool as Andy pulled the chairs together. He placed their towels and his newspaper down to keep their spots. He wanted to have the Beretta handy. He settled onto one lounge and started to read the sports section as if nothing were wrong.

Virginia did the backstroke across the pool to the thrill of two young men watching from the other side. She submerged for a brief sprint, surfacing to see Andy talking to two men. She dove again. When she surfaced, Andy was walking away. One of the men, tall, with dark hair led the way while the other man, dressed like a hotel gardener followed. Virginia watched Andy and the two men disappear around a building near the parking lot. The newspaper was still on her chair. She swam to the edge of the pool and using the polished steel ladder, climbed out. Where were they taking Andy, she thought? Why didn't he say something before he left? It isn't like him to just go off without saying something. What's wrong? The air was already hot and she was almost dry before reaching her chair. Andy had left a note scribbled on the newspaper.

*They have taken me as insurance. You are to wait for instructions. Don't worry. Don't forget to take the paper in with you. The crossword puzzle is in it. The answer to the line that stumped you, I think was razor.*

Virginia picked up the paper. The Beretta was still in it. He wanted to give me the gun, she thought, but what's with the crossword puzzle and razor? I don't do crossword puzzles. What is he trying to say? What's going on? She decided to wait by the pool for a while. Maybe they would come back. What was she going to do now? Virginia picked up the paperback book she had purchased and started to read. She read the same page over and over again. After ten minutes of frustration and worry, she hadn't comprehended anything. The air was getting warmer. She glanced up at the large round thermometer above the pool bar. It read 109. It's still early and already it's hot. She dove back into the pool to cool off. After her brief dip, she settled down again to try to read and wait for Andy.

A shadow suddenly covered her. Virginia looked up. Standing next to her was Mike. A wide brim straw hat was perched squarely on his head. He had a large manila envelope in his left hand. A knot formed in her stomach, goose bumps popped out on her arms. She wasn't going to let him get the pleasure of seeing her nervousness.

"Well, if it isn't my friend from the cabin," she said sarcastically. "And to what do I owe this displeasure?"

"Noth'n personal, honey. You and your boyfriend did a number on poor Gus. He liked you. Roger didn't recover from the ordeal. I figured it was you that shot him from the car. That slug literally tore his shoulder off. He bled to death. Not very nice from someone who wasn't hurt or noth'n."

"Yeah, but you would have had to kill us sooner or later."

"True enough, but we'd had some fun first. I figure I better be careful around you. After what happened to Ms Abbey and stuff, even in that bathing suit you could be dangerous," he said raising one eyebrow and pointing with the envelope. "I'm supposed to give you this and leave. If you follow instructions, your boyfriend will be given back and you could make some money. Have a nice swim." He turned and walked between the oleander bushes that surround the pool, continuing toward the parking lot between the buildings.

Virginia looked around. There was no one close to where she was sitting. Carefully she opened the envelope and withdrew the contents. There were eight by tens of her on the patio from last night making love on top of Andy and her nude standing next to the patio railing looking at the dark golf course. There were two messages. One was a handwritten note from Mike. It thanked her for the show and a picture that he had kept. He also mentioned that he had the negatives. The second note was from another person. This one was typed or done on a word processor. It said:

> *Check out by noon. Retrieve the truck with my merchandise in it. You will be given further instructions then. Don't notify the authorities. You may have some explaining to do to them. Do as you're told and Dr. Clark will be returned, alive and well. Don't and you will get him back in kit form.*

She slid the notes and photos back in the envelope. Virginia glanced around the pool. One of the two young men admiring her in the water was still watching her. The other fellow was missing. She stood up, retrieved the towels, the newspaper with the gun, her book and the envelope and started to walk to her room. She was on the verge of tears. She had been through hell these past few days, lost a friend, saw men killed, someone tried to kill her and Andy, now she lost Andy. A feeling of loneliness washed over her. She noticed the young man at the pool picked up his cell phone and made a call. There were a couple of families arriving as she walked out of the pool area. The splash of the kids hitting the water would have made her smile, but she turned, a small tear formed in her eye. Her dream of marring Andy and having a family seemed empty right now. The walkway to the building of her room was uncrowded. Two gardeners, in pith helmets and light brown shirts, were trimming the bushes. There was a smell of freshly cut grass lingering in the air. A maid pushing her cleaning cart to a storage room gave her a friendly smile. She glanced up at her building. She entered her room and changed into shorts and a red tank top. Virginia threw the envelope from the pool on top of the cloths in her travel bag and zipped it closed. She loaded the suitcases into her car below, drove to the lobby. She went in and checked out. She left the bill on Andy's credit card.

Virginia walked out of the hotel as the valets opened the big doors. She put on her sunglasses and looked around. Nothing seemed out of the ordinary. She climbed into her car, pulled out of the parking lot and turned right out of the driveway onto Bob Hope Drive. Reaching Ramon Road she turned right and headed for the freeway on-ramp. The highway wasn't crowded. Easier to see a tail, she thought. A series of quick glances at the rear view mirror made the hairs on the back of her neck hackle.

"Either I'm getting jittery or I've got company" she said to no one.

The green Ford Blazer stayed with her in traffic. Virginia increased her speed to eighty-five. The green car stayed at the same distance behind her.

"It's not bad enough these scumbags have Andy and want the treasure, now they are following me."

Spotting the Morango Indian Casino, she turned off the freeway and entered the parking lot. The green Bronco followed.

The reservation had a gambling casino off the freeway that catered to travelers going to or from the Palm Springs area and locals. The casino had slot machines, card games and lounge shows. The bright reds and deep greens of the carpets and draperies were an attempt to look like Las Vegas. Neon signs illuminated it at night to attract customers after the big score but more likely to loose it all.

"Gotcha!" she said to herself.

Virginia pulled under the high canopy covering the drive up entrance. A valet came to her car door and started to open it.

"No thank you. Could you please call that police officer over," she said, pointing to a tribal police officer standing at the entrance.

The uniformed police officer walked to her car. "Can I help you?"

"Yes sir," she said in a vulnerable soft voice. "Over there is a green Ford Blazer with two young men in it. They have been following me since I left my hotel. Do you think you could detain them for a while so I can leave?"

The officer looked at the car sitting in a parking stall in the middle of an isle in front of the casino. It had two men sitting in the front. He pulled his radio out of the holster on his belt and spoke into it. Virginia couldn't make out what he said over the roar of the air conditioning and the radio. He stopped talking into the radio, bent down, and looked at her.

"Wait just a minute. Then slowly pull out and head for the exit. If they try and follow, we'll detain them."

"Thank you so much." She waited for a short time then headed for the exit. The green car started to pull out when a tribal police car pulled in front of it. The red and blue lights went on.

Virginia got back on the freeway and drove toward the coast. With out anyone following her, she sped into traffic. The desert rolled past her as she drove past the big concrete dinosaurs along the side of the highway. The gigantic monsters were a landmark to travelers around Southern California. Banning came and went. She turned off of the I10 freeway onto California 60. The windy road seemed to fly by. Virginia's thoughts were of watching Andy walk away with those two men. We sure weren't very smart, she thought, everyone but the cops seemed to know where we were. She checked the mirror every few miles to see if there were any suspicious cars following.

In the City of Tustin, near Irvine, she exited the freeway at Jamboree Street to take city streets home. At two major inter-sections she took the traffic lights at the last second to throw off anyone following. As she approached her apartment house she realized anyone who knew where she and Andy had been, also knew where she lived. This entire running around was useless. A feeling of desperation began to set in.

"Shit. What was I thinking?" she said to herself. "Those guys following me will just come here anyway." Virginia pulled her bag from the car and walked to her apartment. The place smelled musty. Dust was in the light streaming in through the glass patio sliding door. She dropped her bag on the entrance floor and went to the sliding glass door to the patio. She unlocked and opened it. The fresh air seemed to rush in. Next she turned on the fan sitting on the breakfast bar. The room started spinning. Her body slumped. She sat in a heap on the floor, her strength gone. Leo appeared out of nowhere and rubbed against her. She petted his head.

"I guess you've been pretty lonesome. Poor baby." Leo strutted to his overloaded food dish and began to eat. "I see Donna's been spoiling you."

Carefully, she got to her feet, picked up her bag and walked to the bedroom. She dumped the bags on the floor and fell on her bed. "Andy, where are you? Please, God, watch out for my Andy, I need him so." She started to cry. Leo curled up beside her and purred.

A half-hour later, Virginia sat up, dried her eyes and walked to the bathroom. She turned on the light and looked into the mirror. Bloodshot eyes and a tear streaked face looked back. "What a mess," she said to herself. She undressed and climbed into the shower. Steam filled the air. The hot water hitting her body felt like a message. She could feel herself relax a little. As she washed and rinsed her hair, she saw her razor on the shelf. On the side was written *Gillette*. She stood with the hot water running over her starring at the razor. Gillette. Gillette Safety Razor Company. Andy's message said the missing word was razor. Did he mean the person behind the kidnapping was named Gillette? Who was still alive that new of the treasure? Mike? No, he wasn't smart enough. A henchman at best. Who new about the treasure that she was aware of that was Gillette? Dr. Gillette at the university? Couldn't be. He didn't know Abbey. Or did he? The water started to get cold. She turned off the shower, toweled off and wrapped the towel around her waist.

Virginia slowly entered her bedroom in a state of shock and disbelief. She pulled on a pair of jeans, a pale blue tee shirt and a pair of running shoes. She dried and combed her hair; then walked into the kitchen. She opened the refrigerator. There was nothing that looked appetizing to eat.

She picked up her keys and left the apartment. Her car seemed to have a mind of its own as she drove to Newport Beach. She parked near Peninsula Park and walked across Balboa Boulevard to the harbor side of Balboa peninsula and the Fun Zone. She bought a hot dog and chips next to the bumper cars and merry-go-round, and ate them as she walked past shops, restaurants and rides. The smells of the restaurants, sea breeze and engine exhaust from the rides added to a sense of loneliness. The last time she was here was with Andy. Virginia looked at the unique houses and shops on Balboa Island across the harbor. The ferry was a block away. She walked to the boat and boarded as the cars were driving on. The small ferry has one deck that holds three cars and about twenty walk-on passengers. The little pilothouse had one person piloting the ferry.

A deck hand saw to the loading and unloading. Two ferries moved across the harbor in opposite directions to maintain the vehicle traffic from the island to Newport Beach. On this trip there were two cars and a dark blue van. There were only two other passengers without cars sitting on the port side. She sat on the starboard, amidships seats, alone, watching the boats in the harbor. As the ferry slowly glided into its dock on the island side of the harbor, Virginia decided to ride it back. It was peaceful on the water. The cars and van drove off and a new set of vehicles boarded for the return trip. She was the lone pedestrian. The salt air was refreshing as she watched the sailboats slide silently into the harbor.

So far we've been blown up, spied on, followed, shot at, killed people, been kidnapped and now Andy's been taken, she thought. Why don't I just leave the damn truck at the nearest police station? That won't work. They'll put it with Abbey's shooting and Andy and…forget it. Now what? Give it all away? If it will get Andy back, she'd do it. She realized she had walked back to the parking lot without noticing anything around her. The small shops, restaurants, and business were all a blur. She felt like the past hours were a dream. As Virginia walked to her car, she saw the sign displaying the parking rates. There was extended parking for people who took the boat to Catalina Island. A vehicle could be parked here for extended overnight stays. She had to move the truck from the university. This would be a perfect spot. Right out in the open.

She ran to her car. Starting the ignition, she roared out of the lot and headed for the university. She took three lights on what she called late yellows or 'pinks'. She knew the police usually called them red.

She parked her car in a student lot and slowly strolled toward where Andy had left the truck. She took an indirect route through buildings, doubling back a couple of times to be sure she wasn't followed.

Virginia drove the truck out of the parking lot and toward Newport Beach. The truck was stuffy from being closed up. She rolled down the window. The early evening breeze, scented with salt air and eucalyptus cooled the interior quickly. The truck moved through traffic on the peninsula. Virginia watched for anyone following and any police cars that might take an interest. Halfway down the two-lane road, on the peninsula, a police car pulled in behind her then abruptly turned off.

The parking lot was nearly full when she purchased a permit for four days. She parked the truck in the middle of the lot and locked it. Carefully, Virginia walked back to the Fun Zone and boarded the ferry to Balboa Island. The lights were coming on around the harbor. The breeze was dying. The sky had a red glow. She thought of a saying she had learned as a child: "Red sky at night, sailors delight, red sky in the morning, sailor take warning." Maybe tomorrow will bring Andy back, she thought.

Oh, Andy, I miss you so, please stay well until I see you again, she thought as she looked at the boats across the harbor. What are they doing to you? I wish I could take his place. Please God, watch over him until I can get him back. Why did I ever get us into this mess? I'm not much of a girl friend. I hope he'll forgive me. I've got to figure out how to get him back and not get us both killed. So far all I've done is get us into trouble. Andy's been the thinker and gotten me, or us, out of my misadventures. She looked down. Her hands were shaking. She took a deep breath.

Virginia hopped off the boat when it landed and hurried along the waterfront and the glass fronted multi-million dollar homes. Reaching the main street, she hailed a yellow cab and climbed in. Settling back she told the driver to take her to the university.

"Nice night, isn't it?" said the driver over his shoulder.

Virginia looked at his license attached to the passenger side sun visor. His name was Frank Verentelli. Under his Angels baseball cap, she could see his brown hair. He was wearing a khaki short sleeve shirt and jeans. Frank appeared to be in his late twenties or early thirties.

"Yes, you can see almost to Laguna," she answered.

"Terrible what happened there the other day, wasn't it?"

Virginia looked at the back of the driver's head for a second, "What happened?"

"The killing of that poor girl by a hit and run and a double murder a few blocks away. They say it may be a gang thing or robbery or someth'in."

"Do the police have any suspects?" she asked.

"The cops ain't say'n much, but they have said there was a car and truck seen in the area, but they don't have anyth'in reliable. 'Course they usually don't tell everything they know to the news people. Seems funny if you ask me. Them kill'ns and the blowing up of the cave with that professor and his girl friend in the same area not more than a few days ago. Probably connected somehow. What's you think?"

"You could be right," said Virginia. "What did they say happened at the cave that got blown up?"

"Not'n much. A Prof. from the university and his girl friend were exploring the cave for some sort of old treasures. A well to do couple from around Pasadena blew it up. Tried to steal their loot too. The police have it and everyone else is claiming it. The state, the Irvine Company, like they need it, and the couple in jail. Had a picture of the Prof. and his girl friend in the paper." He glanced into the rearview mirror. "She looked someth'in like you."

Virginia looked at Frank's face in the rear view mirror. He was smiling and looking at traffic. I wonder if he knows, she thought. He doesn't seem to have put it together.

The car swerved as the driver maneuvered to avoid a green BMW that cut in front of them. The driver yelled at the car. "Them foreigners shouldn't be allowed on the road, there ought to be a law."

The cab pulled up to the main entrance of the university. Virginia paid the fare.

"Have a nice evening," she said.

"You too," said Frank as he pulled away.

There were a few people walking around the campus but no one paying attention to her.

Virginia walked toward the Humanities building where Dr. Gillette's office was located. She opened the glass door to the building and entered a long empty hall. The offices were closed. The only light came from a couple of florescent lights kept on for security. The cork bulletin boards were stripped of the pounds of notes usually attached. At the end of the hall she found Dr. Gillette's office. On the little cork board next to the door was a note attached under his name. It read:

'On Sabbatical for the Summer and Fall Terms'

"Sabbatical, my ass," she said to herself. "You…you bastard, and your friends have Andy." She kicked the office door, turned and stormed out of the building. Under the swaying trees she marched back to her car.

There on the windshield was a note. Her heart started to pound, her hands got clammy. Slowly she pulled the paper from under the wiper blade; it was a parking ticket. Virginia couldn't control herself; she started laughing. "After all this and I get a fucking parking ticket! This takes the cake!" She climbed in, crumpled the ticket and threw it on the seat next to her. Virginia sat there, numb, staring out at the trees. She started her car and slowly drove home.

Virginia walked into her apartment, threw the keys on the kitchen bar and turned on the lights. The red light on her answering machine was flashing. Now what? She walked to the breakfast bar and pushed the black message button.

"We know you moved the truck and didn't take it to your apartment. That wasn't in the plan. We'll call you with instructions. Follow them to the letter and we'll give your boyfriend back. No police." The answering machine beeped.

Damn it. She couldn't do a single movement without being followed. Where the hell were they? Why didn't she see them. She'd been so alert all day. This was like being in a fish bowl. How many of them were there? Where they watching her now? Virginia pressed the save button. She looked at Leo sitting on a chair. "Why aren't you a watch cat?"

She walked to her sliding patio door, unlocked it and walked to the railing. The air was warm and full of jasmine. They need to keep me and Andy alive if they want the treasure, she thought. What happens when I give them the treasure? Do they lock us up until they make a get-a-way? Do they kill us too? She shivered as a cold chill went up her spine. I need to think of something, Andy needs me. Where are you, Tiger? What do I do now? You've always been there to rescue me from my follies. How do I do this?

She turned and walked into her bedroom. She stripped to a pair of dark blue panties and a loose blue tank top that went to her upper thigh. Sitting on her bed, she looked at the night-stand. Where did I put the little gun I took from Abbey, she thought? I'll be dammed. It's in my car. Shit, the big gun is in the truck at the beach. At least I have mine. She opened the night-stand drawer. Inside was the automatic Andy had given her. What am I going to do with the three of them?

## ~ *19* ~

Lieutenant Kilroy sat in his office, his coat thrown haphazardly over a wooden chair. The overhead lights flickered. He rubbed his eyes with the back of his hands. He looked at Sergeant Rubin across his messy old wooden desk. The chair he was sitting on looked as if it had seen better days.

"You called off the pursuit car Newport PD had on her truck, right?" asked Kilroy.

"Yes sir. We found and lost her in Irvine. The Newport PD found her and was going to intercept when we intervened. She moved the truck. They found it in an overnight parking lot near the Fun Zone. They have an unmarked unit watching it."

"Where did she and Dr. Clark hide it for so long," asked Kilroy. "Any ideas?"

"It appears that they had it parked here at the university," said Rubin as he stood up rubbing a cramp in his leg.

"Right under our noses? We were protecting it and didn't know it? Now that takes balls. How did you find out?"

"The APB we put out on the truck was spotted by an Irvine PD unit not too far from here," said Rubin. "But she spotted him and lost him. We ran a license check on parking permits and found it."

"So she moved the truck to a public place," stated Kilroy. "Nice move." He leaned back in his swivel chair, placed his hands behind his head and smiled.

"She put a Club on the steering wheel and did something to the engine before she left it." Rubin stretched and sat down again.

"Where did she go afterwards?"

"We lost her on the ferry. By the time we got someone on the other side she was gone. We found a taxi driver that picked up a girl of her description. He took her to UCI. By the way, we ticketed her car. The officer didn't realize it was hers."

"I bet she loved that. Void the ticket. She's been through enough. By the way, explain again how the Highway Patrol unit lost her, too." Kilroy yawned.

"It's been a long couple of days, Lieutenant. The Highway boys were following her in an unmarked unit. They didn't think she saw them. They followed her into a casino on a reservation. When she left, the tribal police intercepted them. By the time it was straightened out, she was long gone. Ingenious little thing, isn't she?"

"You have no idea, you have no idea at all. Is she still in her apartment?"

"Yeah. She's there. Seems to be in a daze. We've got men watching her patio, her front door and her car. We don't have a tap on her phone yet. But she isn't going anyplace without our knowing."

"I'm not as confident as you. Her boyfriend has been kidnapped and she has had contact with the suspects. She hid and moved the truck without us knowing where it was, she lost you and the CHP, more than once I might add." said

Kilroy. "She's scared and alone. No telling what she'll do." He twisted in his chair.

"Maybe so, but we have her bottled up pretty tight. Do you want to make contact? We could phone her, or send an officer as a delivery man or something."

"They have probably told her if she contacts the police, they'll kill Dr. Clark. She probably won't cooperate. She's nervous and worried about her boy friend."

"What about the murders at the art gallery her friend owned? Any connection?"

"I'd bet my pension on it," said Kilroy. "But the details I could not even start to guess."

"Laguna PD thinks the car with the bullet holes and the girl in the hit and run and the art gallery killings are related. Our girl couldn't be involved in all that, could she?"

"I don't know. I think she was involved somehow. We may never know if we do something dumb and get her and Dr. Clark killed. Keep the surveillance team in place. Watch for anyone else watching her, too. Part of the team's job, the most important part, is to protect that young lady!"

Raising from his chair, Sergeant Rubin adjusted his shoulder holster and put on his sport coat. "I'll remind the units to watch for anyone else with an interest in Ms. Davies. Why don't you go home and get some rest Lieutenant, We'll let you know if anything happens tonight." He walked out of the office.

Lieutenant Kilroy slowly got up and stretched. He walked out of his office to the back of the squad room. Kilroy looked at a large map of Southern California on the wall. Where will you go next, little lady? You have a lot of people worried about you, he thought. He returned to his office, locked his desk, grabbed his sport coat and walked out, turning off the lights as he left.

# ~ *20* ~

The morning sun peeking through the window found Virginia waking from a fitful sleep. She sat up and rubbed her eyes. The sheet fell to the side as she got up and stumbled into the kitchen. In a few minutes she had the coffee maker humming. She returned to the bathroom to brush her teeth. She turned on the shower and climbed in. The warm water hitting her skin felt good. After drying off she got dressed in a pair of tan slacks, dark red polo shirt. Feeling somewhat civilized; she retrieved a mug from the cupboard and filled it with coffee. The requisite two spoons of sugar were added. Next she set the table on the patio. She retrieved the toaster oven, butter, peanut butter and jelly from the kitchen and took them to the patio. The toaster oven's electrical cord just made it from the table to the wall socket where she plugged it in. She cut some bread for toast. Breakfast was served.

I guess I just sit and wait, she thought. She tossed Leo some toast.

The kitchen clock read ten fifteen as the phone rang. Virginia picked it up with a jerk.

"Hello?"

"Listen carefully," the voice said. "Take the van to 13256 Ada, number 3, Irvine Spectrum. Be there by eleven fifteen. Pull up behind the building and wait."

"How is Andy? I want to talk to him."

"He is fine. Be there and he stays that way."

"If he isn't there when I arrive," said Virginia frantically, "the van goes to the police."

"No police or no Dr. Clark." The phone went dead.

She slammed the phone down. "Damn. I guess I'd better get ready." Those bastards are liable to try anything. Well, I might as well make it hard for them. If they've harmed Andy, I'll…I'll kill them, she thought. She could feel the adrenaline rush through her. Her muscles tightened as she thought of them harming Andy.

The baby Beretta went in her purse. She ran into the bedroom. She tucked her small automatic into her right sock. She fumbled around in the hall closet and kitchen stuffing miscellaneous items into her backpack.

She grabbed her car keys and left the apartment. At the bottom of the stairs she almost ran down a maintenance man.

"Sorry, I'm in a big hurry."

"That's Okay, I understand. Must be life or death by the speed you're going."

She stopped. "Yeah, kinda is. Thanks."

Virginia climbed into her car. She raced through the driveway and turned toward the beach. The drive seemed to take forever. The traffic on Newport Drive was heavy. She pulled into the parking lot and parked three spaces from the van. She opened the door of the van and removed the Club. Reaching under the dash she released the hood. Virginia opened the hood. She removed the distributor cap from her backpack and replaced it. She wiggled under the dash pulling her backpack with her. Virginia removed the articles she had packed and began assembling a makeshift device attached to the accelerator and steering column. Thank God for Duct tape and an engineer boyfriend, she thought. She took a deep breath and started the engine.

Virginia pulled out of the parking lot and drove east on Newport Drive. She crossed over PCH and drove past Hoag Hospital. I should have stopped this madness when I got Andy out of that place, she thought looking at the hospital. The van headed up the 55 freeway. She weaved in and out of traffic. Why was every one going so slow, she thought. The turn off for the 405 came up quickly and she headed south. The traffic was light, so her 70 mile per hour speed didn't seem to be a problem. At Culver a Highway Patrol car swerved in behind her and turned on his lights.

"Shit, Shit, Shit," she said as she pulled over. Her watch read ten forty five. "I don't have time for this." From her rear view mirror she watched the officer exit his car and walk toward her.

"Good morning miss," said the officer. "May I see your license please?"

Virginia pulled her license from her purse and handed it to the officer. He looked at it and walked back to his car. She sat, her hands sweating her heart racing. She could swear that it beat so hard she could see it hit her chest. I hope he didn't see inside my pack, she thought, the Beretta is in there. I don't need this now. What's taking him so long?

"Thank you miss," said the officer handing her back the license and a paper. "Drive carefully." He walked back to his police car.

Virginia realized that he hadn't told her why he stopped her and looked at the paper in her hand.

> We know about Dr. Clark and your treasure. If you are delivering this van to the kidnapers hit your breaks once. The officer will advise us. We will be around to help if and when you need it. Lt. Kilroy

She stepped on the break pedal once. I wonder how much Kilroy really knows? Does he know about Abbey? Where is he? I've got more people watching me than a Playboy Bunny. The police car pulled out into traffic leaving her sitting on the shoulder of the freeway. Virginia tore up the note and stuffed it in her backpack.

"Well, here we go."

She pulled into traffic driving to Sand Canyon Road. She swung off the freeway and drove to Alton. She proceeded to Ada. She was in the Irvine Spectrum Business Park. The buildings were all two story white office or spaces ready for make over into manufacturing or storage units. The van crept up the street as she looked for the address. She found the small complex with 13256 on the side. Unit number three was in the middle, bottom floor. The sign said Orion Import-Export. How convenient she thought. Virginia drove around to an alley in the back. Number three had a big 3 painted on the large garage type door. She stopped the truck. Her watch said ten after ten. There was no one around. Fumbling, she reached under the dash and pulled a wire tight. She was sweating, her hands clammy. She pulled the Beretta out of her pack and placed it on the seat under the backpack. The smell of Italian food filled the air. I must be crazy. Why would someone be cooking here, she thought?

The door to the truck jerked open. Someone grabbed her shirt and pulled her from the truck. Mike and another man were standing there. The second man was tall with dark wavy hair and brown eyes. His muscular arms strained the green tee shirt he was wearing. He had brown pants with a pistol tucked in the waistband. He held her against the truck. Mike looked inside the truck. On the seat, sticking out from under her backpack was the Beretta.

"Well, well, what have we here?" he said pulling the Beretta from under her backpack. "Going to use this little pea shooter on us were you? What else do you have in store for us? Hold her tight, Jack."

He pulled the van door open again and looked inside. The only thing he saw was the backpack resting on the passenger side of the seat. Mike pulled it towards him and dumped the contents on the seat. The backpack didn't have anything of interest. A small notebook, pen, compact, wallet, lipstick and miscellaneous items. He rummaged around and found the magnum behind the seat.

"Well this is more like it. Is this what you shot poor Roger with?"

"He wasn't poor Roger. He was an ass hole who kidnapped us. He got what he deserved. And he shot first," stated Virginia. "Now, where is Andy?"

"In due time, my dear. Search her, she's dangerous even in a towel."

"You kidding?" asked Jack. "She couldn't hurt a fly."

"Well, you lame brain, she's responsible for Gus' and Rogers' deaths and helped kill Ms. Abbey and Junior. Now if you want to be next, it's your skin. Me, on the other hand, don't want anything to do with her."

Jack turned her so she was facing the truck and had her stand with her hands on the truck above her head leaning against the vehicle. Her legs spread apart. Perspiration trickled down her armpit and along the sides of her breasts. Her hands grew clammy against the warm side of the van. He put his right foot inside hers and started the search. He ran his hands across the back of her neck and down her back to her waist. Her shirt was tight, tucked into her slacks. He looked at the small of her back. No bulge. He ran his hand around front. Nothing. Next he slid his hands across her bra.

"Anything tucked in there?" he asked.

"Nothing you'd be interested in."

"Yeah, let's see." He slid his hand over her breasts slowly. Her soft bra was moving with his hand. "Any where else I should look?"

Virginia could feel the rage surging through her. "Where's Andy?"

Jack stepped back. He drew the pistol from his waistband.

"She's clean. Sit down over there," he said pointing, with the gun, to the side of an adjacent building. She didn't move.

"Where is Andy, you creep?" Virginia was thinking fast. Don't show fear. That's what they want, a helpless female. Didn't these jerks ever study biology? Don't mess with the female of the species.

Jack pushed her to the side of the building.

Slowly, she slid down the side of the building. She tucked her legs up against her chest, hands around her ankles. "Where is Andy? Why isn't he here?" she asked softly.

"We thought we'd help our selves to the loot before our partners take it and leave us with almost nothing. We've been through hell for this. Those piss ants ain't done shit. Sorry about your friend, but every war has its casualties."

Rage flared through her body. Virginia watched them like a cat.

Mike walked over and climbed into the truck, starting the engine. He screamed and grabbed for his eyes. Jack heard the scream and turned to see what had happened. Virginia pulled her automatic from her sock and fired. Jack looked at her in disbelief and shock. The first shot hit him in the left shoulder. He dropped the gun. The second punctured his neck. The third shot hit his lower chest. Blood was splattered on the side of the van. The forth and fifth shots hit Mike in his chest as he stumbled out of the van trying to rub his eyes with one hand and drawing his gun with the other. Her sixth shot hit Mike in the center of his chest. Pepper spray had filled the cab of the van. Mike and Jack stumbled a few paces and fell to the ground bleeding.

She opened the truck windows and climbed in. Her makeshift trap was expended. Teary eyed, she drove out of the alley. Her pulse raced. Behind her she could hear sirens. Virginia drove to Alton Parkway and to the 405 freeway. So much for the police help, she thought. Good thing they didn't show up. Andy might still have a chance. Boy, it's a good thing the bastards didn't find my little gun. That Jack was more interested in my boobs than my socks. Just like a man. What a pig. I didn't know that little gun could do so much damage. Andy said something about hollow points or something. He gets a big kiss for this. I hope I get to give him that kiss, she thought. Tears welled up in her eyes. I've lost Abbey, Lord; I can't loose Andy too. Virginia drove back to the parking lot and secured the van. She took her car and drove to the ferry crossing Newport harbor. The ferry chugged across the mirror like surface of the bay depositing Virginia in Balboa and among the multi-million dollar homes. Slowly, almost in a trance, she drove through Balboa and back to her apartment. The trip seemed like a dream, like it never happened.

"Unit fourteen," the radio in Lieutenant Kilroy's unmarked car crackled.

Kilroy pulled the microphone from its' holder and answered. "Fourteen, go."

"What's your twenty?"

"I'm at Alton and the 405 freeway."

"Lieutenant, the Irvine PD requests a 10-38 at 13256 Ada, number three, rear. That's close to your twenty. You are cleared for code three. Lieutenant, I hope your little lady is okay," said the dispatcher.

"Yeah. Me too. Unit fourteen code three, ten four. " Kilroy looked at the nonregulation statue of St. Christopher on his dash board as he replaced the radio mike. "Keep her well, my friend." An ambulance sped by, lights flashing. I hope the ambulance isn't for Virginia he thought. Kilroy turned on the red spotlight and sounded the siren. The car swayed as he raced through the noon time traffic.

The UCI police car screeched to a halt next to a white Irvine PD patrol car. Two other police vehicle were parked at the entrance. Kilroy climbed out of his car and rushed up to a uniformed officer standing next to the entrance to the rear alley.

"Lieutenant Kilroy, UCIPD, who is in charge?" he asked flashing his badge.

"The Sergeant is en route sir. Officers Ford and Williams were the first on the scene," said the officer pointing. "They are over there by the two wounded men."

Kilroy walked the short distance to the two Irvine officers kneeling next to the two wounded men. Kilroy was careful not to step in the blood that was caking on the white cement. Officer Williams looked up at him and rose.

"They tried to heist the van from the young woman. Seems she was too much for them."

"What else is new. What have you got?"

"We've got three guns, a car with interesting markings on it, and paramedics in route. They aren't going anywhere for a while," he said pointing at the men on the ground. "Their names are Mike Singer and Jack Holm. Both small time con men with records that could weigh down a semi."

Kilroy glanced around. "Any sight of the van or Ms. Davies?"

"No sir. She was last reported on the 405 freeway headed north. We were told not to intercept."

"What were they hit with?" asked Kilroy. "Looks like they ran into a cannon."

"A small caliber with hollow points by the looks of it. I don't think they expected her to fight back. Jack there had a gun that he pulled. He must have flashed it at her and didn't expect her reaction. Same with the other fellow. Whoever trained her to shoot did an excellent job. All six of her shots hit their targets. To do something this desperate, she must be scared shitless."

"You're right. I wouldn't want to be in her shoes. For that matter, I wouldn't want to be the guys that have her boyfriend either. Have the sergeant send me the reports on this as soon as possible." He turned and ducked under the yellow police line tape and walked to his car.

Kilroy sat behind the wheel for a minute then pulled the microphone off its clip and pushed the talk button. "Unit 14."

"Go ahead 14," came the voice over the speaker.

"Get me Sergeant Rubin…and fast."

"10-4"

Kilroy squirmed in his seat as he waited. He rolled down the driver's side window.

"Unit 14, we've patched you through to Sergeant Rubin, go ahead."

"Rubin here"

"Time to call in the big guns, my friend. Ms. Davies is up against professionals and she doesn't have any help. We sure weren't much good to her this time. I bet she wouldn't go near a cop now."

"I heard some of the radio traffic. Is she okay?"

"Yeah, but it's not our fault."

"What do you want to do, pull her in?"

"No. And we can't go near the van. That could be the end of Dr. Clark. Boy, I'll be glad when I can retire. Who ever thought a university police would be involved in all this? Like I said, we need to call in the big guns. She's getting close to the real culprits and real trouble, too. This time we can't let her down. Make the call."

"Consider it done."

Virginia walked slowly up the stairs toward her apartment when her neighbor, Donna, stepped out holding a large, brown envelope. Donna was about five foot six, in her mid-thirties, with short silky raven hair and a very pretty face with high cheekbones and full lips. She had flawless olive skin with deep almond colored eyes. She was dressed in a light blue tee shirt and cut off denim shorts that beautifully displayed her curvaceous figure and long shapely legs. Virginia liked her outgoing, warm and friendly manner. The men in the apartment building were always rating her a fifteen on a scale of one to ten. Virginia always wondered how she rated, but didn't want to ask.

Donna and Virginia belonged to the same quilting guild, Quick Stitch Quilters. Virginia met Donna at a quilting class three months earlier. They worked together on some quilt squares, during which Virginia learned that Donna was a travel agent and travel writer for a magazine. She was also looking for an apartment. Virginia told her about the empty unit next to hers and Donna had become her neighbor.

"Hi, Virginia. This arrived a couple of minutes ago for you. The man who left it says they owe you one." She handed the envelope to Virginia. "You don't look too good, are you coming down with something?"

"Thanks for the message," Virginia said waving the envelope. "You're right, I'm not doing too well. Thanks again, and thanks for watching Leo."

"That's okay. I love Leo. Hope you don't mind, a couple of nights he slept in my apartment."

"No. That's wonderful. I'm sure he appreciated it. I know I sure do. Thanks again."

Virginia unlocked her door and shuffled in. She poured herself a glass of white zinfandel and plopped on the couch. She took a sip of the wine and tried to relax. It didn't work. The envelope rested on the coffee table. There were no markings except the word VIRGINIA hand lettered in black ink.

She tore the end off the envelope and pulled out the contents. Inside was a note from Andy saying he was okay, so far. Clipped to it was a photo of her that he had in his wallet. She was topless at a beach in Mexico. She thought of when the photo was taken. That trip seemed so long ago and yet like yesterday. How romantic, the grilled lobster, the warm sand and the people. The natives liked them, the other three couples were fun. Then there was the uptight religious couple that stormed off when she and the other girls went topless on the secluded beach. Life seemed so simple then. Why was Andy still carrying it in his wallet? She told him she didn't want these pictures flashed all over when he opened his wallet. At least it was one of the ones of her topless, not one of her nude, that he carried. She hoped. Then again, there was one of her topless in his den for the world and anyone who entered his den, to see. Then there was how they met. What difference did his wallet make? It wouldn't be the first time she was seen topless. Funny, all I want now is to see my Andy and his stupid baseball cap. I wonder where the pictures that Mike took went, she thought? Next was a note from his kidnapers. It read:

> You did a nice job on the two rats. The police have them. They also have the gun that was used in the Laguna Beach murders with their finger prints on it, and Ms. McQueen's gun. Their car also matches the one that killed the girl the same night. Paint, and all that stuff the police use. Your gunfire brought them out of the safety of their donut shops. You did us a big favor. Sorry about the traffic ticket. Be more careful next time. Bring the van and yourself to the public boat landing at Newport Beach near Mc Duggal's Bar and Grill. Come at nine thirty tonight. The gate will be open. Wait in the truck. Like before, NO police. We'll trade Dr. Clark for the treasure. We are watching.

"I bet you are watching," she said as she stuffed the notes back in the envelope. She put her feet up on the table and sipped on the wine. The warm air and the smell of a barbecue drifted into the apartment from the patio. It felt soothing on her body. Virginia looked out the window at the palm trees moving slightly in the breeze. The big leaves looked like elephant ears. I'd better get my act together she thought. Can't go out tonight with a buzz.

She got up. The world was unsteady. She glanced at the light fixture hanging from a chain over her dining table. It wasn't moving. Well, it can't be an earthquake, so it must be me.

Moving unsteadily into the kitchen, she put on a pot of French Vanilla flavored coffee. Virginia made a sandwich and poured a large mug of coffee. She took them to the bathroom. Her bathtub was large for an apartment. She turned on the water and poured in three capfuls of bubble bath. In the bedroom she selected a pair of denim pants and a green tank top with spaghetti straps to wear later. She undressed and slid into the tub. The water gently caressed her skin as she ate the sandwich and sipped her coffee. The world started to settle down. She thought of Andy and the last time they were in the tub together. He sat there in that silly baseball cap. She chuckled. I'd give anything to have him here now, even with that crazy hat, she thought. They better not have hurt my Tiger.

The water started to get cool. Slowly she pulled herself up and climbed out of the tub. The earth was stable. Virginia dried herself with a big fluffy bath towel and applied baby powder. The smell took her back to a time when life was simple and any hurt could be cured by a kiss from mom. She went into the bedroom and dressed.

Retrieving the automatic from her pack in the kitchen, she tossed it on the bed and searched the dresser for the box of bullets. Virginia sat on her bed with the gun. She released the clip and pulled the slide back. A bullet flew out of the magazine. Now it's empty, she thought. She carefully loaded bullets into the clip as Andy had shown her. She inserted the clip and pulled the slide. A shell was loaded, ready to fire. Virginia removed the clip, loaded another bullet and reinserted it into the pistol. She set the safety. Seven shots she thought. The extra shell might come in handy. Virginia went to the vanity and combed her hair and applied a little make up.

She walked out on her patio and looked at the pool area. She scanned the gardens and pool. No one suspicious was lurking around. These guys must be good. The last batch of bums we had to deal with was inept by comparison. They were so bad we could see them. I wonder if Lieutenant Kilroy's boys are around too? I need a plan, she thought.

Virginia turned on the television. The news was on. The weather was going to be the same tomorrow as today, warm and sunny after the evening and morning fog burned off. Heavy fog tonight near the coast. She started for the bedroom when the announcer started a story about a shooting in Irvine. Virginia stood frozen as she watched a vidiocam of the scene of a shooting in Irvine. On the ground were Mike and Jack. Paramedics and police were everywhere. The reporter was saying that this was the scene of an apparent attempted robbery. The intended victim got away after shooting the robbers. Police were not giving out information on the alleged victim or what the target was. Police reported that the robbers had guns in their possession at the time but had not fired any shots. According to paramedics, both robbers were in critical condition. No names have been released as yet.

Virginia turned off the television. So far the police are playing it cool. I hope it's the Lieutenant behind it, she thought. She still needed a plan.

"Did he say heavy fog tonight?" Virginia thought for a moment. "God, it just might work!"

She picked up the telephone and dialed Donna's number.

# ~ *21* ~

Virginia loaded a large duffel bag into her Toyota. It wouldn't make any difference if anyone were watching, she thought, they couldn't see inside. At four o'clock, she climbed in and started off for Newport Beach. She could see the fog coming in over the hills. Every block or two she glanced in her rear view mirrors to see if anyone followed. So far so good. She ran a couple of red lights to throw off anyone following that she hadn't seen. At Baker Street she changed direction and headed for Bristol Street. She turned north and drove to South Coast Shopping Center. This place is big enough to loose a 747, she thought.

Virginia carefully parked the Toyota on the first floor of the two story parking lot next to Nordstroms. She locked the car and walked slowly into the shopping center. Virginia casually meandered from store to store making no effort to hide. She stopped to watch the merry-go-round in center court. Next, she went up the escalator to the second level. She strolled down the wide aisle to a store specializing in outdoor wear. A half-hour later she walked out. Her hair was done up under a baseball hat. Her oversized red shirt and brown baggy pants effectively hid her body from view. She looked like an ad in Field and Stream. A shopping bag hung from her arm. No purse was evident.

She weaved her way through the crowd to Nordstroms and exited on the second floor to the parking structure. Virginia looked around then spotted the green Geo Prism with her duffel bag resting in the back seat. She pulled a key from her pocket and climbed in. Donna was a great friend. She could picture anyone following her now trying to make sense of the route Donna was taking in the Toyota. Donna would be dressed in a green tank top and denim pants and a blond wig under a baseball cap. At a distance, the two women looked a lot alike. She had come out of the dressing rooms a short time after Virginia went in. Now, Virginia was headed for the harbor. Her plan was taking shape.

She parked the car in a lot near a restaurant and walked, with the box from the store, to the Fun Zone. Virginia found the boat she wanted and rented it for two days. It was a small white inboard motor boat with seats for four people. She started the engine as the dock boy untied the thirty-foot inboard and threw the rope on the foredeck. Virginia slowly motored the boat about a mile and a half to the pier next to the boat landing. She tied the boat and locked the ignition. Withdrawing a roll of masking tape she taped the key under the seat. She climbed on the pier and hiked back to the Fun Zone. Virginia found a small seafood restaurant, Captain John's, and ordered dinner. The restaurant was small. It was decorated like a pirate den, compete with treasure chests and pieces of eight. The server dressed as pirate. Virginia laughed as she watched him lift his eye patch to see. She sat at an outside table and ate her fish and chips washing it down with a Sam Adam's beer. After dinner, she went into the restroom. A few minutes later she emerged wearing her original clothes. She added a gray UCI sweatshirt. The new clothes were now tucked in the box.

Virginia ambled back to the Geo and exchanged the box for the duffel bag. The crowd at the harbor was increasing. Diners came in search of a seafood meal at restaurants overlooking the harbor filled with yachts and small boats. The big vessels, used for the ride to Catalina Island, were tugging at their moorings as passengers boarded for the last trip to the island for the night. Yachts with smokestacks lined the far side of the harbor. Must be nice to have that much money, she thought.

The fog was settling in. The air was damp with the smell of salt air. The temperature had dropped drastically in the past hour. The breeze had increased to a slight wind. She threaded her way through the people toward the parking lot with the van. She stopped at a bench to watch a couple standing at the iron railing along the water. They were holding hands. The woman's head was resting on his shoulder. Virginia's heart fluttered in her chest as she watched. Andy…I love you so…please be okay. Hold on, I'm coming. Never screw with the female of the species. Especially when pissed off, she thought.

Virginia continued toward the van. She opened the front driver's door and pushed the duffel bag inside. Withdrawing a small vile she squirted the contents into the locks on the side and rear doors. Next she pushed the small automatic into her right sock and pulled her pant leg down. She started the van. Her hands started to sweat and her stomach knotted. It was nine o'clock. The fog had thickened. The lights from the shops by the bay were blurred. She slowly maneuvered her way up Newport Boulevard to the turn off for the boat landing. Virginia saw a husky man with dark hair and a mustache, in a blue turtleneck sweater standing next to the curb between two parked cars. He pulled the two orange cones from the street and motioned for her to park there. She pulled the van into the space and killed the engine. The man walked around the front of the van and opened her door. He held a small semiautomatic with a round cylinder attached to the front. A silencer. She had seen them in movies.

"Just get out slowly and walk to that boat at the end of the pier," he said. "Don't do anything stupid. Leave the keys."

Virginia slid down from the van, closed the door and edged her way to the boat. The white yacht was about sixty feet long. There was a small boat secured to the second deck with a boom to lower it into the water. The superstructure had a rotating radar and various radio antennae. The main salon was lit up. There was a tall muscular man at the top of the gangway. He motioned her up. Virginia climbed the gangway holding the guide ropes. She felt like her knees were ready to buckle.

"This way Ms. Davies." He pointed to the stern of the yacht. "You are expected."

Virginia ambled onto the stern deck. The drapes to the salon were drawn. Light streamed out from around the edges of the curtains. The door to the salon opened and Dr. Gillette walked out. He was dressed in an opened-collared green dress shirt with dark blue slacks and deck shoes.

"Welcome aboard the Cassandra, Virginia. Come inside please."

"Where is Andy, you bastard?"

"I know you feel betrayed, my dear, but that's life. You will be reunited with your lover shortly my dear," said Dr. Gillette. "First we must secure the treasure and see what kind of deal we can make."

Virginia entered the salon first. The walls were polished wood paneling. Overstuffed tan chairs and plaid couches were arranged around the sides. At the far end of the room, on the port side, stood a wet bar. To the right was a wooden door. The floor was covered with a rust colored thick carpet. The drapes were solid dark green. There was a tall, blond man behind the bar in a short white jacket. A muscular man with a bald head in a Rugby shirt and jeans stood next to the rear door. He had a gun tucked in his belt. On the couch sat an Asian man of medium height dressed in a deep green polo shirt, expensive looking tan wool slacks, and brown loafers. He wore a heavy gold chain around his neck. Virginia caught the flash of his Rolex from across the room. A gold statue Virginia recognized from the cave rested on the table in front of him.

"Let me introduce Mr. Andrew Chang, a leading seller of antiquities and works of art," said Dr. Gillette. "Mr. Chang, this lovely lady is the famous Ms. Virginia Davies."

"Very nice to meet you my dear," said Chang raising up from the couch. "You have caused us much perplexity. It is an honor to finally meet my adversary. I owe you a debt for eliminating the two rats that double crossed me."

"They're still alive," said Virginia. "They can talk to the police." For crooks, they are polite, she thought, even stuffy, what bastards!

"That would have been a very bad situation, for all of us," said Chang. "However, that little detail is being taken care of as we speak. Bring Dr. Clark up, will you please, George?"

The man standing in the rear of the room opened the door and disappeared down the corridor. In what seemed like an eternity to Virginia, he returned pushing Andy into the salon ahead of him. Virginia rushed to Andy and flung her arms around him. She bent her head back and looked into his eyes. They seemed glassy and far off, like he wasn't there. Something was wrong. The last time she had seen him like this was after his wisdom teeth were pulled. He was drugged. As she pulled him close, she kissed him. Her neck tightened. These sons of a bitch will pay for this.

"Okay, That's enough of that for now," said Dr. Gillette. "After what happened today and seeing her ability to get out of tight places, I suggest we search her. She's a little Annie Oakley. I don't want to test her marksmanship here. Search her George."

Virginia whispered, "misdirection time again," as she was pulled away from Andy.

George pushed Andy down on a chair. Virginia was shoved to the center of the room. George approached her carefully.

Virginia pulled her sweatshirt off and threw it to Andy. Every eye was on her. Virginia's heartbeat quickened. She smiled.

"Do I look like I have a weapon on me?" she asked as she slowly turned around. "Anyway, you have the treasure. Let Andy and me go. That was the deal."

"No. You don't seem to have any weapons. But, while you're our guest, we need to insure that you are defenseless. You seem to come up with something every time you are in a tight spot. You're right, that was the deal. However, we can't just let you go. You know enough to have the police all over us in short order," said Dr. Gillette. "Search her, George."

"Funny, I didn't think it would be that easy," she said sadly. A knot formed in her stomach. Her heart felt like it was going to hit her chin. She had to keep them from the automatic in her sock. Virginia swallowed hard, this wouldn't be the first time she done this, but this time her and Andy's life depended on her ability. Her hands turned sweaty.

George edged closer. He hesitated for a minute, not exactly sure how to search a girl in a tight top and pants.

Virginia smiled at George. "It's okay George. I'll make it easier for you."

Virginia slowly turned around and with clammy hands, pulled the tank top out of her pants. She raised it up just below her breasts. Facing Dr. Gillette and Mr. Chang, she removed her top, exposing a shear lace bra.

"See any weapons?"

She reached around back, unfastened the snaps and removed her bra. She held it out in front of her, smiled, and dropped it on the carpet. All eyes followed it. Virginia felt in control. Small beads of perspiration formed on her brow. Next she unfastened her belt and pants. She slowly wiggled them down past her hips and let them fall around her ankles. She stood in the middle of the room in a pair of French cut black panties. Her forehead was hot, her heart pounded, blood raced everywhere.

She smiled. "Satisfied, gentlemen?"

They sat without speaking for a minute. George stood about five feet away. He looked like a bass, mouth opening and closing with nothing coming out. Men were so defenseless with a nude woman around. For all their big talk, they're pussycats at a time like this. Jerks, she thought. Virginia slowly bent down and pulled her pants back up. With a decided wiggle, she pulled them over her hips and fastened the belt. She slowly bent down and picked up her top. With prolonged gestures she pulled it over her head and tucked it into her pants. She picked up her bra and went to Andy. She sat next to him. Thank goodness they missed the gun. The last thing on their minds was my socks. She thought of Mike and Jack. Thanks for the rehearsal.

The door to the salon opened and the man from the gangway stepped in. His eyes were narrow and his nostrils contracted reflexively. He definitely looked upset. The knuckles on one hand were bruised.

"She put something in the door locks. We're having a hell of a time. Should we just rip it open?"

"No!" yelled Chang. "Do you want to attract attention and the police?" Turning to Virginia he said, "What the hell did you do?"

"A little super glue goes a long way."

"Shit!" Chang threw an ashtray across the room. "You are a pain in the neck, a royal pain. I thought you'd do something like this. You and your boy friend won't be going anyplace soon. George, take them to Dr. Clark's cabin while we sort this out. I'll deal with you personally, young lady."

George pulled his gun and motioned for them to head for the door. They walked down the hall to a polished wooden door on the right side of the corridor. Andy opened it. Virginia and Andy entered the stateroom as George closed the door. Virginia heard the lock turn. This had better work, she thought. There is no plan B. Andy sat on the queen size bed under a red draped porthole. The room had polished oak walls with a painting of a sailing ship on one wall. An oak dresser with a mirror stood next to the door. A small closet was on the sidewall. Next to the closet was a small wood desk and padded chair. The floor had a green carpet with a wide rust border. Virginia sat on the bed next to Andy. He still seemed doped.

"How do you feel?" she asked.

"Like I'm in a daze. Everything seems in slow motion." He pulled Virginia close. Her head rested on his chest. Andy smelled the apricot shampoo in her hair, felt her warmth. She was there. He could feel her breasts moving against his chest. It seemed like a dream.

"I've got to get us out of here," she stated as she pulled back and looked around. "I think I have a plan."

"That's scary. By the way, nice strip tease back there, but did you really need to do that?"

"You bet. If George had searched me, he would have found this." She raised her leg and pulled the small automatic from her sock. "This way, they were concentrating on the rest of me and didn't think of my ankle. Most men are perverts at heart. Show them some boob and they can't even remember their phone numbers. Present company excluded, of course. I must be getting pretty good at it by the way things are going. Anyway it worked so far."

"I'm not exactly in the prime of condition. Can't think straight," slurred Andy. "What are we going to do? On second thought, I may not want to know ahead of time."

"Very funny. Our first objective is to get the hell out of here."

Virginia straightened up and surveyed the room. No bathroom. How convenient she thought. Here we go again.

Virginia stood up, took a deep breath, went to the door and banged on it. She called out to George. A few minutes later George arrived. He unlocked the door and with his nine millimeter drawn, he slowly opened it. Virginia's heart raced. She stood four feet back from the door so he could see her. As he entered she looked at him with sedate expression. He looked at Andy sitting on the bed and put the gun in his belt.

"What do you want?" he asked.

"I was going to ask to use the bathroom, but I'll settle for that gun," said Virginia as she swung the little automatic from behind her back. She aimed it straight at his head.

George looked at her in shock. "Where did you get that?"

"In my sock, and carefully drop your gun on the bed. I'd hate to mess up such a pretty boat. But for what you've done to Andy, I'd happily blow all of you into little pieces. I'm getting pretty good with this, too."

"So I've heard."

George dropped his gun on the bed as Virginia motioned him into the room.

"We didn't see your socks when we searched you, did we?" asked George.

"No. As usual, you men were more interested in my top than my ankles. Nice of you to oblige. And, by the way, you didn't search me. I showed you what I wanted you to notice and you did. Now lay down and put your arms behind you. Tie him up will you, please, Andy?"

"With what?"

"That," said Virginia pointing to her bra.

George lay face down on the bed while Andy tied him with Virginia's bra.

"Now that's a nice touch," she said. She picked up the nine millimeter as Andy stuffed part of a pillowcase in George's mouth. Virginia searched his pockets. The keys were in his back pants pocket.

"Let's go," she said pulling Andy by the arm.

Virginia and Andy slid into the corridor. The carpeting will help keep noise down, she thought. She locked the cabin door.

"Is there another way out besides the main salon?" she asked.

"Yeah," Andy mumbled as he pointed. "Down that way a couple of doors."

They hurried to the outside companionway door. Virginia peered out the window. It was dark and foggy. She cracked open the door and listened. The gentle sounds of the water lapping against the side of the boat were mixed with muffled music from a radio. They slid out and quietly shut the door. Virginia took the lead down the companionway, hugging the wall, toward the stern and shore when the yacht trembled as the engines started. God this better work she thought. The yacht started to move. The damp salty air had a definite chill in it. Virginia shivered.

"Who goes there?" a voice called from the fog in the direction of the bow.

Virginia didn't answer. She and Andy bent down and hurried aft. A shot rang out as the bullet roared past them. Virginia turned. She raised the nine-millimeter automatic and fired three shots in the direction the voice and bullet had come from. A door opened. She heard footsteps on the walkway above her. Soft light filtered through the curtains from the main salon. Virginia could hear Chang yelling orders to someone inside. The rear door to the salon opened. A figure rushed from the light onto the aft deck area.

"Jump!" she said, pushing Andy head over heals into Newport bay. She fired one more shot as she heard his splash. She jumped in the water behind Andy. The automatic flew out of her hand as she fell. The water was cold. Cold to the bone. Her body went rigid as she sank into the dark water. She felt her small automatic slip out of her belt into the bay. Her body convulsed with the cold. How was Andy handling the cold in his drugged condition? Where was Andy? She couldn't see three feet in front of her. She couldn't hear any splashing or sounds of swimming. Fear griped her like a vice. Voices were emanating from the Cassandra as it moved away. A gun fired. She could hear the bullets hit the water a few feet away. Six or eight more shots rang out over the water. The men on the yacht couldn't see them in the water. They were shooting blind. Did they hit Andy? After all she'd been through, he just had to survive. She turned around and collided with Andy. He was face down in the water. Virginia turned him over and slowly swam away from the retreating yacht pulling Andy with her. Hang in there, big boy, I need you, she thought as she struggled. I'll never make a lifeguard. This is tough. Through the fog, she heard a soft voice. Barely an audible sound, more like a whisper.

"Virginia. Virginia is that you? Please be you…p l e a s e."

It was Donna in the rented boat.

"Over here," she said, spitting out seawater. "Over here."

Donna followed Virginia's voice. Skillfully she pulled the boat next to Virginia and Andy. As Virginia pushed and Donna pulled, they managed to get the half-awake and half-drowned Andy into the boat. Virginia climbed in. She could hear police sirens getting louder.

Donna tossed her a couple of heavy blankets. "Put these around you and Andy before you freeze to death." She steered the boat toward the center of the harbor and aimed for the rental dock. Virginia stared at Donna. She was dressed in baggy brown corduroy pants and a dark blue fisherman's bulky wool sweater. She seemed right at home at the controls.

"Thanks. Good timing." Looking at the blanket she was wrapping around Andy she said, "By the way, where did you get these?"

"Thought you might need them tonight. It was going to be a bit chilly and that water is damn cold."

Virginia wrapped the second blanket around herself as she started to shiver. She pulled the blanket tighter and tucked the ends of Andy's blanket under him.

The red and blue lights from the police cars looked like diffused beacons in the foggy night. For the first time Virginia heard the baritone sound of a foghorn at the entrance to the bay. The yacht was in the main channel racing toward the harbor entrance. It was maneuvering without running lights. Virginia could barely see the outline as the fog swallowed the Cassandra into the night. They motored in silence somewhere behind the yacht. The lights from restaurants lining the bay added a diffused eerie light to the bay. Motor boats, yachts, and sailing vessels swayed in their slips like ghost ships in the dark.

Donna turned the boat toward the boardwalk. "I think we belong somewhere around here," she said. "How's Andy doing?"

"He's coming around, I can't...what the hell is that?" said Virginia looking at the bright lights in the fog. The Cassandra was lit up.

A voice boomed from the direction of the lights ahead of the yacht.

"This is the United States Coast Guard. You on the Cassandra, stop your engines and prepare for boarding. Get everyone out on the fore deck with their hand on top of their heads. Refuse to obey and we will fire."

Virginia and Donna looked into the light. There, ahead of the Cassandra, was a large Cutter. She had a big deck gun on the bow. Virginia could barely see the small zodiacs that were pulling away from the Cutter heading for the Cassandra.

"I wouldn't want to argue with that," said Donna. "Let's get you two to shore. I think we may need to get Andy to a hospital."

Donna found the dock and pulled into their mooring stern first like an experienced salt. The fog swirled around the pilings and other boats.

"Remind me to ask how you seem to handle this boat like it was part of you," said Virginia. She shivered again. "God, that water's cold," she said blowing on her hands.

"Hello. Let us give you a hand," said a voice from the dock.

Virginia looked up. Standing on the dock were two men in suits and two uniformed Newport Beach Police officers. One of the men in a suit was Lieutenant Kilroy. Donna tossed the stern line to one of the uniformed officers. He took the line and tied off the boat. Virginia passed the second rope to Kilroy. He secured the line to a cleat on the dock. The boat secure, the second uniformed policeman jumped into the boat to help Andy onto the dock. Andy sat on a bench with the blanket around him. Virginia and Donna climbed on the dock. Virginia checked the boat in while the police officers examined Andy.

"Ms. Davies, this is Special Agent Wickman of the U.S. Customs Service," said Lieutenant Kilroy. "He is very interested in the booty that the Cassandra is carrying."

"Nice to meet you…I think. It's cold and I think Andy needs a doctor. Could we talk later?"

"The officers have called the Paramedics. We can all go to the hospital and talk while the docs look at Dr. Clark. Why don't you ladies ride with us? We'll bring you back to your cars later."

"I'm sorry, Lieutenant Kilroy, this is Donna Boletti. She's a friend. And our life saver." said Virginia.

"Under the circumstances, I'm glad you're here. We weren't much help protecting this lady or Dr. Clark." He said as they started toward his car.

"Oh! Wait a minute, I'll have to move my car," said Donna. "It can't stay where it's parked much longer without a ticket."

"I'll take care of that," said a uniformed officer. "No one will touch your car or Ms. Davies'." They told him where their cars were parked and the license numbers.

The paramedics arrived. A fire engine pulled in behind the paramedic van and blocked the road. The firemen lowered Andy to the stretcher and examined him. An intravenous bag was attached to his left arm as the medics talked to the hospital. They injected some drugs Virginia couldn't identify into the tubing. The ambulance attendants loaded him into a waiting ambulance along with one of the paramedics. They transported him to Hoag Hospital. The fire truck took the lead in front of the ambulance. Donna and Virginia followed the ambulance, in Lieutenant

Kilroy's police car. The paramedic van and the Customs Service Agent's vehicles brought up the rear of the caravan.

"While Dr. Clark is being taken care of, why don't you fill us in on your adventure?" stated Lt. Kilroy.

"How much do you already know?" asked Virginia. *They probably have enough information to lock Andy and I up for the rest of our lives.*

"Considering what you've been through, and the fact that you inadvertently helped capture a smuggling ring, I think I owe you that much," answered Kilroy. "We picked up some two bit hoods trying to rob Ms. Mc Queen the evening you were blown up in the cave. She told us where you were and that Charles Jameson was there to get the rest of the treasure. She also said that the robbers told her that Jameson was going to kill you. We arrived at the cave too late. Jameson and his girlfriend are now resting in the company of the Sheriff."

"So, you thought we were dead. How did you figure out we were alive?" asked Virginia shivering. She pulled the blanket tighter.

"We thought you were dead until credit card usage was reported. We contacted your parents. They told us you and Dr. Clark were alive. We had no idea where you went. The Laguna Beach Police put a trace on the university credit card. There was also the matter of a couple of killings in Laguna. A witness thought someone looking like you was seen near the murders. The Sheriff was interested in a car found in Laguna the night of the murders. Seems it had bullet holes in it. And, it seems it was seen near a cabin belonging to Ms. Mc Queen." He reached for the sleeve of his sport coat and removed a piece of lint.

Continuing he said, "There were more bodies there, too. Dr. Clark's and your fingerprints were at the cabin. The Sheriff doesn't know how long they'd been there. Now, presto, you turn up in Palm Desert. We had the Riverside County Sheriff put a stake out on you. As they were arriving, the call for officers came in from the hotel. The stake out team watched as the hotel security people and another team of uniformed officers took the low life that was watching you away. At the pool the next day, they saw Dr. Clark talk to some men. He seemed agitated. When he left with them, one of the detectives tried to follow. They got away. We lost them. The second officer stayed at the pool to watch you."

"They must have been the two young men I saw while swimming," said Virginia pacing the floor, dragging her blanket. Her eyes took on a haunted look as she glanced at the doors to the treatment room.

"That was them. They watched you check out and notified the CHP to tail you. You must have spotted them. They had fun trying to explain themselves to the Tribal Police."

"Great, I shanghighed my body guards, " said Virginia in a cracking voice. She sat down in a green upholstered chair and tucked her legs under the blanket.

"We picked you up at your apartment. We managed to loose you when you moved the truck. Hiding it at the University was a cute trick.

"Yeah, but I got a parking ticket in the mean time."

"I had your ticket canceled. We didn't know where you put the truck. When you went to get it for the first try at trading it for Dr. Clark we found you. The Highway Patrol helped with the traffic stop and the note."

"That scared me. The police were all I needed," said Virginia. "Even at that, you guys weren't much help when I needed it."

"Because of the location, we couldn't get close without endangering you. When the Irvine unmarked units heard the gunfire, they responded," said Kilroy. "You took off like a scared rabbit."

"No shit!"

"What we found when we got there was a policeman's dream."

"How so?" asked Donna as she leaned forward in her chair.

"What we found were two injured suspects with guns. It looks like one belonged to Ms. Mc Queen. The other may have been the gun that killed her, along with an accomplice, and a man at her cabin. Obviously…they did the terrible deeds. There was a car there that belonged to one of the men. It is being examined for possible involvement in a hit and run in Laguna the night Ms Mc Queen was killed. I don't think I want to know where you were that night."

"I heard the two men who tried to rob me are dead. Is that true?" asked Virginia.

"Yes, someone got to them in the hospital. They won't be testifying. Who told you that?"

"Mr. Chang, from the yacht."

"Chang told you, tonight?"

"Yeah."

"That could implicate him in a double murder. The DA will love that."

"By the way, how did you manage to bring in all the horsepower tonight?"

"We had you followed. You two did a good job with the switch at South Coast Plaza. That caused us to follow both of you. We picked off one of their people trying to follow you…or Ms. Boletti as it were. He said he never saw the stop sign. When the officers noticed his gun, they took him out of the picture. When you rented the boat, Customs notified the Coast Guard."

These guys are pretty good after all, thought Virginia. Kilroy was there at the end. How about that? The good guys won after all.

Turning toward Special Agent Wickman Donna asked, "How do you fit in?"

"We have been trying to get something on Mr. Chang and his associates for some time," said Wickman. "Ms. Mc Queen was under suspicion along with Dr. Gillette. But, we had nothing concrete. The ring smuggled art and antiques into the country and sold them to private collectors and some museums. The antiques or art was usually stolen. These types of crimes are difficult to solve. Mr. Chang, while appearing very polished is ruthless and a killer. The Lieutenant notified us of your treasure and what was happening. We agreed to cooperate. We had agents on that cutter that stopped them." He looked down at his pager. Smiling, he got up and went to the pay phone in the corner of the waiting room.

Kilroy looked at Virginia and Donna, "You two pulled off a feat that has stumped law enforcement for years. You not only saved Dr. Clark but also managed to have Mr. Chang and Dr. Gillette get caught with the antiques on their boat. With what we have learned and the kidnapping of Dr. Clark, they won't be walking around much. You two, however, risked your lives. You should have called us to help you."

"Like in Irvine?" said Virginia with a coy smile.

"By the way," interjected Wickman as he walked back to the group, "The agents on the Cutter just called. They have Chang's records, complete with names, dates, items sold…everything. The U.S. Attorney and the IRS boys are going to have a field day with that. Tax evasion will put them away for a real long time."

The door to the emergency room opened. A doctor shuffled into the room.

Looking at Virginia he asked, "Are you here with Mr. Clark?"

"Yes," said Virginia standing. "How is he?"

"He'll be fine. The drugs they gave him will wear off in about twenty-four hours. He has the constitution of an ox. The disposition of one, too. He doesn't like our company and wants to go home."

"Great! Any special instruction?" asked Virginia.

"Just rest and fluids. Someone will be wheeling him out soon." He turned and went back in the emergency room.

Turning, Virginia asked, "What's next, Lieutenant?"

"First we take Dr. Clark home. Agent Wickman will do that. I'll return you two to your cars. I want you both to come into my office at the university sometime tomorrow to help fill in the details, that I and I repeat, I, think we need. I want you to think about the questions and answer just what's asked. Understand?"

Virginia and Donna looked at each other then together said, "We understand, sir."

Andy appeared in a wheel chair pushed by a serious looking orderly. He still seemed dazed. "I may be a little dull right now, but didn't we just go through this exercise? I'm getting tired of hospitals. To the gates of this place, please, James!"

Virginia patted Andy's head and looked at the orderly, "He's this way when it's time for finals too. Don't take it personal." She walked along side of the wheelchair holding her blanket off the floor as the others followed.

Andy was placed in Agent Wickman's car for the drive home. Virginia kissed him and closed the door. Andy was waving his arms and talking fast. A big grin appeared on his face, like a kid who got away with the cookie jar. The Customs Officer nodded his head and put his red light in the front window as they turned out of the parking lot. Virginia smiled as she and Donna got into Lieutenant Kilroy's police car. He did it; he got the red light on, what a smooth talker. The fog looked like smoke as they made their way to the beach and Virginia's and Donna's cars.

As the police car pulled away from the parking lot, Virginia turned to Donna.

"I don't know how to thank you for tonight. You were wonderful."

"Don't mention it," said Donna. "How often does a girl get to go boating at night, in the fog, get shot at, rescue friends, and explain the evening to the police, in a hospital." She started to laugh.

"Well, are you game for one more little adventure?" asked Virginia.

"I've gone this far, why not. What do you have in mind?"

"Call me first thing in the morning and I'll explain. I'm going to Andy's tonight to make sure he's okay. Here, I'll give you his number."

Virginia retrieved a piece of paper and a pen from her car and wrote Andy's number on it. "You're not working tomorrow are you?"

"No. Even if I were, this would warrant a days sick leave. The travel business has been a little slow lately."

$$\sim 22 \sim$$

Virginia walked on the patio. Andy was sitting at the redwood picnic table, in his brown terry cloth bathrobe, eating an English muffin and drinking coffee from a Laguna Playhouse mug. The sun created a rainbow in the sprinkler in the lawn.

"You're not planning on doing anything today, right?" she asked.

"Yeah. Just me and the TV. I'm feeling a lot better except for the headache. The doc said to expect it but I can't take anything for it. I'll be okay. Only the good die young. Who was on the phone?"

"Donna. I told her to call this morning," she said. "We have a couple of things to do, including talking to Lieutenant Kilroy. I need to use the truck, is that okay?"

"Sure. Go ahead."

Virginia bent over and kissed him. "I was worried about you Tiger. I love you, yeah know."

"I know. I love you, too. After what you went through to get me, I'd be a damn fool for letting you get away. Even if you are a little nuts, life around you isn't boring."

Virginia headed for the truck parked in the driveway. She tucked her pale blue blouse into a pair of tan slacks and slung her brown backpack over her left shoulder. She climbed into the truck, opened the sunroof, and drove out of the driveway. A quick glance around didn't reveal any unusual activity as she pulled away. Virginia chucked; looking over her shoulder has become a habit. Seems funny now, she thought.

Pulling into the driveway of her apartment house, Virginia spotted Donna waiting. In her red blouse and jeans, she stood out like a beacon against the greenery around the apartment building. A brown leather purse hung from her left shoulder.

"Are we going to see Lieutenant Kilroy?" she asked, climbing into the truck.

"Yeah. I thought we'd get it out of the way first. I called and he said he'd be there waiting for us. From what he said, it shouldn't take long."

Virginia and Donna spent the next four hours talking to the lieutenant going over the details. The police didn't want to press the issue about the cabin. They figured that there was a problem between the low lives that were at the cabin the night of the shootings and the attack on Gus. Since the gun used at the cabin and at Abbey's shop seemed to be the same, the ballistics tests should confirm it, and Mike had it when the police found him, it seemed like a reasonable assumption. There was no gun to compare to the bullet fragments in Mike and Jack. It would be hard to prove that Virginia had anything to do with it, except that she was there about the time the police heard gunfire.

Anyway, it would probably be ruled as self-defense, so why bother to push the issue.

"Do you want to get a bite to eat before we head for our next project?" said Virginia.

"Thought you'd never ask."

Virginia drove to Pacific Coast highway and turned south. The fog had lifted. The afternoon sun was bright and warm. The ocean was calm, and the breakers were small, about two to three feet. Traffic in Laguna Beach was light. She parked the truck on a side street. They walked to a little Italian restaurant, El Cappo, and took a table overlooking the ocean. Virginia ordered an antipasto salad and ice tea. Donna ordered a Caesar Salad and ice tea.

Donna drew circles in the white tablecloth with her fork while watching the ocean below. "Where are we going next? " she asked.

"Have you ever had a funny feeling that something wasn't right?" asked Virginia. "You know, that feeling in the pit of your stomach? Well, when Abbey, Andy and I were taking the treasure from the cave I had one of those feelings. So in order to cover myself, I didn't load all the treasure into the van."

Donna's eyes grew. She tilted her head. "You're kidding? Didn't anyone notice? Does Andy know?" She dropped her fork. Her hand went to her mouth as she stared at Virginia.

"Abbey made a comment. She said that for all our work, she thought there should be more stuff. Andy said it was probably fatigue from moving the heavy gold pieces. The stuff she took to the safe was what I ended up with in the van that I used for Andy's release. Only it almost backfired."

"So, we're going for the rest of the treasure?" asked Donna. "Where is it?"

"In another cave near the one we took it out of."

"I take it the Customs Service and the police don't know of it's existence either."

"Right," said Virginia. "They think the treasure that Jameson and Chang had was all of it. There is no record of the total amount, so for all practical purposes, it doesn't exist. We're going to go get it. And, we can have some fun with it until we turn it over to the Irvine Company. "

"I can't wait to see it. A real honest treasure, not something from Disneyland."

"Yeah. I wish we could keep it, but it really belongs to the Irvine Company. When the investigation is through, they'll get it all. It was on their land."

Lunch was served. They ate their food watching the ocean and a handful of people walking on the beach. Virginia thought of Andy and the men on the Cassandra. A sudden chill ran up her spine as she thought of how close they came to getting killed.

Virginia drove up Laguna Canyon Drive to the parking lot and the start of the trail.

"Hang on, it's a rough trip from here on," she said.

The truck wound slowly up the trail. Small rocks pinged against the bed of the truck as it swerved up the dusty road. Donna closed the sunroof. Branches of thistle and small scrub bushes scrapped against the sides of the truck.

Donna looked out the window at the drop off as they rounded a corner. "Oh shit! I hope you know what you're doing," she said griping the handle above the glove compartment, white knuckled.

The truck bounced into the clearing. Virginia parked it under a large spreading oak. She sat for a minute looking at the entrance to the cave where she and Andy almost died. The pained expression on her face told volumes. Donna just waited.

Virginia hopped out of the truck and looked in the back. Tied to the side was a canvas tarp and rope.

Pointing up the hill she said, "Grab the flashlight from behind the seat will you please? That little opening under that tree is our destination. Let's go, this could take some time." She looked at the ground. The last time she had seen it from the outside, the only tracks were of the two trucks, small animals and Andy's, Abbey's and her footprints. Now the area was trampled with tire tracks. It looked like a small army had been there.

Virginia and Donna hiked to the cave. Donna turned on the light and swung it around.

"I don't like snakes," she said. "I met a rattle snake when I was young. I was about ten. It was in a woodpile. I was getting some firewood for my dad. The snake rattled and scared me. I fell backwards as it struck. It got my boot. Fortunately, it didn't get through the leather to my foot. My dad killed it and took me to the hospital. I haven't liked snakes since." Donna was sweating.

Virginia and Donna beat the bushes around the cave with long sticks. There were no snakes. They bent over and entered the cave. Virginia led them around a curve and into a small side fissure. She shined her light into the back. Gold glittered in the beam of light. Donna stopped. Her eyes grew.

"A girls second best friend, after diamonds of course. If this is what you hid, how much was left? This is wonderful!" Donna abruptly stood up. "Oh shit," she said as she bumped her head on the roof of the cave. Some small rocks fell around her.

"Let's get this loaded and out-a-here, "said Virginia picking up a small statue. "I don't have fond memories of this place. It gives me the creeps,"

Half an hour went by slowly. Virginia and Donna were covered with dust. The truck bed had a half dozen small gold figurines, medallions, a couple of masks, some bracelets, knives and two necklaces. They sat on the tailgate to rest.

"I won't be needing the gym today," said Donna. "This was quite a workout. That stuff is heavy."

Virginia draped the canvas tarp over the gold. Donna tied one end of the rope to a tie down at the rear of the truck. Virginia wound the rope across the tarp and secured it to another metal loop at the front of the truck bed. A noise was coming from the road. Virginia and Donna stood frozen for a second.

"Damn," said Virginia. "We don't need visitors now."

Virginia grabbed her backpack and withdrew two small yellow cylinders. She tossed one to Donna. Donna looked at it and nodded her head. They stood up and closed the tailgate.

A black, Ford, four wheel drive, pick up truck entered the clearing. The driver swung it around kicking up a dust cloud. The Ford stopped twenty feet from Virginia. The doors opened and two men in their mid twenties climbed down. A beer can tumbled out of the driver's side. They were both wearing white tee shirts and blue jeans. Large knives were fastened on their wide western belts. Both driver and passenger had short dark hair. They were about five foot eight.

"Well, lookie here Frank, a couple of little pretties for us to play with," slurred the driver.

"Yeah," answered Frank. "And it looks like they've been busy. What's ya got there, girls?"

"Non of your damn business, " said Donna in a piercing voice.

"Spunky too," said Frank. "I think they need a little taming, what do you think, Paul?"

Paul walked closer to Virginia and stopped four feet from her. "I like this one."

"Good, 'cause I like this one," answered Frank as he strutted toward Donna.

Donna thrust her shoulders back. Her firm breasts pulled on the fabric of her blouse. Frank's eyes widened. Virginia did the same. Her thin blue blouse stretched over her ample chest and lace bra. The sight had the same affect on Paul. Both men stared for a second.

"Now!" yelled Donna.

Donna swung her canister from behind her back and shot a stream of pepper spray straight into Frank's eyes. Virginia followed with a stream of spray in Paul's face. The men screamed in pain as they grabbed their faces. With the backs of their hands they rubbed their eyes. Frank stumbled away. He ran into a tree and fell to the ground. Paul backed into his truck.

"We'll get you for this, you dumb bitches," he screamed.

He stopped rubbing his eyes. As his hands came down, Virginia shot another stream of pepper spray in his face. He opened his mouth to scream as Virginia shot a blast of liquid in. His face became red as he grabbed his throat. His knees buckled. He fell on the ground gasping for air and trying to rub his eyes again.

Donna walked to the back of the truck and knelt down next to the right rear tire. She pulled a small pocketknife from her pocket and unscrewed the air valve. Air came hissing out. She got up, dusted her pants off and confidently walked back to Virginia.

"I think it's time to go," she said.


Virginia piloted the truck down the dirt road. The rocks pinged off the undercarriage as she flew around the bends. At the bottom of the road she bounced the truck into the paved parking lot and stopped. She held the wheel and starred straight out the front window.

"This life is going to kill me," said Virginia. "Nice job back there. You're one rough mama."

"Those creeps needed a lesson. I thought of what you told the police and figured we could distract them long enough to get the first shot. Worked too."

"I didn't realize you had it in you. What will Dean think of you?"

"Dean thinks I'm somewhat of an uninhibited nut. But we need to keep them interested, right?"

"Wait until those characters can see again, and get a load of the flat tire. They'll be fuming. Did you notice any spare tire on that truck?"

"Nope," said Donna with a smirk. "I'd love to see how they it get out of there. I just insured that they wouldn't be following us any time soon."

"I would love to hear the story they'll be telling their friends," said Virginia laughing.

Virginia turned the truck around and drove out to the highway. As they approached Irvine, Donna twisted in her seat.

"Are you sure you want to take this to your place or Andy's? The police or customs people could visit you and how would you explain all this," she said pointing to the rear of the truck. "We can turn it over to its owners later."

"I didn't think about that. You're right. I'll take it to Andy's storage space. It isn't too far from the campus and the keys are here on his key ring. We can put it in there and call the Irvine Company to arrange getting it to them properly. Thanks."

Virginia drove to the storage lot. Andy's space was number 27. She fumbled with the lock and opened the door. The room was about a third full. Donna untied the tarp and pulled it back.

"As we unload it, take one of the necklaces you would like and put them aside," said Virginia.

The unloading took half the time that it took to load the truck. Donna walked to the front gate to buy a couple of soft drinks. When she returned Virginia was loading two gold necklaces in the truck.

Donna strolled up to the truck and handed Virginia her soda. She looked in the truck and saw the necklaces. "What are they doing here?"

"I saw the way you looked at them and figured you'd like to have one tonight to tease the guys."

Donna stared at Virginia. "Good idea. I know Dean's never seen a real treasure before. It'll be fun."

"I'm sorry it isn't the real thing, but I got you a statue that looks like one in the treasure." She pulled a small statue from behind the seat and gave it to Donna.

Donna took the statue and examined it. It looked just like a couple she had seen in the truck. She put down her soda can and gave Virginia a hug. Teary eyed she said, "Thanks, I really didn't do that much. Last night was an adventure and I got to help a friend. You didn't have to do this."

"It isn't much. I wish it were the real thing."

"It's beautiful. I'll remember last night every time I look at it. This is sure sweet of you. Thank you, very much."

Virginia locked the door to the storage room and climbed back into the truck. She wound the truck out of the storage yard and nosed it toward Irvine. Donna turned the radio on to a rock station and sang all the way to the apartment house.

Virginia pulled the truck into a visitor-parking slot across from the pool area. Donna said good-by and went to retrieve her mail. Virginia climbed the stairs to her apartment. She needed to change and call Andy and feed Leo.

Andy answered the phone on the third ring. Virginia asked, "How are you doing, Tiger?"

"Fine. I'm feeling better by the minute. Where did you two go all day?"

"I'll explain tonight. Would you mind if I invite Donna and Dean to join us in a little barbecue tonight? We could use the spa."

"That would be fine. After what you two did last night, I couldn't object to anything."

Virginia called Donna and invited her and Dean to Andy's house for the evening. "I have an idea that should be fun," she said giggling. Donna listened and agreed.

# ~ *23* ~

Virginia turned off the ignition and got out of the truck. She pulled her backpack and Andy's blanket out of the truck. She unlocked the front door, dropped the backpack and blanket on the floor, and went seeking Andy.

He was sitting in his family room, in a blue tee shirt, jean shorts and another UCI baseball cap watching television. The movie was **Road to Hong Kong** with Bob Hope and Bing Crosby. Virginia saw him and started to laugh. She never thought she'd be happy to see that cap, until now. As far as she was concerned, he could wear it with a tux. Then again, he probably would. On the coffee table in front of him was bowl of popcorn and a Dr. Pepper. He looked up.

"Hi. Where's your friend? Is she bringing Dean? That's his name right?"

"Yes, that's his name, and they'll be along soon. How are you feeling?"

Andy looked at her with a cheerful grin. "I'm doing good. I feel like a dope sitting here while you're off talking to the police and doing God knows what. By the way what were you doing?"

"I'll tell you later. Lieutenant Kilroy said he'd be around to see you in a few days. He needs to get some things straightened out first. I'm going to change into my bathing suit and start the corn and beans. Why don't you start the barbecue?"

Andy went to the patio and uncovered the gas barbecue. He turned on the gas bottle under the barbecue, lifted the lid and pushed the igniter. The flame shot up. He lowered the lid and returned to his movie. Why does she think that's so hard, he thought. Women. I'll never understand them, especially her. Then again, it's more fun wondering what she'll do next.

Virginia retrieved her pack and went to the bedroom to change. She put on her dark blue bikini. Virginia removed the gold necklace from her pack and tried it on. The gold disks and leaf were suspended on intricately wound gold cord. The necklace formed an inverted triangle with the widest portion around her neck. The gold flowed down her chest, a star shaped object lying between her breasts. The light from the window reflected off the centuries old gold.

It seemed to weigh more now than when she placed it in her pack. She looked in the mirror on the dresser. She ran her hands over it slowly. A tingling sensation ran through her fingers. This magnificent necklace was centuries old. It hadn't seen daylight in years. Now it was on her neck. Who had worn it before? Had a young maiden worn it before being sacrificed? She turned slightly, admiring the workmanship, the intricate details in the gold. This was part of a treasure many people had lost their lives over. Now, part of it was hers, at least for tonight. The light reflected off a gold leaf. It cast a beam across the closet door.

Virginia looked at the necklace. She had it, but at what cost. Andy could have died. She lost a friend. She thought Abbey was a friend anyway. People had tried to kill her and Andy. She looked down at the gold and sighed. Was it all worth it? Virginia unfastened the necklace and placed it back in her pack. Wait until Andy sees it, she thought. For that matter, wait 'till Dean sees Donna's. He hasn't a clue as to what's been going on. It could be fun springing this on the poor lads.

Virginia walked through the family room to the kitchen. Andy was in front of the television laughing at Bob Hope. She removed the hamburger from the refrigerator and formed the burgers for Andy to kill on the grill. You get your meat one of two ways with Andy at the barbecue, she thought. Rare or nuked. She prepared the beans and set them on the stove. Her rattling the pans in the lower cabinet brought Andy to the kitchen.

"What are you doing?" he asked, his head turned to the side.

"Where did you hide the pan for boiling the corn? It isn't here?" asked Virginia.

"It's in the garage. I'll get it for you. And don't ask."

Virginia straightened up and started to husk the corn as Andy returned with the pot. She watched as he washed and dried the big pan. Sheepishly, he handed the pot to Virginia.

"Nice bathing suit" he said with a child like smile.

"This old thing?" she answered. "It's your favorite." She decided that whatever he was doing with the pot must have been one of his experiments that didn't work and was best left alone. "Thanks for getting this for me." She kissed him on the cheek.

Andy went in the bedroom and changed into his bathing suit. He returned to the family room to see how his movie was doing. The credits were running. Virginia had placed the corn in the pot of water and turned on the gas. When she turned around, Andy was there. He had a purple and green surfer bathing suit on with a blue tee shirt. His hat was missing.

"Where is your cap?"

"It didn't match."

Virginia started to laugh. "It didn't match? Have you looked in a mirror? That's not all that doesn't match. What am I going to do with you, Dr. Clark?"

The doorbell rang. Andy went to the front door and opened it. Donna was standing in the doorway. She had on a red bikini top with a pair of matching shorts. In her left hand was a large cloth bag with wide straps for handles. Inside were beach towels. Standing behind her was Dean. He had khaki shorts and a red tee shirt that matched Donna's bikini top. Donna smiled.

"Hi Andy, How are you feeling?" she said.

Andy stepped out of the way and motioned them in. "Good. Come on in. If it wasn't for you, I don't think Virginia and I would be here."

"Andy, this is Dean. He's my other half. He's a programmer at Campus Vision."

Donna put her bag in the bathroom off the family room and went to help Virginia. Andy and Dean walked out on the patio. Virginia brought out two beers and the hamburgers for Andy and his new 'assistant chef' to cook.

The smoke followed the chefs around as they tried to look professional. The flames lapped at the underside of the burgers. Dean helped place the patties that looked done on the upper shelf of the cooker to keep warm as Andy tried not to make them into slabs of carbon.

"I think the Marquis De Sade invented the barbecue," stated Andy.

They ate dinner on the patio. Andy probed Dean for details of his work.

"Programming always fascinated me, but I never really got into it. I think it's amazing what you guys can do. We use the computers at the university for everything from writing reports to simulation models, but these are nothing compared to what you do."

Dean was explaining a game program to Andy as they went to turn on the spa. It was getting dark. Andy turned on the underwater light. The bluish light shown up into the night as it cast ripples on the side of the house. The air was warm and quiet.

"Seems hard to believe that last night it was extremely foggy at the coast. Look at it now," said Andy.

Looking to the west, Dean said, "By the looks of that fog bank hanging on the hill over there, I bet the beach areas are getting more tonight. That's what nice about living inland a little."

Virginia and Donna were finishing cleaning up. Donna joked about the paper plates and plastic dinnerware and cups. Easy clean up. Virginia and Donna walked out on the patio where the two men were sitting.

"Why don't you two get in.?" said Virginia. "We'll get some wine and glasses and be right out."

Andy and Dean tested the water, removed their shirts and settled into the swirling warm water. The bubbles felt like little fingers on their bodies.

"Have you noticed how funny the girls have been acting after dinner?" asked Dean. "Donna is a real handful. She's always up to something. With the way she was acting tonight, I'm beginning to wonder what we're in for."

"After what we've been through the last few days," said Andy, "I don't even want to think about it. Virginia gets into enough trouble by herself."

"Yeah. Between the two of them I'm surprised that they haven't been tossed out of the apartment house. Being next door neighbors and both liking to sun themselves topless, and in bikinis, I've wondered about people that live there with small kids."

"There aren't any kids there," said Andy settling back in the spa as the warm water bubbled over his shoulders. "And the manager is a single man in his early sixties who likes both of them. I think the only people there that would be upset are the females. I'm not even sure of that. Some of their swimsuits are about the size that a husky mosquito could take off with from a very short runway. Did Donna tell you about the wet tee shirt contest that they had a month ago during a Saturday pool party? She and Virginia were finalists. A red head won."

The patio lights went out. The spa light partially lit the yard, casting moving shadows. The sliding screen door opened and Virginia and Donna stepped out. Virginia had two large candles, the flames dancing as she walked. Two glasses were in her other hand. Donna carried two wine bottles and two glasses. They slowly walked to the spa. They were wearing matching gold necklaces. The rounded points at the bottom of the necklaces were resting between their breasts. The gold contrasted with their bating suits. Their skin glistened in the pale light. Virginia set the candles and glasses down. She skipped over to the light switch and turned off the spa perimeter lights. The candles flickered an eerie light around the spa. Donna stepped into the water and poured the wine. Andy and Dean sat among the tinny bubbles and stared. Virginia slid into the spa, picked up her glass and raised it.

"To the conclusion of our adventure and to very good friends," she toasted.

The others raised their glasses and drank to the toast.

"First," said Andy. "Where did you two get those necklaces? What is all of this? Where have you two been all day today?"

"The necklaces are part of the treasure that I hid when we were loading the stuff for Abbey to take to her shop." Virginia stopped talking and poured more wine. She continued, "If you recall, Abbey commented on the fact that she thought there should be more. There was. I hid it. We went and got it today. I loaned that necklace to Donna and I kept this one, to tease you boys."

"You had a plan? How did you know for certain that we'd get out?"

"You men are so predictable, I didn't count on all the shooting though. It was just a hunch."

"How much of the treasure did you save?" asked Andy.

"I'd guess about 600 to 800 pounds. We put most of it in your storage locker. I figure we can call the Irvine Company and deliver it to them. What do you think of our necklaces? They'll go back with the rest of the treasure tomorrow."

"I love them. How about you?" said Andy nudging Dean.

Dean was staring at Donna. "Yeah, I love them too. Is that real gold? What's going on?" He reached over to Donna and lifted the necklace. "This is heavy."

"The treasure that we discovered was basically split into three sections. One the police found when the cave, with us in it, was blown up. The second was the treasure that Abbey had. That's what I used to try and free Andy. But some of the treasure I hid in case something went wrong. These," she said lifting the end of her necklace, "are part of the treasure I hid."

Dean bent closer to Donna's necklace and stared, "You mean this is really part of a buried treasure? For real? Wow!" He looked at Donna then at Virginia. "I don't know what to say."

"Don't say anything, you big lug. Have more wine," said Donna with a silly grin.

Andy and Dean poured more wine in all the glasses.

"These necklaces are getting heavy," giggled Donna. She reached up and unfastened her necklace. Virginia's followed. Donna handed her necklace to Virginia. She placed them on a chair near the spa. The two girls slipped back into the warm water.

"I have a bit of news to add," said Andy. "The newspaper called today. They want the story about the treasure and my rescue." He looked at Virginia. "I told them you were the person to talk to. They'll be here in the morning. And you, my dear, received a call from a Dr. William Smithe at the Southbrook Museum on Friday. He wants to talk to you about a position at the museum." He looked over at Donna. She was getting sleepy. "I think you two need to spend the night. You're not in shape to drive."

"Good idea," slurred Donna. "Shall we tell them about the little misadventure we had today as well?"

"What misadventure?" asked Dean.

Andy looked at Virginia, "Don't tell me you two got into more trouble."

"Not exactly. While we were at the caves getting the remainder of the treasure, a big, black, truck came up the hill," said Donna. "Two young punks wanted to get cute. We changed their minds and left them there."

Dean became serious, "What did you do?"

"We used pepper spray and Donna let the air out of one of their rear tires." Virginia stood up and stepped out of the spa. Turning she added, "Then, we drove off like a bat outa hell!"

She grabbed her towel and started to dry off. The reflection of the light and ripples of the water reflected off the windows and upstairs blinds of the rear neighbors house. She saw the blinds quickly move as she glanced toward the house.

"I've had too much wine or your neighbor back there has been watching us. Probably both. His blinds keep moving."

Andy glanced around. "He'll have a tough time, the trees are pretty dense."

"If I can see him, he probably can see us, or at least me right now."

Donna looked up. She got a mischievous smile on her face. "Let's give him something to talk about. We can be the talk of the neighborhood."

Before Andy or Dean could move, Donna was out of the water and standing next to Virginia. They looked at each other, and started to seductively dry themselves off.

Andy and Dean jumped out of the water. "You don't have to put on a show! Do you want the whole neighborhood upset with me?" said Andy as he went for Virginia. Dean headed for Donna. The two girls ran into the yard with Andy and Dean in pursuit. Virginia ran by the pool equipment and turned off the light. Donna had evaded Dean and was behind a tree, staying just out of reach.

After a few minutes of playfulness, Donna sat down with a thud. Looking up at Dean, she said, "I'm pooped. Let's go to bed."

Virginia admitted that she was tired. She looked at Andy, "I think we gave your neighbor enough of a show for tonight, let's go, too."

Andy and Dean picked up their towels and started to talk about computers when Virginia and Donna walked by.

"Good night boys," they said together.

"I don't think we could get two more stubborn women if we tried," sighed Dean.

"Yeah. And I don't think we could get two more uninhibited ones either. What are we to do with them? Love them I guess. I wouldn't trade Virginia for all the money in the world."

"Yeah, can't live with them, and we sure as hell don't want to live without them. Good night." Dean followed Donna to the spare bedroom.

Andy found Virginia in the bedroom pulling down the covers. She was wearing one of his oversized tee shirts with a buffalo on the front.

"You two were something tonight. The neighbors will run me out of town on a rail. But, I love you anyway."

Virginia scampered across the bed and put her arms around Andy's neck. She looked up into his eyes and kissed him.

"Good night, Tiger. I'm sorry if tonight got a little out of hand. It felt good to be free and not worried about you." She climbed into bed and beckoned him to slide in beside her.

"I'll turn out the lights," he said changing into a pair of boxer shorts and a black tee shirt. "The adventure is finally over. I hope. You need to call the Irvine Company tomorrow, don't forget. That, and Dr. Smithe. By the way, I need to see the Dean tomorrow about a new grad student. I'm to oversee his thesis. Oh…as far as tonight, don't ever change. I love you just the way you are."

"With or without my clothes?"

"Either way."

## ~ **24** ~

The morning sun illuminated the kitchen through the open bay windows. Virginia sipped a cup of coffee with the comic strip in front of her face. She lowered the paper as Donna ambled in. She had her bathing suit on and a towel draped around her neck.

"Where is the coffee? Does your head feel like a roasted marshmallow too?"

"Sit down. I'll get you some. Sugar's on the table," said Virginia. She got a mug from the cupboard and filled it with coffee.

Donna looked at the steaming cup for a minute then slowly raised it to her lips and sipped. "Ahh, that's good. I needed this."

Virginia leaned close to Donna and said, "How much wine did you have?"

"More than I want to remember. I think. Dean will be right down. He's taking me to breakfast after I change into real clothes. What are you up to today?"

"Well, for openers I'll get cleaned up and wait for the news-paper people. While I'm waiting I'll call the museum for an appointment with Dr. Smithe. Then I need to contact the Irvine Company about the treasure in Andy's storage space." Virginia put her cup down and glanced out the window. "I'll be around my apartment later to change for the museum. It probably wouldn't be a good idea to mention what we picked up yesterday to the paper or the museum."

"I agree." said Donna stretching. "We don't need the government or anyone else trying to get it." She finished her coffee.

Donna got up from the table. "I don't know how you trained Andy to be so cool. I still have Dean in training." She removed her top and tossed it and her towel over a chair and chuckled. "I'll get my purse and stand here like this when Dean comes down. Watch his expression. It's fun teasing him. Sometimes he can be real uptight." She picked up the necklace and put it in the bag with the towels and her shorts.

"The hard part was getting Andy to relax when I was that way around men. I'll get you one of my tee shirts for the ride home if you want one, " added Virginia.

"No. The top and shorts got me here so they'll get me home. But, I'll get a rise out of him first."

Dean lumbered down the stairs. When he reached the bottom step, Donna walked by.

"Are you ready to go?" she asked smiling.

Dean stared at her with his mouth open. "Where do you think you're going like that? Anyway, all the windows are open. All the neighbors can see you."

"I'm going home. You're driving. I don't care if the neighbors can see me. I usually sun myself like this at home, without any complaints, I might add," said Donna. "Anyway, the last time we went to South Laguna for the afternoon you didn't object." She put her top on and laughed. "I told you he'd react." She wiggled into her shorts.

Dean looked exasperated. He rolled his eyes, his chest rose and fell with a big sigh. He took Donna's hand and squeezed it. Looking at Virginia he said, "Thanks for the evening and the spa. And, thanks for the treasure you shared with Donna. Imagine; real treasure like you read about in books. We'll see you and Andy later. By the way, were is Andy?"

Virginia walked to the front door and opened it for her guests to leave. "He's at school seeing the Dean about a grad student. He left early. I think he'll go see Lieutenant Kilroy while he's on campus. I bet the Dean will be full of questions about our adventure as well."

Donna and Dean shuffled to the car. Donna waved as they drove off.


Virginia finished combing her hair when the doorbell rang. She darted down the stairs to the door. She stopped in the front hall to look in the mirror. Her blue blouse was tucked into a pair of jeans. She was bare foot. She smiled, turned and opened the front door. Facing her was a reporter in a dark brown business suit. She judged his height to be about six three. Dark hair and tan complexion. The second man was shorter and built like a football player. He held a camera in his left hand.

"I'm Jason Scott, reporter with the Orange County Herald," he said presenting his card and credentials. This is Frank Holm. He's a photographer with the paper. Are you Ms. Davies?"

"Yes." Virginia answered looking at Scott's credentials. They seemed genuine. "Please come in gentlemen."

She escorted them to the living room. "Can I get you something to drink?"

"No thank you, we've had all the liquids we can stand for the morning," answered Jason.

"Yeah. Any more coffee and I'll blur every picture today," said Frank.

Jason and Frank sat in two wing chairs opposite the long green and brown couch that Virginia had taken. She sat with her legs tucked under her and her left arm across the back of the couch.

"You have some questions?"

Jason watched Virginia for a second. "We have reports from people in Newport Beach about a shooting the other night. The police, customs and the Coast Guard captured an international art theft and smuggling ring that was involved. We have it on good authority that you were involved with it and saving a professor at the university. There is believed to be a tie in with the discovery of treasure in Laguna Beach and your assumed death. Can you elaborate?"

"I can tell you part of it," she said as Frank took a picture of Virginia on the couch.

"We found a faded, partial map in an old clock. After researching it we found an area near Laguna Beach that looked promising. Further exploring turned up the treasure in a cave. Fortunately the cave has an underground river in it. During our extraction of the treasure we were held up," said Virginia, "The cave entrance was blown up and we, Dr. Andy Clark and I, were left for dead. The treasure that was removed from the cave was taken into custody by the police along with the people that tried blow us up. We escaped through the underground river." She repositioned herself in the opposite direction. "We managed to secure part of the treasure that was removed earlier. The people on that boat you mentioned kidnapped Dr. Clark. I used the remaining treasure to try and secure his release. It didn't work out as planned but we escaped and they were caught. Got all that?"

"There are a few aspects we would like to clarify," answered Jason.

Frank took two more photographs.

Jason looked at Virginia and smiled. "Before we go on, I'd like to ask one question that is haunting everyone that has heard of your adventure. Did you manage to keep any of it?"

"To be honest, we did manage to save some of the treasure. It's safely locked up at this time. I'll be contacting the Irvine Company as soon as you leave so they can claim the artifacts. As for anything for ourselves, if we did, do you really think I'd tell anyone? I'd have more instant friends than I ever imagined, the IRS all over me, and people with real or imagined claims to it suing me. For the record…no."

A half-hour later Jason and Scott left the house. Virginia watched them get into the newspaper's minivan and drive off. She walked back to the living room. They seemed like nice fellows she thought. She looked at the room. The short hairs on the back of her neck bristled. I'm getting paranoid. This is ridiculous. Virginia went to the wing chair that Jason Scott was sitting in and probed the cushion he sat on. Nothing. She looked around and under the chair. Nothing unusual. She got up and went to the chair Frank used. She probed this chair as well. Exasperated, she sat down on the chair.

Why am I doing this she thought? She started to get up when she saw the small shinny metal object under the edge of the end table next to the chair. Her heart throbbed. She felt her face flush with heat. Her hands were shaking. Will this never end? She reached for the little device under the table and pulled it loose. It fell free into her hand. She looked at it. Her hand shook as she carefully set it on the table. It was round and metallic. It seemed to have a cross hatched section with a screen covering it. It was about the size of a quarter and about a quarter-inch thick. What should she do with it? Why would the newspaper people leave it? She felt the rage race through her body. You can't even trust the paper anymore. The telephone rang.

Virginia jumped. Her heart missed a beat. Tears started to form in her eyes. The room became cloudy. The phone kept ringing. Virginia ambled into the kitchen and picked up the telephone.

"Hello".

"Hello yourself," said Andy. "Are you all right? What did you do to the alarm system? My portable monitor just went bananas."

"Your what?" said Virginia.

"The alarm system has sensors in various parts of the house. Even though it is off, it monitors itself. If someone tries to tamper with a sensor, it alerts me. When it went off a minute ago I got worried. What happened?"

Virginia sank into a kitchen chair. She felt like a wet dishrag. "Did you have a sensor or whatever under a table in the living room?"

"Yeah. It's a motion detector. Plugs into a small socket under the table. When the system is on, it looks for motion in that part of the house. Why?"

"I thought it was a bug left behind by the news guys that were here earlier and panicked. I pulled it out of its holder. I'm sorry. Just jumpy."

"It's okay. Just slip it back. Get some rest. You need it. Are you seeing the museum people today?"

"Yes, at one. Want to come by my place later? We can go out for dinner. I want to show you your storage locker too."

"Sounds good to me. Take it easy. Your nerves must be pretty shot by now. Try and relax. I'll see you later. Knock'em dead at the museum."

Virginia went back into the living room and plugged in the little sensor. Next she telephoned the Irvine Company. They agreed to send an armored car for the gold the following day. She looked at the clock on the dining room wall. Almost time to get ready. I think I have everything. Her briefcase was on the table. Virginia opened it. Letters of reference, resumes, copies of reports and research she had conducted were all organized. She closed the briefcase and headed for the bedroom to change.

## ~ **25** ~

The air-conditioned air rushed at her as she opened the massive wooden doors. Virginia walked into the Southbrook Museum. She was wearing a dark blue, straight, knee length skirt and matching blazer, with a white blouse. Her brown leather brief case held her resume, letters from professors and her wallet and comb. To the right was a counter with a short pudgy woman behind it. On the front of the counter was a sign stating admission was three dollars. The woman smiled. Virginia walked to the counter.

"I'm here to see Dr. Smithe. Can you direct me, please?" asked Virginia fumbling for her wallet.

"You must be Ms. Davies. Dr. Smithe is expecting you. You don't need to pay anything," the woman said. She reached in a drawer and pulled out a badge with a clip on it. Virginia's name was on the front in bold letters. "Please put this on. This way security won't get upset seeing you in authorized personnel areas. Go to the right past the Neanderthals and up the stairs. Dr. Smithe's office is on the right. Can't miss it…Good luck honey."

Virginia thanked the woman. She pushed her way through the turn-styles and wondered past the exhibits of the Neanderthals, stone tools and cave drawings to a small staircase. The museum was large with multiple display cases, statues and skeletons all around her. The ceiling towered high above her. In the center of the room was a pendulum swinging? It was knocking down little pegs in a circle around it.

There was a thick red rope across the opening to the stair well. Virginia unhooked the rope and entered the small space. She rehooked the rope and climbed the stairs. She felt butterflies trying to get out of her stomach. Her hands started to sweat. Shifting her brief case, Virginia rubbed her hands on the sides of her skirt then opened the door to the director's office suite.

Virginia entered the office suite. There were love seats on either side of the door with small coffee tables in front of them. Each held out of date magazines. Just like a doctor's office she thought. The wall on her left had large certificates framed in massive dark mahogany. The opposite wall had framed photos of people in different parts of the world at archeological digs and in front of displays. In the center of the room was a large dark wood desk. Behind the desk was a slim woman with dark brown hair in a tan suit. The nameplate on the desk said Ann Bowels. She looked up from the papers on the desk as Virginia entered.

"Good afternoon, Ms. Davies. If you'll take a seat, I'll try and find Dr. Smithe. Heavens knows where he's wondered off to this time." She pressed a button on a small black box on her desk. Virginia watched her.

"This little thing-a-magigge buzzes his beeper that I got him. This way I can find him without running all over the place. He'll be right back, I'm sure. Can I get you anything? Coffee, soda?"

Virginia declined the offer and sank into a sofa. Well, at least it seems to be a relaxed environment, she thought. She tried to control her heart. It started to pound in her chest. I don't remember being this nervous in the underground river. Get hold of yourself girl. I wonder what Dr. Smithe is like? As she reached for a magazine the office door burst open and a short pudgy man in blue Docker pants and a red Polo shirt rushed in past Virginia.

"Is she here yet, Ann?" he asked, panting for breath.

"Right behind you, doctor."

He straightened up and turned. Red faced, he smiled, and walked toward Virginia, reaching out his hand. His thin, grayish-black hair had straw sticking out of the back.

Taking Virginia's hand he said, "Hello, my dear. I'm Dr. William Smithe. The museum director. Please come into my office." He turned and led the way through a door behind Ann's desk. Smithe brushed the straw from his hair.

After taking a chair in front of Dr. Smithe's big polished oak desk, Virginia glanced around the room. There were bookshelves on the wall to her left filled with various sized books and folders. Next to a coach was a Big Sur style Burylmaple coffee table. The wallpaper on the wall behind Dr. Smithe was a brown cloth. On it were framed diplomas, awards, and photos. One photo was of the President of the United States and Dr. Smithe. There was one of him with a Cardinal. The wall to her right had a painting of an English village. It was centered above a heavy wooden table covered with artifacts, brushes and a magnifying glass. She turned to look at Smithe.

"The magnifying glass is there because visitors think us stuffy museum types are suppose to use them," he said with a chuckle. "It was nice of you to come on such short notice. Thank you."

"I'm afraid you have the advantage on me, sir. I am interested in a job. I'll finish my thesis in September and need to find a job. I don't understand how you found me."

Dr. Smithe looked at Virginia with a big grin. "We have a mutual friend. You know Lieutenant John Kilroy of the university police, I assume."

"Yes. I think I drove him to drink. I'm not sure he's a big fan of mine though."

Smithe assessed the young woman in front of him.

"Well, for your information, he thinks highly of you. Seems you managed to out fox some very nasty criminals and most of the police in Southern California. According to him, you led the police to one of the largest art theft rings in the world. Something the major police agencies couldn't do."

Virginia could feel the heat radiating from her face. She glanced at the floor for a second. Her eyes returned to Dr. Smithe. He was smiling.

"And, again according to our friend, you got the top bananas. The good lieutenant said you're very loyal too. And you did some very strange things to save your boyfriend. He recommended you as an associate of this museum. He thinks you'd make a good detective too. Said that you and your friends uncovered the lost treasure we've been reading about. Quite a set of accomplishments, if I do say so." Smithe leaned back in his chair and put his left leg up on the corner of his desk.

"He said that?" asked Virginia. "Wow. How do you know him? If I may ask."

"I worked at the New York Metropolitan a number of years back. Our friend, John, worked for the NYPD in the art theft detail. We became friends. I even attended his wedding. A few years ago I got this position and moved out here. He brought his family, his wife Sue and little girls, Tracy and Kelly, to visit and go to Disneyland. I'm Kelly's godfather by the way. That's the girls in that photo over there," he added pointing to the table. "He decided he didn't do cold real well after that. He landed a position with the university police and moved here a couple years ago." Smithe brushed something off his shirt. "We are still close friends. I help him on cases once in a while, when I can. This packing straw gets everywhere."

"I didn't know he ever worked for the New York Police," said Virginia. "He never talked much about himself. He was there when we got away from the guys who kidnapped my boyfriend. I guess I led him on quite an adventure."

She removed a resume from her case. Handing it to Dr. Smite, she said, "What is the position you have open?"

Smithe glanced at her resume. He rose from his chair and walked to the small couch in the corner and sat down. Virginia shifted in her chair.

"Your professors think highly of you, too. A Dr. Green can't say enough good things and showed me some of your work. He was thrilled that you managed to catch the thieves, including a colleague of his at the university." He shuffled some papers. "Ahh, here it is. A Dr. Gillette." He settled back in the seat. "The position is Associate Curator of North American Studies. This museum is interested in not only pre-Colombian history, but in the history and folklore of the Americas. There is a wealth of knowledge that is being lost due to lack of study and interest by families as they become more diverse. I also understand that you're becoming something of an aficionado of quilting. That's going to fit in very well with the position. As you know, quilting is a big part of our heritage. We want to capture it and preserve it for future generations. We have not just inherited the past, but we are borrowing the Earth and setting up the future for our children and future generations."

He looked at her with wide, deep blue eyes. "This museum is well endowed and will provide an excellent salary, benefit plan, office and support for your work and any future studies you may take." He leaned forward. "There would be some travel too. Would you be interested?"

Virginia stared at Smithe for a minute. This was more than she ever dreamed of. She loved history but what did a history major do after college…teach. This could be rewarding and may pay more than teaching. She liked to travel, especially on someone else's money.

"I'm…I'm very interested," stammered Virginia. "Would you like my references and samples of my work? It sounds like you already have checked me out."

An hour later Virginia was in the museum personnel office. The offer was excellent. She signed the papers. She was now an official Associate Curator of the Southbrook Museum. Her photo ID card said so. She walked out of the front doors with her new ID, keys to the museum and her new office. Virginia liked her new office. She thought it was the size of a bedroom. A small window looked out on a park across the street. She had a desk, work table, office chair with a work stool and two casual chairs. The walls were cream colored and bare. The floor had rust carpeting. A computer table was next to the desk. Dr. Smithe assured her a computer, with modem and printer, would be installed in the next two days. A large bookshelf and filing cabinet were next to the door. Overall, you've done all right, she thought.

I have some place to finish my thesis and move my books and stuff to, she thought. Wait'll Andy hears about this. Me…A curator. The gods must be smiling at me today. The way things have gone; someone up there seems to like me. The gods and

Lieutenant Kilroy, imagine, they say it pays to network, this proves it. Wait until I tell mom and dad! Her heart raced as she thought of all the things that she still needed to do. Virginia felt like she was walking on air as she ventured down the street to her car. From now on, she'd park in the staff parking lot. Virginia pulled the protective paper off her staff-parking sticker and pasted it on the right side of the front window. She stood back and admired it. The red and blue colors seemed extra vivid as the sun reflected off the surface. She climbed in and started her car. She eased the car out of the parking space into traffic and drove home. The late afternoon sun warmed her neck as the breeze drifted in through the open sunroof. Her spirits were flying high. If I could only persuade the Irvine Company to exhibit the treasure here at my museum. What a way to start a new job.

## ~ *26* ~

Virginia made dinner reservations at the Golden Sloop restaurant in Newport Beach. She ordered a table overlooking the Newport Harbor and the yachts. She took a shower and selected an outfit for the evening. She thought about Andy. Would he be as excited about her news as her folks had been? How should she let him know? She could wear her new badge. She could just tell him. She was giddy as a schoolgirl that finally got a date with the star football player. What's the matter with me, she thought, I know Andy. Why am I acting this way? The news about the treasure was as big. That was easy. Maybe because this was her first R E A L job. All the others were part time or temporary. This one was real and she got it because of what she had done. That was it, she thought. She'd better call Andy and make sure he would be on time. Now where was that phone?

She wrapped a towel around her waist and went to the kitchen. She found the portable phone next to the sink. She dialed Andy as she glanced out the window. The sunset cast a red glow to the building across the pool. The pool area was almost empty. Two young men were sitting at a table talking while the redhead from across the hall from her was swimming laps. The men watched her. It was nice to see things normal again. Andy's answering machine went on. Virginia hung up. He's probably on his way. I'd better get dressed.

As she turned the telephone rang. Virginia jumped with a start. "Hello?"

"Hi," said Donna. "How'd it go at the museum?"

"Great, I got my dream job. I'm officially an Associate Curator. Matter of fact, I'm on the payroll as we speak." She told Donna about Dr. Smithe and Lieutenant Kilroy, the museum, her new office and the job. "Dr. Smithe has a project for me as soon as I finish my thesis."

Virginia finished talking to her and hung up as Dean arrived to take Donna out for dinner. They were going to a restaurant in San Clamente.

Virginia ran to the bedroom to get dressed.

Andy arrived. He waited in the living room. That seemed strange. He always liked to tease her and try and enter when she was dressing. She became apprehensive. What was wrong? She looked at herself in the mirror. Everything looked OK. Her blond hair was flowing over her shoulders contrasting the black turtleneck. The gold chain belt hung at an angle from her waist above her black slacks. The simple gold necklace seemed to glow.

Virginia opened the door and stepped into the room. Andy stood up. He was dressed in a dark suit with a red and blue regimental tie and had a large bouquet of flowers. He looked handsome. She took the flowers and gave Andy a kiss. Virginia placed the flowers in a vase on the dining table, turned out the lights and shut the door behind them as they strolled hand in hand to the parking lot.

"Have I got news for you Dr. Clark."


Virginia sat down at the table as Andy pushed in her chair. The Golden Sloop was a large restaurant with a New England motif. The open wood beans were painted blue. The wood walls were off white and tan. Large paintings of three masted sailing ships adorned the walls. On high shelves were polished brass ship fittings, compasses, lights and cleats. The tables and chairs were heavy dark oak. The last of the sun cast an orange hue over the calm harbor waters. The slips were full of sailboats of various sizes with an occasional power craft. Seals, watching from lichen covered rocks on the breakwater, slithered, one by one into the calm blue waters of the harbor. A large cabin cruiser, The Lady Lee, was berthed just outside the window next to their table. Andy stared at it for a while.

The last time I was here wasn't a real good experience," said Andy. "Just think, all that fog, the drugs and then getting shot at, all in one evening. If it wasn't for you, I'd probably been shark sushi. I get a chill just thinking about it"

"I'm sorry. I didn't think. Newport wasn't a good idea," Virginia whispered." I wanted tonight to be special. I'm so sorry…"

"It's okay. If I weren't here with you, it would be different. Now, tell me about your day and your meeting with Dr. Smithe."

The waiter arrived. He was dressed as an eighteen hundreds sailor. "May I take your order?"

Andy ordered crab cakes for an appetizer. For dinner he ordered Yankee pot roast and clam chowder. Virginia ordered orange roughie and baked potato with a dinner salad.

Virginia looked out the window at the view, then back at Andy. He looked terrific tonight.

"The news people were quite nice. I bet they get the story all wrong though. They took pictures and everything. It's the first time I've been interviewed. It was like being a celebrity. It was fun," said Virginia. She fiddled with her napkin and gazed at Andy. "I'm really sorry about the alarm. I had no idea you added the motion detectors."

"You gave me a start. After all we've been through, I kinda panicked when the alarm sounded. I was just glad you were okay. How'd it go at the museum?"

Virginia shifted in her chair. "I met Dr. Smithe. He is cute. Kinda eccentric, absent-minded but with a real zest for life and the museum. He's been everywhere. He flew a single engine plane over the North Pole, canoed down the Mississippi and Colorado Rivers, explored the pyramids. He's been to South America and Africa and everything."

"Look at this," She reached into her purse and pulled out a booklet on the museum. Her arm thrust across the table to hand it to Andy. "The museum, that is Dr. Smithe, wants to spend more museum assets on American history and folklore. That's where I come in. Isn't it wonderful?"

She dug into her purse again and pulled out her new museum badge.

"See, it's official. I'm a curator! And guess what? Lieutenant Kilroy was the one who recommended me to the museum. He and Dr. Smithe were friends in New York. Smithe is even one of the lieutenant's kids godfather. How about that? Small world. I thought Kilroy would only want me out of his life." She sighed and settled back in her chair. "I'm sorry, I've been doing all the talking."

"So the good lieutenant was behind it. I had no idea he was from New York. That's terrific. After all you…we…put him through, he went to bat for you. We need to invite him and his family for dinner or something," said Andy.

"I have a question, honey. When you came over tonight, you seemed to be preoccupied. You didn't come into the bedroom and tease me. Is anything wrong?" asked Virginia.

"No, not with us. I met with the Dean today. Besides having to coach a new grad student, I inherited two new classes. We're short handed and being the youngest and newest Prof., I get the short end of the stick. They still expect all the research, but now I have more than I've had before. It's a little depressing, that's all. It's all the new stuff at school and getting over our adventure that just got to me."

Virginia ran her tongue over her lips. "I'm sorry about the meeting with the Dean, I wanted tonight to be special. When you came in and were different and not your normal, mischievous self, I was concerned. And then I get us reservations at the harbor. I bet the last place you want to be is at the water."

"It's okay. I just want to be with you," said Andy with a sheepish grin.

"Good. I want to be with you, too. Now that that's settled, I have some other news," stated Virginia. "I talked to the Irvine Company. They'll be picking up the treasure tomorrow. All that work and loosing Abbey and they get the treasure. Doesn't seem fair somehow."

Andy reached for her hand. "I know how close you and Abbey were. I'm sorry about what happened. I still see that night in dreams. Are you sure you're okay?"

"Yes. Funny thing is I never figured that business was that bad, and that she was selling illegal art stuff. She always joked about the business and using her dad's money that he left her. She always seemed to have money, even a BMW. I thought she was doing well. I never dreamed she was an international crook. Her or Dr. Gillette."

Dinner arrived. Virginia and Andy ate while taking in the view of the harbor lights.


As Virginia and Andy walked out of the Golden Sloop, Andy said, "Ya know, the treasure you and Donna slipped by everyone is worth over a quarter of a million dollars as just plain gold. As the artifacts that they are, they must be worth many times that. Now we have to give it to the Irvine Company. After everything you've been through, it doesn't seem fair."

"Bit I don't want to become like Abbey. Anyway, I never owned it, so it's not like I've lost something that was mine. And, we get the credit for finding it. The people at the company are allowing the treasure to be displayed at our museum." answered Virginia. "I don't know when they'll make an announcement."

They strolled past a bank of newspaper dispensers next to the parking lot. Andy glanced at the headlines as they passed. He stopped in his tracks. Virginia turned. Andy was bending over straining to read a story on the front page of the evening edition of the Orange County Register.

"What are you looking at?"

Andy rose and sifted through his pockets for a quarter. He inserted it into the dispenser, raised the lid, and removed the paper. Folding it over he handed the paper to Virginia. "This. Read it, you're a celebrity."

Virginia looked at the paper. The headline read:

### Irvine Company to Display Pirate Treasure at Southbrook Museum

The Irvine Company spokesman today disclosed that the Pirate treasure uncovered days ago on the Irvine Ranch would be released from police custody. The treasure consisting of rare Aztec statues and other artifacts will be put on display at the Southbrook Museum. The exhibit will open September eighth according to Irvine Company and Museum officials. According to the Museum Director, Dr. William Smithe, nothing like it exists outside of New York and Mexico City. "This is a great honor for our museum," stated Dr. Smithe. Ms. Virginia Davies, Associate Curator at the museum and a friend from the university, Dr. Andrew Clark, were instrumental in finding the rare collection. The pair was almost killed during the discovery.

Andy turned and drew Virginia close. As the lights cast a golden glow in her hair he could smell the apricot shampoo in her hair. He lifted her head and gently kissed her. "For tonight, let's not think of treasures and adventures. Just for tonight."